THE HOUSE
on P STREET

PEGGY CHERNOW

Other novels by Peggy Chernow

Despicable Lies

Second Chances

Trapped

Dangerous Attractions

Destiny

Secrets

Loss of Innocence

A Remarkable Woman

Lost & Found

The Pastry Chef

ISBN: 979-8-9862028-8-4

Published by Noble Way Media

To best friends.
There is nothing better.

CHAPTER 1

Dawn Sutter was seated in the showroom of her internationally-acclaimed design company's expansive 110,000 square-foot showroom. She was cataloging and admiring the newest collection of expensive Italian furniture, and a huge assortment of new accessories, throw pillows, lamps, and electrical fixtures that she had recently accumulated for her clients. Her unique business provided a much-needed service that eliminated the need for middlemen and endless shopping excursions. It was a one-stop, all-inclusive, luxurious design experience, vastly different than any that her competitors offered.

Dawn's long list of affluent customers included busy, accomplished people, world-famous athletes, Wall Street geniuses, Supreme Court Justices, Congressmen, Senators, and professionals who valued their time and could afford to pay for the convenience of finding all their decorating needs under one roof – whether they were building or renovating an entire home or refreshing a single room. Her award-winning company, Sutter Interiors, provided everything a customer could want without having to travel all over town or around the country to look for a special fabric color or a one-of-a-kind furniture piece. When a client hired her firm, with its twelve talented decorators, it was an easy, convenient, hassle-free experience for them.

Her knowledge of the latest styles and trends, and her access to hundreds of vendors in all the trades, provided everything imaginable for a discerning consumer under one roof. A client could sit with a cup of coffee or a glass of champagne and with Dawn's skilled guidance, select anything they could possibly want – marble slabs for countertops, tiles for backsplashes, one-of-a-kind drapery or upholstery fabrics, period or contemporary wall papers, cabinet handles, pulls and knobs, shower heads, or paint colors for an entire house. If a customer required something Dawn did not presently have, she made sure it appeared in her showroom within forty-eight hours.

She stopped her cataloging long enough to take a short break and glance through the morning edition of *The Washington Post*'s style section. Always on the lookout for potential new customers, she used any means at her disposal, whether from actual factual accounts or from juicy gossip columns. Both yielded new leads. The local and community newspapers often announced marriages, deaths, divorces, scandals, and bankruptcies before they were known to the general public. Tabloids and *Page Six* in the *New York Post* were also a good source of potential information. Dawn read them religiously and was often the first to discover a new business opportunity for herself. Once she had a lead, she was relentless in following it up.

Today's bold-faced headline announced that Britt Holmes, a presidential hopeful, and distinguished, fifty-two-year-old popular senior senator from Delaware and one of DC's most handsome and eligible widowers, had recently become engaged to a pretty young socialite, Charlotte Randolph from Richmond, Virginia. Her blueblood forefathers claimed pre-Civil War ancestry and had owned an Antebellum house with a huge wraparound porch, Greek inspired columns, large windows to let in the breezes, and high ceilings. They had been affluent plantation owners before the Yankee Army decimated their crops, torched their land, and confiscated their property. But they had been wise and anticipated the war coming. They buried a fortune in gold and cash and some expensive artwork in a vault beneath their fruit orchard before the troops arrived, and they were able to retrieve their treasures after the war ended.

Since that time, Charlotte's relatives had reinvented themselves to fit into the ways of "the new south." What remained of the plantations had been sold to developers for housing tracts or shopping malls, and the gracious lifestyle of that era had never been restored to its previous grandeur. Charlotte's father, Ralph Randolph, saw an opportunity and moved to DC when she was eight and he opened a small but exclusive art gallery, The Randolph. Over the years it provided a substantial income and prestige for his family. Occasionally a skeptical customer questioned the origin of one of the gallery's paintings and demanded proof of authenticity, but he always managed to persuade them of the work's intrinsic value and avoid a scandal. Excellent forgeries hung side-by-side on his gallery walls and no one, even the most discerning buyers, could tell the difference. Over the years Ralph became such an expert at deceiving his customers and inflating the price of his pieces that even he had difficulty telling his originals from the fakes. He blurred the fine line between truth and fabrication in his business as well as in his private life.

After Charlotte, under some duress, accepted Senator Holmes's marriage proposal, Ralph was ecstatic and hired an exorbitantly expensive wedding planner to arrange an elaborate ceremony in the rotunda of The Capitol with a lavish reception to follow at The Chevy Chase Country Club in suburban Maryland. It was going to be the most ostentatious and flashy wedding that the DC area had seen in decades. Over 450 guests were to be invited including the current President of the United States and the First Lady, and many important art aficionados from all over the country. Ralph wanted the affair to be a glitzy, over-the-top event that would cement his place within Washington society and showcase his lovely daughter as potentially the next First Lady of the land. He had high expectations for her and her future husband, and even more grandiose ones for himself. He planned to ride their coattails to even greater financial heights. His not-so-secret agenda was to be named as the US ambassador to London or Paris. Being the father-in-law of the future president was a way to guarantee that would happen.

As a pre-wedding gift to his young bride-to-be, Senator Holmes had surprised Charlotte with the purchase of an historic, 18,000-square-foot mega-mansion on P Street in the affluent and prestigious Georgetown section. When she pouted and announced in exaggerated tears that the crumbling old house was not to her taste and she preferred something more modern, he gave her an exquisite emerald necklace as a consolation prize and an unlimited budget to furnish and decorate the house. She still was not happy, but her Mama convinced her that she could hardly refuse such a generous gift and that she must make the best of it.

Britt's infatuation with the twenty-two-year-old southern beauty, thirty years his junior, was due mostly from loneliness…and extreme pressure from her father. He had dated frequently during the five years since his wife's passing, but women his own age were primarily involved in their own lives and those of their grandchildren. He was not willing to place himself in second or third place. Charlotte was different. She was free-spirited, lively, and unpredictable. Having such a beautiful young lady on his arm was ego-boosting and made him feel young and alive again. After his wife's death, he had not planned to remarry but circumstances changed. His reasons for wanting Charlotte to become his wife were not readily apparent to friends or outsiders. They guessed correctly that he was lonely and flattered by her attention – but there was much more to it. For his ambitious personal goals to be achieved, he knew that it was imperative that there was a photogenic and aesthetically pleasing Mrs. Britt Holmes by his side. To his calculating mind, his choice of a child bride would bring him increased attention from the press and would keep him in the public's eye until the next election…all desirable outcomes for a presidential hopeful.

After reading about the engagement, Dawn dropped the newspaper in disgust, shaking her long, brunette hair at male frivolity. *Men and their frigging penises,* she thought disdainfully. *What would the world be like if they were disciplined enough to keep their pants zipped?* There would have been no love child born to Arnold Schwarzenegger's maid, no Monica Lewinsky and her blue dress, and no Stormy Daniels and her alleged payoff from Donald Trump. *Wouldn't the world have been better off?*

She brought her attention back to the task of the moment – securing Senator Holmes's and his fiancée as her newest customers. If she was smart, Senator Holmes's engagement could enrich the bottom line of her interior design business. If he agreed to hire her to redo his new house, it would be a major coup, a publicity bonanza. Why not add his name to her list of distinguished clients? According to political rumors, he had a good possibility of becoming the next leader of the free world.

Looking carefully at his picture, Dawn thought that the handsome senator could easily have been the star of the popular television program, *The Golden Bachelor.* Britt Holmes's impressive credentials and physical appearance put Gerry Turner's to shame in every way. And Theresa, as nice as she appeared to be, was no match for the lovely Charlotte Randolph.

"Lolly," Dawn used the office intercom to call her assistant and closest friend. "Please find out where Senator Holmes usually dines when he's in DC – at which restaurant – and when he's expected there next. Then make a reservation for two on the same date and time. Discreetly request a table near his. You'll be my plus one."

"Oh dear, not again." Lolly laughed, knowing her friend's nefarious intentions well. "Are you on another reconnaissance mission? Chasing after another new client?"

"You bet, and this time I plan to land one of the biggest fish in Washington's political swamp. If I do, it'll be great for business."

"There's no 'if' about it. It's simply 'when' the poor, unsuspecting man falls under your spell. Count me in. I'll make some calls. In the meantime, Cora Withers, the mayor's ex-wife, just wandered into the showroom with an armful of decorating magazines. She doesn't have an appointment. Should I greet her, or will you?"

"You take her, please. I need to research the house that the senator recently bought. I want some new ideas to make it spectacular before I accidentally, but on purpose, meet him in the restaurant. If memory serves, I think that house once belonged to Jackie Kennedy's distant cousin and that I sold it to her about ten years ago."

"I'm sure you did," Lolly grinned. "In the last two decades, you've sold almost every house in Georgetown, some more than once. I think that was the last house you sold before changing careers and we started this business. Remember, I've been diligent and recorded the particulars of every house or apartment you've ever listed or sold, and they're all filed alphabetically in the beige metal cabinets against the back wall of the supply room. Just think what a fascinating book they'd make if anyone took the time to go through them and could read your illegible scrawl."

"Don't disparage my unique handwriting," Dawn objected humorously. "I learned my penmanship at a posh boarding school, and it's served me well ever since, but I admit, sometimes when I'm in a rush it can be a tad difficult to decipher."

Lolly smirked; her point proved. "A tad? When you have a second, I need you to decode the latest invoice you want to send the Simpsons. I can't make sense of your boarding school scribble."

"Really? After all these years? Just do your best," Dawn chuckled and headed to the supply room. Lolly had been her best friend since elementary school and no matter the circumstances, she always made her smile.

CHAPTER 2

Dawn leafed through the photos of the P Street property. She had previously sold it to Lara Kennedy Chapman. At that time, the rooms had been traditionally furnished with threadbare, odd-sized, oriental rugs scattered haphazardly over dark, hardwood floors and a veritable garden of mix-matched upholstered chairs and overstuffed sofas in colorful flower patterns completed the look. Elegant decorating had not been one of Lara's passions. She preferred comfortable furniture where she could put her feet up on the tables and her many rescue dogs could sprawl out next to her. In checking the online pictures of the ten-bedroom listing by Sotheby's, Dawn realized that not much had changed in all these years. The senator was going to have to spend lots of money to bring the house up to twenty-first-century luxury standards and she was counting on being the person to help him do it.

She sometimes still missed the thrill of finding the perfect home for the right buyer and putting them together. Selling residential real estate has always been satisfying and lucrative work. However, she and Lara Chapman had not remained in contact over the years, but the house had great potential and back in the day, she would have killed for the listing. She saw that it had sold for full price in only two days, and for cash...no mortgage. She studied the listing brochure and recognized the realtor.

He was Thomas Joseph Kennedy, a relative. Keeping the hefty sales commission on the 16-million-dollar home in the family coffers was probably important to Lara. Her family was known for being frugal and had apparently passed that concept onto future generations.

Dawn noticed some new watercolor paintings hanging on the walls and many pictures of the former president, and first lady displayed on various tables, but otherwise the home's décor had not changed. The kitchen needed total gutting; the appliances were antiquated, and the cabinet doors had yellowed and were misaligned. The eight bathrooms and three powder rooms were only a step above disgraceful, with peeling wallpaper and old-fashioned plumbing fixtures. Lara had obviously allowed the house to fall into deplorable disrepair. Owning a show place had not been one of her priorities. She was earthy, into rescuing dogs and cats, saving endangered birds in Africa and the sea turtles in Florida. Her only hobby had been gardening and growing prize-winning hybrid roses.

Dawn knew that for Senator Holmes and his child bride, a complete redo of the home would be absolutely necessary. From his reputation, she was aware that he was a driven, determined man, eager for more power and notoriety and out to impress his colleagues and constituents. There was nothing understated or self-effacing in his character or about his ambitions. She expected that he would settle for nothing less than the best, and his new home would reflect that and make an impressive statement to the world. Dawn was confident that if given the chance, she and Sutter Interiors could do the job to his complete satisfaction. And, if his political ambition were realized, she might have the chance of a lifetime – to redecorate the White House.

CHAPTER 3

Dawn took all the information on the P Street home and went back to her office to spread the papers out on her drafting table. She needed to refresh her memory about the layout and floor plan, the room sizes, ceiling heights, thick, intricate moldings, and chair rails, and to try to find a more up-to-date way to feature the home's distinctive architectural features and modernize its insides.

The house had good structural bones but needed a skilled facelift with shots of Botox here and there. She wanted to come up with a plan for an ambitious renovation, so that when Britt asked her for her ideas (and she was determined to set the stage for that to happen), she would be prepared and entice him and his fiancée to hire her on the spot.

Dawn's business rivals were impressed by her phenomenal success but behind her back, they suspected that she sometimes used questionable methods to secure new clients. She, however, thought of herself as merely ingenious and creative. She knew no other way to conduct business and believed in the old adage that the early bird catches the worm. She was tenacious and did not wait for a hapless deer to wander in front of her headlights, but instead, loaded her ammunition in advance and waited strategically for the right moment to pounce. Dawn was always organized and that characteristic, whether good or bad, helped her outshine and outsmart her competitors, making her a successful businesswoman. She was not conniving or underhanded, but as her childhood Girl Scout leader had taught her…she was always prepared.

To start, she looked at the drawings and decided to tackle the main rooms first. She felt that each should reflect the senator's sophisticated taste and subtly reveal his close attention to detail while sparing no cost to achieve perfection. She was astute enough to know that Britt would, at the very least, be solicitous of Charlotte's opinions and want to please her. Dawn, even if it was not her first choice, had to allow for some southern touches that would appeal to the young girl, soon to be the mistress of the stately house. Dawn had to win her over, first and foremost. Charlotte was the key to the senator's pocketbook and a huge commission for Sutter Interiors.

Two hours later she took a break and called Lolly into her office. "How did it go with Mrs. Withers?" she asked curiously. "She can be very opinionated. Did we land her as a client?"

"I think so. She's a bit flustered by the cost of some of the furniture, but she's going to speak to the mayor and see if he'll advance her the money as part of her divorce support. She claims that they have a cordial relationship and she's hopeful that he'll agree. We'll know in a few days, but I have a good feeling about it."

"Great job, Lolly. But now I need your help with this P Street project."

"Oh, now it's already a project, and you haven't even met the owners yet," she chuckled. "You certainly have big kahunas." Laughing, she pulled up a chair.

Dawn took off her reading glasses and smiled warmly at her friend, revealing her big, sable-brown eyes and a wrinkleless forehead. At forty-eight, she was still a beauty, many people thought of her as a

Natalie Woods look- alike, and age had given her wisdom, not facial lines or brown spots. She tucked a wayward strand of brunette hair back into its French casual twist. "I'm always optimistic. But I'm not much into southern décor. All I think about is tall, Waterford crystal vases filled with forsythia or magnolia branches and delicate China tea cups on white frilly lace doilies. Am I wrong? Have I seen too many issues of *Southern Living?*"

Lolly laughed. "There's more to it than that. Don't be so myopic. What do you have in mind?"

"Well, I know to win Senator Holmes over, I'll have to seduce his bride. I remembered on the house's floor plan that there's a long porch running along the length of the back. Lara's only used it to store patio furniture when not in use. I was thinking that I could redo it…paint the inside and the floor a bright color and add interesting light fixtures, ceiling fans, screens, or even sliding glass doors and floorboard heat units to make it usable year-round. An old-fashioned gliding sofa in the center facing several high-back cushioned rocking chairs would be a nice touch. A rope hammock at one end of the room and a built-in bar at the other…a mint julep station, so to speak, would complete the room. What do you think? Would that be enough to win Charlotte Randolph over?

"Well, it's a damn good start. All you're missing is the baked apple pie and sweet tea."

"Any other suggestions?" Dawn rubbed her hands together in concentration. "I'm sure half the design companies in the country are vying for his business."

"Maybe a Sisal rug on the floor?" Lolly suggested thoughtfully. "And by the way, Senator Holmes has a reservation for two this Saturday night at the Wise Owl. Now we also have one there at the same time, a mere two tables away. I told Tony, the maître d', that we're relatives of the senator's bride-to-be and want to surprise her on her birthday. Maître d's love to suck up to customers for big tips, and especially to congressmen and senators. He was only too happy to agree to my request and offered to give her a complimentary cake."

"Is it really her birthday? How convenient."

"No, but Tony doesn't know that. Besides, if you run true to form, we won't be staying long enough for dessert. Mission accomplished before the entrees are served." Dawn was predictable and Lolly knew her so well.

"One can only hope," Dawn grinned. "See you in the morning. I'm off to Chic Hair for highlights and a trim. Call my cell if you need me."

She picked up her new sky-blue Louis Vuitton handbag, her latest present to herself, and jauntily headed to her car. Since there was no husband or man in her life at the moment, she frequently spoiled herself with new purses and expensive jewelry. *Why not?* For all the hard work and long hours she put in, she deserved it. She had no children or close relatives to inherit her money, so why not spend it on herself? Lolly was the sole beneficiary of her will except for a few charities. Dawn claimed that she planned to enjoy life to the fullest and die poor.

Feeling very hopeful that by this time next week she could count Senator Holmes as a client, she was elated. Maybe his P Street home would finally bring her the professional recognition she had always craved. The more excellent work she did, the better her chances of receiving the coveted American Society of Interior Designer (ASID) Award or the Designer of Distinction one. So far both accolades had escaped her, although her showroom's walls were filled with flattering magazine and newspaper articles and numerous citations and plaques crediting her creative and imaginative work. She was positive that redesigning the Senator's home would bring her well-deserved fame in the industry, but first, she would have to give the performance of her life on Saturday night.

CHAPTER 4

The week dragged by endlessly but by Saturday evening, Dawn was as prepared as she could ever be and anxious to make her move. She and Lolly took an Uber to the Wise Owl, deliberately arriving ten minutes late for their dinner reservation. Dawn knew that it was customary in DC for popular restaurants to hold reservations for fifteen minutes before they gave away the table to someone else. She wanted to make an entrance, to attract attention to herself, but only after Senator Holmes and his fiancée had been seated.

Lolly followed the hostess into the room and Dawn strolled behind her, as if she was walking the red carpet at the Oscars. She was dressed in a creamy, perfectly fitted, beige Dior silk pantsuit that clung provocatively to her body's enticing curves and left little to the imagination. She wore four-inch red Louboutin strappy heels that accentuated the shape of her legs and made her appear taller than her five-foot-six frame. Her Tiffany gold and diamond studs glistened in her ears and were her only jewelry and she carried her favorite red Chanel bag. Most heads in the restaurant turned to admire her as she walked by. She looked like a sophisticated model and her statuesque presence seemed to fill every corner of the room. She relished the attention but pretended not to notice.

Senator Holmes looked momentarily away from Charlotte as Dawn entered the room. He was an expert at making grand entrances and calling attention to himself. It was one of the practiced talents that made him such a formidable fundraiser and a skilled politician. He recognized a like-minded person when he saw one. He glanced appreciatively at Dawn, nodding his head almost imperceptibly, giving her his approval.

She pretended not to notice him, and took her seat at the table with Lolly, promptly ordering a glass of champagne from a hovering, solicitous waiter. She and Lolly kept up a lively conversation throughout their Caesar salad and lobster bisque courses, totally ignoring his table. Dawn reached into her bag and pulled out a small notebook and her cellphone. She began pretending to show pictures on it to Lolly, who nodded appreciatively, making occasional comments while Dawn took notes. It was a scene as well acted and rehearsed as any in the theater, but this choreographed performance was for a specific audience of two.

Just before the entrée was served, Dawn stood up, having inconspicuously loosened the strap on her right shoe under the table. She grabbed her phone and began walking slowly towards the ladies' room, directly past Senator Holmes's table. As she approached him, his eyes landed on her face and with one furtive glance, he quickly took in her entire deliciously toned body. She looked up at him shyly and pretended to stumble. Losing her balance, she tripped forward over her hanging shoe strap, and fell indelicately against his table. Fighting to regain her balance, she deliberately dropped her phone on the tablecloth in front of Charlotte. Wine, water glasses, and silverware went flying. The Senator jumped up to help her while Charlotte, looking stunned, began quickly mopping up the spilled drinks with her dinner napkin.

"Oh, I'm so sorry," Dawn blushed, looking earnestly into his eyes. "Forgive my clumsiness. My shoe strap must have come unfastened." She grabbed her ankle and grimaced. "I think it's broken or at least badly strained."

Britt looked around for the nearest waiter. "Please bring this woman a chair. She might need medical attention." He turned back to Dawn who was leaning against the table for support, being careful not to put any weight on her injured ankle. "I'm Britt Holmes," the Senator introduced himself. "This is my fiancée, Charlotte Randolph. "Here," he looked at Dawn sympathetically. "Please take my chair. The waiter will bring me another."

"I'm so sorry to interrupt your evening. Of course, I recognize you, Senator Holmes. I'm Dawn Sutter. And this," she said by way of explanation turning behind her, is my best friend and personal assistant, Lolly Hamm. Right on cue, Lolly had run to Dawn's assistance when she saw her friend begin to fall.

"Are you all right, Dawn," she asked, feigning concern.

"I think so. My ankle's throbbing and I'm about to die from embarrassment," she answered sheepishly, staring at the floor, pretending to be mortified by the commotion she had caused. Most of the other diners had witnessed the scene but returned to enjoying their meals.

Charlotte jumped up and gently helped Dawn into Britt's seat. "My goodness, let's get some ice for your foot. My mama always says ice cures most things…that, and a stiff shot of bourbon." She spoke with a deep southern drawl and genuine concern. Dawn could not help but smile. The woman was delightful.

"You're right, my dear." Britt nodded to Charlotte. "Bourbon fixes almost everything." He asked the flustered waiter to bring a napkin filled with ice for Dawn's ankle. "Please join us, with your friend, of course." He nodded to Lolly politely, but his undivided attention was purely focused on Dawn. "Let's sit and enjoy a drink together and give the ice a chance to work. I'm sure you'll feel better in a few minutes."

"That's very kind of you. I really hope so. I can't afford to be laid up because I have a presentation to make in the morning." Dawn indicated her cell phone. "I was going over the details with Lolly before this happened."

"What kind of a presentation?" Charlotte asked. She thought Dawn was one of the most attractive women she had ever met and was curious about her. She wondered who Dawn was and what did she do for a living?

"I'm an interior designer," Dawn spoke softly. "I own Sutter Interiors on M Street. Perhaps you've heard of it? I'm about to take on a huge home transformation for a very important client and I have to be at my best. The owners are difficult and very opinionated. They challenge me on every decision, but I believe I've come up with some wonderful ideas that even they can't shoot down."

"How interesting," Charlotte said sincerely. "I'm not much into decorating but I know what I like. May I see?" She reached for Dawn's phone and glimpsed a picture of a lovely, screened-in porch. "Oh my, that's beautiful. I adore porches. They remind me of my childhood home. We had a big wrap-around one in Richmond. Can I see some more?"

"I'm afraid not," Dawn answered primly, taking the phone back. "I hope you understand but I take my client's privacy very seriously and can never reveal anything personal about them or their homes. It's a pledge I make to them when they hire me. Complete confidentiality is my motto. My goal is that everyone's home must be completely original, not a copycat of some magazine picture. Each should tell its own personal story – not showcase my decorating skills. A beautiful home must truly represent the personality of its owners."

The senator was impressed. He carefully lifted the makeshift ice bag off Dawn's ankle. "I think we caught this in time. There doesn't seem to be any swelling." He touched it gently and she pretended to flinch. "Maybe you should go home and prop your foot up on some pillows."

Dawn nodded, seductively smoothing her pant leg down and removing her other shoe. "I think it's safer if I walk out of here barefooted," she explained with a hint of a smile. "You both have been very kind. Again, I apologize for interrupting your evening. I think I'll take your suggestion and go home to elevate my ankle. Hopefully I'll be able to walk properly by the morning."

She rose carefully, smiled warmly at Charlotte and the senator, and with Lolly's help, limped dramatically to the door. Handing the maître d' her credit card, she asked him to charge the senator's dinner to her Amex and expressed her regret for causing a disturbance. "The food I ate before I tripped was delicious, and I'll definitely be back." He accepted her card and a fifty-dollar tip.

"That went well," Lolly grinned as they waited on the sidewalk for an Uber. "Picture perfect, in fact. You never cease to amaze me. Acting really should have been your career."

Dawn smiled playfully. "Now all I have to do is wait for the senator to call in the morning." She put her high heels back on as the car service arrived. "Do you want to go somewhere for a bite to eat? I'm still hungry."

CHAPTER 5

The next day, Dawn paced around the showroom, waiting impatiently for Senator Holmes's phone call. She assumed he would reach out to her that afternoon, believing she was busy in the morning with her so-called client presentation. She was not wrong. At 1:30 p.m., the office phone rang, and he asked to speak with her.

"Good afternoon, Dawn," he said brightly. When she picked up the line: "It's Britt Holmes."

"Oh yes, of course," she answered, trying to sound as if she had not been expecting his call.

"Charlotte and I are wondering about your ankle and hoping your morning presentation went well."

"Oh yes," she said, smiling to herself. "Thank you for checking on me. It did go very well and my ankle's a little sore but it's fine."

"That's good news." He sounded relieved. "We were worried that you might have a hairline fracture."

Dawn remained quiet and waited for him to speak. In her experience, negotiating real estate contracts and complex interior design arrangements, the first person to speak usually lost. Silence was golden.

Britt began again. "Last night, in the midst of your ankle trauma, Charlotte saw a picture on your phone of what appeared to be a southern-style screened porch you were creating for a client. She liked it very much and said it reminded her of her parent's home in Virginia. As you may have heard, I recently purchased an older house on P Street in Georgetown and now I need to find a decorator to handle the renovation and the furnishings. We'd both like you to come by the house as soon as possible and take a look. We think we'd enjoy working with you." He paused and took a deep breath. "It might be a little challenging because Charlotte is quite young and has no definite style preferences. I'm much older – thirty years in fact – and quite set in my ways with very traditional leanings. I'm willing to compromise a little to make her happy, but only a little. As you may have heard, I've been exploring a future presidential run, and want my home to reflect my personality with particular atten-tion to the history of our forefathers, excellent craftsmanship and, of course, elegance. It must be a real show place, *Architectural Digest* cover worthy, but with private, cozy spots where I can relax. It must also have spaces for me to do elegant formal entertaining. Money is not an object. I want the best of the best. Are you interested?"

What designer wouldn't be? "Yes, of course," she answered, trying to sound casual and hide her excitement. "Actually, I sold that same house to Lara Kennedy over ten years ago, so I'm very familiar with it. However, I'm completely overwhelmed with previous commitments right now," she fibbed. "I can't possibly see you for another week or so...if you can't wait, I'll certainly understand. I could refer you to someone else." She crossed her fingers and held her breath. Playing hard to get usually worked, but this was a huge gamble.

He took a long time to speak – her entire professional future hinged on this bluff. She could not appear anxious or too willing to drop every-thing for him. It was the kind of reaction that he had come to expect, people groveling and sucking up to him. Dawn was not going to fall into that trap or become one of his groupies. She believed that for a professional relationship to work, she had to be the person in charge. By nature, she was not dishonest or conniving; on the contrary, she was straitlaced and a rule-follower, except when it came to securing clients. There, she was a little more creative in her approaches than most of her colleagues. Her results were proof enough that her methods worked.

* *

Dawn had been self-supporting since age twenty when her parents died in a freak small plane accident leaving her no money and some sizable credit card debts. With no husband or family to help her, she was forced to drop out of Georgetown University and immediately acquired her real estate license. She made a success of herself, relying solely on her own intelligence and her wit. At twenty-three, she set out to prove her worth to herself and to her co-workers, and she did. Thirteen years later, as one of the most successful agents in the area, she decided to change professions and went to school to become an interior designer. At age forty, she fearlessly started her own business, Sutter Interiors, with a wallet full of debt but an iron determination to succeed. As she began to make a name for herself in the industry, it was not the money, but the look of happiness on her clients' faces and their grateful praise at the end of their project that motivated her. She had made enough money over her career and invested it wisely so that it was secondary now. In some cases, she barely charged anything just to see a smile on a client's satisfied face or to work with someone she admired and wanted to get to know. Pride in her work and pleasing people inspired her the most.

Dawn had never had a husband or any children. She enjoyed dating and loved socializing with her many friends, but she was married to her career and perfectly happy with that arrangement. She did not feel that she was missing out on anything, especially when she listened to one dis-illusioned girlfriend after another, disparage their husbands or ramble on and on about their nasty divorces. If she felt a maternal need, she would spoil her several Godchildren, but she had never wanted to be a mother. Parenting was not in her DNA. She preferred to spend her time visiting famous designers around the world and learning from them, rather than sitting in a high school auditorium to watch a child tap dance or play the flute. "Each to her own," she said whenever anyone questioned lifestyle. "Each to her own."

She also believed in paying life forward and was grateful for every-thing she had. Volunteering weekly at a center for distressed women, she often used her own money to buy the frightened girls new clothing, tele-visions, books, or games to distract their children from the abusive men in their lives. She kept that philanthropic side to herself, and few peo-ple knew of her generosity. Occasionally when she saw a client's budget maxing out, she reduced her prices but never owned up to the practice. Only Lolly knew.

* *

Britt listened to Dawn's excuse about being so busy and sighed deeply. He was surprised and a little annoyed. He had expected that she would willingly drop everything and come rushing over to his house. He was not sure if it was her professional services as a designer or the beautiful woman herself that he wanted... but he definitely wanted to see her again, under any guise. He was not used to being rejected. "I, we, will wait for you. When can you get around to us?" He sounded irritated but resigned.

"If you leave your contact information with my secretary, I'll call you as soon as I can clear my schedule, probably at the beginning of next week."

"I guess that'll have to do." He was not happy. Britt Holmes was a man who knew what he wanted and how to get it. Not being the one in control was new to him, and he did not like it...not one bit.

"All right then. Thanks so much for calling. I'll be in touch." She hung up before he could extend the conversation. She grinned. *So far, so good.*

She had an enormous smile planted on her face when she shouted into the intercom. "Lolly, I think I just landed the future president of the United States as our newest client."

CHAPTER 6

Dawn had been extremely busy all week meeting with clients and collaborating with her other designers. She made special trips to the Washington Design Center twice in search of specific fabrics and unique wall coverings to add to her collection for different jobs and she was looking for a specific size of marble end table and a comfortable bedroom settee for another.

Running her business was time consuming but she could easily have put a visit to Britt and Charlotte's home on her schedule. She had chosen not to. She wanted to make them wait so that they would be anxious to see her and seriously consider her suggestions. Over the weekend, she spent numerous hours poring over the house's original floor plans which she obtained from Lara Kennedy's file, and she devised preliminary furniture layouts to scale. The more Dawn worked on them, the more creative and excited she became. The house had spectacular architectural features and with the right improvements and décor, it could be everything the senator wanted and more.

She waited until Monday afternoon before reaching out to Charlotte. Working closely with the woman of a couple was usually the first and best choice. She could, in most cases, cajole her partner into going along with Dawn's ideas. In this case, she understood that Britt would be the final decision-maker, but she wanted Charlotte to feel valued and heard. There must be no jealousy, no pulling rank between designer and client or the results could be disastrous. For a smooth finish, she needed Charlotte on her side…to be her ally, not her adversary.

"Hi, Charlotte," she began cheerfully when the bride-to-be picked up her phone. "It's Dawn Sutter. I've been busy working on ideas for your home and would like to schedule a time to visit the house in person. It's been years since I've been inside. I'd like to meet with you and the senator at the same time."

"Oh, I'm so glad to hear from you Sweetie," Charlotte said in her soft southern drawl. "We're both so anxious to get started. I know Britt has a hectic schedule this week with hearings and there's an important vote on the floor about some immigration thing. I didn't really pay attention." She sighed. "Government is a very boring and complicated business."

"Yes, I suppose it is," Dawn answered, rolling her eyes at Charlotte's naivety. *How could the possible future First Lady care so little about politics?*

"Should I check with Owen Marshall? He's Britt's chief aide. I can ask him about a date, or we could just make one and hope he can join us?"

"Of course I would like the senator's input, but I understand how busy he is. Suppose the two of us plan to meet first and once we've made a few basic decisions; we can include him…unless he insists on being there."

"Oh, that would be perfect. Mama's given me loads of magazine clippings and lists of questions to ask you."

Oh Dear, Dawn thought with dismay. *Now I'll have to deal with Charlotte's mother too.*

"Are you free at noon tomorrow? I can meet you then." Dawn suggested.

"Sure," Charlotte replied enthusiastically.

"We'll go through your ideas. And if you find that the senator is available then, you can ask him to join us, but we'll be fine, just the two of us at this initial meeting. If we go forward with this project together, we'll be meeting and talking together all the time. You'll be sick of me at the end."

"Oh, my goodness. I doubt that and for sure, we'll go forward. Britt said not to tell you, but he's not even interviewing anyone else. He says he knows your professional reputation and he wants you and only you."

"How nice." Dawn smiled to herself. "I'll see you tomorrow."

Well, that went well, she thought. She would have preferred to have a private one-on-one with Britt, but it was a sensible move to humor Charlotte. At present, her opinions seemed to matter to him, but Dawn suspected that might change in time.

CHAPTER 7

Dawn parked her silver Mercedes sedan on the street and leisurely strolled up the pathway towards the front door of the stately brick home on P Street. She admired the beautiful red and white azalea bushes in full bloom and the weedless green grass on the neighbor's lawns. In comparison, the senator's yard looked unkempt and trashy. She made a mental note to suggest a landscaping company to Charlotte. The house, when finished, should be beautiful inside – her job – but also have gorgeous curb appeal – a professional gardener's job. The two must come together to create the right image.

The front door swung open before her hand reached the doorbell and Charlotte rushed out, falling heavily into Dawn's arms. "Welcome, welcome. Thank you for coming." She tugged off her silk Hermes neck scarf, mopped her forehead, and stuffed it hastily into her pocket. "It's so hot and stuffy inside. It makes me perspire and Mama always says that a lady must never sweat in public – except in the gym," she giggled. "It's so good to see you again."

"And I, you," Dawn answered, a little flabbergasted by the unexpectedly exuberant welcome. "It's nice to see you again too, Charlotte." She tried to extricate herself from the young woman's firm grasp, while clutching the two oversized canvas bags she'd brought with the Sutter Interiors logo embossed on them. "Can we go inside please? These bags are heavy."

"Oh sure." Charlotte blushed. "Of course, come in. But I have to warn you, this place is a mess. Somehow, I managed to make a pitcher of my mama's sweet tea for us and bought us some brownies. I set everything up in the library. We can talk there. It's the only room in this mausoleum that has any furniture. Britt bought the God-awful stuff in that room from the seller, but he threw everything else out. At least we'll have somewhere to sit."

Charlotte looked distastefully around the library and winced. "My clever fiancée had his congressional staff come here a few days ago to hang a TV on the wall for me. I'm not much of a reader," she admitted candidly. "Anyway, his people set up a desk area so Britt can get some work done when he's here and they put together a makeshift bar with his favorite drinks, Diet Cokes, Maker's Mark Bourbon, and Kistler Chardonnay. He jokes that the room is his temporary mancave. Everything in it, in the whole damn house for that matter, except the TV, is old, dark, and dingy. I think it's depressing and creepy. I have no idea why he loves it so much. Sometimes I hear strange noises and they frighten me. Britt thinks I'm being ridiculous, but Mama says ghosts hang around and haunt old houses after someone dies in them. Once they're entrenched, they're hard to get rid of. I bet one's living upstairs." She shivered and gulped down her tea. "Do you believe in ghosts, Dawn?" Charlotte's green eyes were wide with fear. "Did anyone die in this house that you know about?"

"I don't think so," Dawn stifled a chuckle, "but I'll do some research if it'll make you feel any better. Britt may know something. Have you asked him?"

"Oh no. I wouldn't dare. He'd think I was a little crazy like my Mama. But I would appreciate you checking into it for me...just between us girls, of course."

"You have my word. I'll be very discreet, but could we talk about this house now and what you and Britt would like me to achieve here for you."

"I can only speak for myself," she answered. "I hate this house more each day and yet Britt tells everyone that he bought it to make me happy. That's not true. He can surely tell a little white lie when it suits him. He knows I've always wanted to live in a wide-open loft somewhere with soaring ceilings, contemporary art, and lots of skylights. My father owns an art gallery, and he could fill the walls with beautiful pictures. But Britt thinks lofts and modern art are for hippies and not grand enough for his tastes. His plan is for us to move in here after we get married. But right now, and unless you completely change this place, you couldn't pay me a wooden nickel to sleep a night here."

"You like this place that much?" Dawn chuckled. Charlotte Randolph was going to be a handful and needed lots of TLC to bring her around to loving what Dawn suspected Britt wanted to do with his home. "I'll do my best to make you love this house when I'm done," she promised gently as Charlotte made a horrified face.

Dawn was afraid that she might have finally met a challenge that she could not meet. She suspected that Charlotte, with all her silly, southern belle charms, was formidable and strong as steel. Dawn did not want to put her to the test.

She did, however, agree that some of Charlotte's observations about the house were correct. The entire place was rundown, shabby, dreary, and smelled of dampness and mold. She looked up at the yellowing ceiling plaster between the dark wood beams and saw the telltale signs of water intrusion. *How could Lara have neglected the house so horribly? It was unconscionable.*

Once she and Charlotte had settled in, and had made a polite attempt to drink the sweet tea and engage in some polite small talk, Dawn became all business. "As the Senator – by the way – may I call him Britt? Senator Holmes is a bit of a mouthful to say in every other sentence."

"Sure, Sweetie. Whatever you like. I'm not the formal type."

"Okay, then, as Britt must have shared with you, this home was built in the late 1700s and designed by the architect of The US Capitol. It became a showplace for politicians, statesmen, and visiting dignitaries, and during the Truman administration, it was used as an additional guest house for the White House in much the same way that Blair House is today. Supposedly, Presidents Washington and Adams, the Shah of Iran, and even Robert Frost, the poet, spent time here."

"So, I've been told." She stifled a yawn. "They're welcome to it. I think they were all a bunch of old fuddy-duddies."

"Maybe," Dawn snickered, "but history has its place in this world, and this house exudes it, whether you like it or not. One doesn't often find homes in this area on so much land with two formal parlors, a portrait gallery, a formal dining room able to seat twenty guests and a backyard with a proper English garden and a private maze. It's almost too big for a private residence and more suited to being an embassy. I can see by look-ing out the window that the previous owner, while she let the rest of the landscaping go to ruin, kept her rose garden in tip-top shape. And look around this house. There's such exquisite craftsmanship and architectural details in every room."

"Oh sure. You mean like the rusty sinks that choke and gurgle and the disgusting toilets that barely have enough water pressure to flush?"

"That too." Dawn could not help but laugh. Charlotte was refreshingly honest. "All of that can be fixed, I promise, but we first need to concentrate on the theme of the house…what we want it to say about Senator and Mrs. Britt Holmes to anyone walking through the door."

"I'm not sure what you mean by that. My Mama always says that a house should be welcoming, and that the furniture and floors must shine like diamonds. She doesn't tolerate a speck of dust anywhere. And there should always be the smell of freshly baked cookies or pies in the air. I don't believe she ever said anything about it having to tell a story. That sounds pretty odd to me."

"You're Mama's only partially right, at least in regard to historical homes. Properties of this caliber should reflect their heritage, acknowledge, and honor the kinds of people who lived in them previously, and be a stepping-stone into the future. A newly renovated historical house should maintain its original elegance and opulence but provide all the modern and luxurious conveniences available. It can, as your mother pointed out, also smell of delicious cookies or pies," Dawn conceded with a genuine smile. She was growing to like Charlotte but was having a hard time imagining her ever loving this house – no matter what she did to improve it.

"By modern conveniences do you mean stuff like running water and central heating and air conditioning?" Charlotte made another face. "I should hope so. But after you're done, we can make up a story, if you think it's important."

Dawn realized that Charlotte had no idea what she was talking about, so she dropped the subject for the time being.

"Can you show me what you brought in your bags? Are they drawings or pictures? And I've been thinking, I definitely want a screened-in porch, a large hot tub, and a fire pit for roasting marshmallows."

Dawn exhaled deeply and deliberately kept her facial expression bland. She brought out a few pictures of room layouts she had drawn over the weekend and began to explain her fundamental 60/40 philosophy...60 percent of a room's floor space should be filled with furniture and 40 percent left open. As she continued, she could see Charlotte's eyes glazing over in boredom.

How did Britt end up with this child-like woman? He should be with someone much more sophisticated. What made him choose Charlotte from all the eligible women in the country? How could he hope to become president with her as his first lady?

Charlotte was sweet and nice enough, but she had the attention span of a gnat and clearly no interest in politics or interior design. *Was she even in love with Britt? Why had she agreed to marry him? They were so different - a very odd, mismatched couple. There had to be more to the story of their romance.* Dawn was very curious but did not have time to probe into the senator's love life. Her only task was to redo his home.

"Maybe I should leave all this decorating stuff to you and Britt," Charlotte suggested uneasily. "How about if I talk with Mama, and we make a list of the things I want, and then you and Britt can take it from there. He's into all this stuff and I'm just not." She rose, clearly uncomfortable and wanting to be something else. "I'll tell Britt what we decided, but I have a Pilates class in an hour. Thanks for coming. Good meeting."

Dawn frowned, crunched up her face and began to gather up her materials. This get-together had clearly been a waste of her time. She would call Britt tomorrow and insist he meet with her. If he wouldn't take the time to come to her, then she'd schlep everything to his office. It was going to be all but impossible to deal with Charlotte, who had no idea

44

about the importance of Britt making a statement and projecting that image with his home decor. *A hot tub, and roasting marshmallows? Really?*

"I'll work everything out, so you and Britt will be happy here. Enjoy your class. I'll be in touch." Dawn spoke through clenched teeth.

"Good, here's the key. I won't be needing it. Just pull the door closed when you leave." Charlotte was out the door with a flaunty wave. "Hope you don't run into the ghost."

Dawn shook her head at the folly of youth and then took out her tape measure and her phone. She decided as long as she was there, she should spend a few hours wandering throughout the house, taking videos of the rooms, and making verbal commentaries and written notes. The house was old and in dire need of renovations, but it was a magnificent structure, and she was sure that she could transform it to far better than its original splendor, as long as Charlotte didn't throw a monkey wrench into her plans. She had to ensure that did not happen.

She was busy the next day and did not have time to call Senator Holmes until the late afternoon. "I met with Charlotte yesterday," she said with no preamble. "I'm afraid it didn't go so well. You and I need to talk."

"I suspected as much. Your place or mine?" He did not seem surprised by the frustration he detected in Dawn's voice.

"It's getting dark, and the house has poor lighting, so I suggest my showroom or your place. I'll need to spread floor plans out on a table and show you some drawings."

"I'm heading home now to my condo in the Watergate. Come to my place. I have a rare night off and Charlotte's having dinner with her parents, so the evening is ours." He gave her the address.

He hung up smiling.

She hung up grinning.

CHAPTER 8

Two hours later, Dawn arrived at The Watergate complex and made her way to Britt's condominium. She had taken the time to shower, fix her hair, and change her clothes. Dressed in a short navy and white linen dress with matching navy ballet shoes, she looked refreshed and sexy. Carrying her signature red Chanel bag and two canvas work satchels, she juggled them carefully as she reached for the knocker on his door.

"So I won't trip again," she explained with a giggle when she saw him looking curiously at her shoes. "I'm completely recovered now. It turned out to be nothing, only an embarrassment, but otherwise we might never have met, so I owe this meeting to my stilettos."

He smiled warmly, his eyes taking in every detail of her appearance, and he offered her a drink. She politely refused.

"Business first. I'd rather have a serious discussion about the house and afterwards I'll be happy to have a drink."

"Okay, then." He led her to the dining room table and removed the centerpiece. He liked that she was singularly focused on the job. "You can spread everything out here."

She reached into her bags and pulled out several stacks of paper, and two books of fabric samples. "I warn you; to do this right, we'll have to meet many times during this project and tackle one room at a time. But for tonight, I'd like to go over some basic simple premises so I'm sure I know exactly what you and Charlotte have in mind, the kind of statement you want the house to make, and naturally any budgetary restrictions I must abide by."

"The budget will not be a stumbling block as long as you keep me well-informed and use common sense. But I warn you, I detest plaids. Please keep that in mind. Do you have a contract for me to sign?"

"Yes, right here." She reached into her purse and pulled out an envelope. "It's our standard employment one, but don't you want to see my ideas first?"

"That won't be necessary. I know in my gut that you understand exactly what I want. I'm very busy and have a lot of traveling and schmoozing to do in the next year, so you'll be left pretty much on your own. I'll check in with you from time to time, but you'll have to make many final decisions if I'm unavailable. Do not concern yourself with Charlotte. Do you agree?"

"I guess so," she answered in surprise. "You don't know me at all. How can you be so trusting? Aren't you afraid I'll make a costly mistake?"

"No, because I'm good at reading people and know how to delegate. Dawn, you must trust that I know what I'm doing, in much the same way I'll have to trust what you're going to do. Now, with that out of the way, can we proceed?"

She nodded somewhat reluctantly and realized that as much as she had orchestrated for it to happen, she was not the one in control. The power in their dynamics had shifted in his favor.

"Here," he smiled and handed her a black leather briefcase, flipped open the catch and told her that it contained half-a-million dollars in cash. "This is my deposit to show my confidence in you. I know you won't let me down. I have also included a POA, my power of attorney, so you can sign any necessary papers on my behalf. The only stipulation I have is that the house must be finished by the end of the year…no extensions, no exceptions. This is April, so that gives you eight months. I plan to officially announce my candidacy for the presidency sometime in the fall and enter the primaries in January. I want to be living in the P Street house before then. Can you adhere to that timetable? It's an absolute deal breaker."

She nodded. "Yes, it will be tight, but I'll do whatever I have to in order to make it happen." She looked at the briefcase, dismayed. "Frankly, I've never seen so much cash, not even in a casino." She fingered the money gingerly. "It's customary to pay by check or with a credit card. How can I walk around town with half-a-million dollars?"

"Carefully," he grinned, "But seriously, no one will know what's in the briefcase, but you must guard it well and you take it to your bank first thing tomorrow morning."

"Thank you," she managed to say, fighting the compelling urge to leap into the air and shout giddily to the heavens. This was by far the biggest job she had ever undertaken and the biggest deposit she had ever received…and also the most unusual. If she had not been so excited about redoing his house, she might have listened to the warning bells that should have gone off in her brain. *Why wasn't so much cash a red flag to her?*

He ignored her obvious surprise at the money in the briefcase and continued talking. "I want the house to show my genuine interest in our country's history and especially in our forefathers. The furnishings must fit in with my serious side but show a little whimsy. I have constituents and donors all around the country that I'll need to entertain and impress there. In the meantime, I have to win over an entire nation and convince them that I'm presidential material. Living in this magnificent home will help me project an image of stability and hopefully instill confidence, very unlike what's happening with my opponent, our ditzy incumbent who spends most of his time on vacation."

"That sounds like a well-rehearsed campaign speech," she said diplomatically. "But I understand your point."

He paused for a moment and shifted position. "You'll find, once you get to know me better, that I have a great appreciation for finer things in life. I'm not stuffy or pretentious. My home can't be too glitzy…no solid gold plumbing fixtures or chairs that resemble royal thrones everywhere, like the ones on display in Trump Towers or in Mar-a-Lago. Class with understated dignity is how I would describe my style. My goal is for a plumber, an electrician, a Supreme Court justice, or a Pulitzer Prize author to feel equally comfortable and welcome home in my home. I know you're the perfect woman to create that atmosphere."

"I'm flattered," she answered modestly, but was a little overwhelmed. This was a dream job, the chance of a lifetime. "I hope I don't disappoint. I truly believe that I understand what you need but that's quite a wish list for me to create in one mere house."

He winked. "I know. But that's exactly the reason I hired you. I've been told by many people that you are one of the very best in the world at what you do…so I'm counting on you to do it for me."

She noticed he only talked about his image, his dream for the house and had not mentioned Charlotte once. Did he not care what his future wife wanted?

"I'll do all that I can." She began to point to the schematics she'd drawn and wanted to show him more of her ideas, but he continued talking over her. It was as if he was reading a speech on a teleprompter and could not shut it off.

"There must be rooms that are designated specifically to accommodate elegant cocktail and dinner parties, and there should also be a state-of-the-art catering kitchen in addition to the regular household one."

"Yes, I've already thought of that, and I've also added a full summer kitchen with a large bar-b-que area on the back patio for spring and summer outdoor events."

He smiled in appreciation. "This house has to be a real home, not just a staged setting. I need inviting and cozy spaces where I can relax. Show me what else you have in mind." He pulled up a dining room chair and gave her his full attention. He sat so close to her that she could smell his Old Bay cologne. It was intoxicating and his body so close to hers made it hard for her to concentrate.

She took a deep breath and looked down at her drawings. "When I first start a house, particularly an historic one like yours, I ask myself, what can I keep and what needs to be changed or discarded. I've spent considerable time in all of the rooms and made a list. I'll go over it with you at a later time. For now, let me say, the house, which by the way, you should name, has great potential. I can make it everything you and Charlotte want and more."

He smiled. "Go on. I think you're right. A named house signifies that it's important. Do you have any suggestions?"

"I haven't given it much thought, but Heritage House comes to mind."

"Not bad," he grinned. "It's worth considering. I can visualize the brass plaque mounted to the threshold now."

"I'm glad you like it." She moved away a little to regain her focus on the project and away from the heat she felt generating from his body. "But I must warn you that the design process never really ends. There'll always be room for change and growth going forward. You can redo color

51

schemes and buy different furniture if you tire of what you have selected, but the bones, the skeleton of the home, should remain pretty much as-is with the exception of taking down a wall or two to repurpose a room. As an example, I think enlarging the present kitchen by taking some square footage from the adjacent four-car garage will make perfect sense. Also, enlarging the primary bedroom suite by including the extra guest room and bath next to it would be a huge improvement. But more about that later. Let me start with showing you a sketch of what I think we should do with the two formal parlors and the gallery hall between them. See if you like my ideas and we'll start there."

An hour-and-a-half later, they were still poring over her designs. Britt was thrilled with what he saw. Dawn had a vision and sense of style that was matchless. She had captured his wishes precisely...down to the smallest detail, and her eye for blending architectural details with more contemporary features was extraordinary. Her concept of a portrait gallery, which would display oil-on-canvas paintings of the most prominent and influential American presidents, lined up in chronological order, and interspersed with painting of historical events like George Washington crossing the Delaware and the Battle of Gettysburg, was inspiring and surpassed his wildest expectations. His gallery would look like a mini–Smithsonian Museum and make a great conversation subject.

"This is going to be spectacular! I'm so energized and thrilled by what you've done. We've got to have some champagne to celebrate the beginning of this transformation and then we'll continue."

"Only if you twist my arm," she laughed and followed him to the bar. With practiced ease, he uncorked the bottle. They sat on leather stools there, enjoying the bubbly, and continued talking about the house, his political ambitions, and his upcoming fundraising trips. Occasionally their knees touched, or he brushed his arm against hers and she felt sparks like little electric charges. She wondered if he felt them too. She should not be having these thoughts about a soon-to-be-married man. It was disconcerting but she was caught up in his charisma. It was magnetic.

"I'm not sure that Charlotte's as big into history and traditional furnishings as you are." She approached the topic carefully, treading lightly. It could be a touchy subject. She wanted to sound him out a little about his fiancée and their different tastes, but she had to be cautious, not confrontational or catty.

"Yes, I know. But it's because she's so young and has been completely sheltered by her parents. Her naivety and innocence are what I like about her the most and it's also my greatest source of irritation. She hasn't learned much about our country's beginnings or its history. I wish her parents had given her a broader education – a more realistic view of the world and the US's place in it. Instead, she was raised to believe that if something didn't happen in the deep South, then it didn't happen at all. She honestly believes that the Civil War was about Rhett Butler and Scarlett O'Hara. I want to change that myopic focus and teach her the ways of the world, but it's been slow going."

"You mean something like what Professor Henry Higgins did with Eliza Doolittle in *My Fair Lady*?"

"Yes, exactly." He laughed. "I'm a theater buff and often reference plays or musicals in my speeches. But, as I recall, Eliza Dolittle wanted to better herself and learn. I'm not sure Charlotte does. She's happy to spend her days drinking sweet tea or gin fizzes with her friends, shopping and taking endless Pilates and spinning classes."

"So, what," Dawn asked delicately, "with all your differences, ever made you propose to her?"

His eyes widened. Dawn Sutter was one bold lady. No one else had ever had the nerve to confront him so directly about his feelings for Charlotte or his reasons for proposing to her. His friends joked and skirted around the issue. They insinuated that he was letting his pecker lead him, not his common sense. They were wrong. She was pretty but he was not sexually enamored with her. No one knew the real truth about their relationship – no one, except Charlotte and her father.

He looked at Dawn, who until tonight had been a practical stranger, and could not believe how comfortable he felt with her and that he was tempted to confide in her, of all the people he knew. Instinctively he believed she was honorable, and that he could trust her. He had struggled with his decision to marry Charlotte and the stress of it had given him recent heart palpitations. A cardiologist prescribed a mild antidepressant, but the pills did not work. He was still conflicted and torn between what he needed and what he knew was right. Lately he made some difficult and questionable decisions. *Had his engagement to Charlotte been one of those?*

"My friends tell me I'm crazy," he admitted candidly. "They say Charlotte's too young and unsophisticated for me and that I'm in a pro-verbial middle-age crisis. Also, that if I'm to be president one day, and I admit, that's a big 'if,' but something I really want, I'll need someone more polished and worldly by my side. Believe me when I say that at the time, I thought I had no other choice than to propose and now I'm stuck. I made a precipitous decision. But I keep going back to the fact that frankly, I don't think I can win a national election as a single man. There hasn't been a widower in the White House since our twenty-eighth pres-ident, Woodrow Wilson. The public likes the image of a happily married couple, with a few children thrown in on the side. Not that I'll have kids. Fifty-two is too old to begin fatherhood. It would not be fair to either a child or to myself, no matter how much domestic help and nannies that I can afford to hire or how much my wife wants children."

Lost in thought, his body tensed, and his facial expression stiffened. He seemed to withdraw into private thought. Taking a huge swig of champagne, he refilled his glass. Abruptly changing his mind, he dumped the bubbly into the sink and reached for a bottle of bourbon instead, momentarily forgetting or choosing to ignore that Dawn was there. She sat quietly, watching him and wondering what was going on and why his demeanor had changed so suddenly from relaxed to anguished, maybe even frightened at the mention of his wedding to Charlotte.

Britt finally looked up, noticed her bewildered expression. No pithy comments or wise words of wisdom came to mind. He had unwittingly started something that he was not prepared to finish, at least not yet. "I have time," he swallowed hard. "It's seven months before the wedding. It's scheduled for November 10. A lot can change between now and then."

"Yes, I suppose it can," she mused, uncertain what to say next. She suddenly felt uncomfortable and out of place. Minutes before they had been enjoying friendly conversation and been so attuned in their thoughts on the house, but something had radically changed. "Do you still want me to redesign your house?" she asked nervously. "Should I continue with my presentation?"

"Yes, to your first question but not tonight. I'm sorry but I suddenly feel wiped out, and I have a lot to wrestle with and resolve. Talking to you has made that very clear. Can we take this decorating business up again in a few days?"

"Certainly. I'll begin applying for the necessary building permits and proceed with what we've already discussed until you call me." She hurriedly stuffed her papers and fabrics books randomly back into her bags, sensing he wanted to be alone. She glanced apprehensively at the brief-case full of money. "Should I really take this to the bank?"

"Yes," he nodded, still lost in private thought.

She made her way to the elevator door. "Thanks for the champagne. I hope I didn't upset you by asking about Charlotte." It was all she could think to say. "I didn't mean to overstep. She's a very nice person. I just don't picture her as the First Lady."

"No, no, you didn't speak out of line. I've had the same thoughts, just not had the gumption to say the words out loud. Believe me, you're a breath of fresh air, a rarity in my world." He sighed deeply. "Sometimes it takes a stranger to point out the obvious. My relationship with Charlotte's a touchy subject and one that I have to resolve one way or the other soon. Good night, Dawn. Thank you – for everything."

She left feeling strangely dispirited and oddly unsettled.

CHAPTER 9

Dawn was usually tired after her long days of dealing with clients and their particular needs, so most nights she fell into bed and slept soundly, but not this night.

Her meeting with Britt left her feeling uneasy and bewildered. It had started off well. He had obviously been pleased and more than liked her suggestions. Then, she stupidly opened her mouth and rudely asked about Charlotte and the reason for their engagement. That was when his attitude and demeanor abruptly changed. *Why had she been so nosy?* Her curiosity might have cost her a huge commission and the bragging rights to the most ambitious and prestigious project she had ever undertaken. But she thought with a ray of optimism, she still had his briefcase of money by her bed, so all might not be lost.

Tossing and turning, she vividly recalled the entire evening and their lengthy conversations. *What had Britt meant when he mentioned that the wedding was a long way off and that things could change? Was he getting cold feet about making Charlotte his wife or remarriage in general?*

Under the sheets, she moved her vibrator over her legs and up between her legs. She moaned with pleasure as she recalled the sensual feeling of her knee touching him. *Had she imagined it? Was she seriously becoming infatuated with the handsome senator from Delaware. Could he possibly feel the same way?* She shivered at the thought and after satisfying herself, she put the vibrator away and eventually fell into a fitful sleep. She dreamed about wearing gorgeous ball gowns and hosting diplomatic dinners for foreign dignitaries and heads of state in the White House State Dining Room as President Britt Holmes's popular and much-beloved wife.

In the morning, with her first cup of coffee in hand, she scanned the newspapers as was her usual daily habit and saw a blurb about a well-known investment banker's upcoming divorce. She sometimes wished that she was still in real estate. A costly divorce usually meant selling one jointly owned property and purchasing two new individual ones… three transactions from one marriage on the rocks. Dawn's interior design business was more lucrative but much more time consuming and difficult. She made a mental note to reach out to the soon-to-be ex-wife and offer her Sutter Interiors decorating services and her sympathy about the divorce.

A few hours later Lolly led the usual morning briefing with the other designers and then pulled Dawn aside. "When I came in today there was a message on the answering machine for you from Senator Holmes. I'm surprised he didn't call you directly. You met with him yesterday, didn't you?"

"Yes, last night actually." Dawn was puzzled. "But I'm truly not sure how it went. What did he say?"

"That he's going away and would be in touch."

"Well, that sounds okay. He did warn me that he'll be doing a lot of traveling. In the meantime, I guess I can get started on construction estimates. He's put me in total charge of the project, which is awesome, but he's given me an almost impossible completion deadline of November. We're going to have to personally go to the city and pull a lot of strings and call in some special favors to get the permits issued quickly enough.

THE HOUSE on P STREET

We'll need to yank our people off other jobs and switch them to the P Street house to finish it up on time."

We'll need to yank our people off other jobs and switch them to the P Street house to finish it up on time."

"Where there's a will, there's a way."

"Easy for you to say," Dawn chuckled. "I'll be the one doing the yanking. But you're not wrong."

"It was the last line of his message that confused me." Lolly raised her eyebrows. "He said that under no circumstance should you meet with or talk to Charlotte in his absence. He was insistent that you avoid her completely until he can speak to you again. She's going to live in that house. Wouldn't you think she'd want some input? It doesn't make any sense?"

"Yes, she should definitely have a say in what happens there but honestly, there's something a little off between those two. I can't put my finger on it, but he doesn't act like a man who's madly in love and planning a life together with her. He told me that I was to make all the decisions when he was unavailable. He never mentioned running any ideas by Charlotte or getting her approval. It's as if her wishes don't matter – a strange way to start a marriage."

"That is odd," Lolly agreed. "But you never know what goes on behind closed doors. Maybe they have an arrangement?"

"Possibly," Dawn said soberly, "but there's one more thing. He gave me a deposit, but it was in cash, piles, and piles of hundred-dollar bills." She indicated a black crocodile briefcase sitting on a table next to her Chanel purse and sunglasses. "He instructed me to deposit the money into our business account today…" and before she could explain anything further, her cell phone rang. She glanced at the caller ID.

"Oh shit," she moaned. "Now what am I supposed to do? It's Charlotte Randolph."

CHAPTER 10

Dawn let the phone go unanswered. After three more calls within the hour, she lost her patience and waited until Charlotte finished her latest message and then pressed "play" on the voicemail icon.

"Hi, it's Charlotte. Britt had to go out of town so I thought you and I could meet and talk some more. I have a great idea that I saw on *HGTV* yesterday. I want you to design a chicken coop for our backyard so we can have fresh, organic eggs every day. Saddie, the senator's cook, makes a delicious spinach omelet. Chip and Joanna Gaines built one for one of their customers. I saw it on the Magnolia Channel and took a picture. I'm sending it to you now. Can you have lunch with me so we can talk? We don't need an English garden or a damn maze…but a bunch of chickens and maybe a rooster would be so cool. Call me soon, Sweetie, please."

Dawn looked at her phone in horror. She could not help herself. She burst out laughing. *What had Britt gotten himself into?* Against her better judgment and contrary to Britt's wishes, she texted Charlotte right back. "I'm so sorry, but I'm tied up with customers all this week, so lunch won't work. While I like most of Joanna's ideas and watch *Fixer Upper* occasionally myself, I don't think a chicken coop will sit well with your neighbors. Georgetown is not Waco. You may need to rethink that."

A chicken coop, really? Dawn could not stop laughing. "She pictured Senator Holmes dressed in a three-piece suit, carrying a little straw basket around his yard, collecting eggs every morning before he set out to cure the problems of the world?"

"It would be quite a photo op for the tabloids," Lolly snickered. "I can see his face now on the cover of *The Legislator Times*."

"I predict Britt would not be happy about that image. It's not what he had in mind for himself. Now that I've had time to think about it, I realize that he and Charlotte are so different...not only three decades apart in age, but they seem to have little or nothing in common. They're almost caricatures of country bumpkin meets city slicker."

"Why then do you suppose he wants to marry her?"

"I'm honestly not sure he does. I picked up some strange vibes when I talked to him about it. He said things could change in the future but then he clammed up and sent me home. He's out of town now so I can't ask him, and I'm left with only my speculations and curiosity. However, I really wonder why he doesn't want me talking to Charlotte. I need to straighten this mess out before I waste any more time on their renovation."

"It does seem strange, but for now, can we put Charlotte and her weird ideas aside. I need to go over details of the Thompsons' job and invoice the lighting company for their fixtures."

"Sure," Dawn answered, as her phone rang again. Charlotte, it seemed, would not take "no" for an answer.

* * *

Dawn spent the rest of the morning in the office catching up on paperwork and revising carpet selections for a client who had suddenly changed her mind about the six oriental rugs she'd had ordered to be custom made for her townhome on Capitol Hill. Dawn was trying to figure out if she could use any of the expensive rugs in her other projects. If so, it would save time and the inevitable hassle and expense of returning them overseas. It was too late to cancel the order. The woven masterpieces were already sitting on a cargo ship awaiting clearance into the port of Miami, to be unloaded and transported to DC.

She thought that they might work in Britt's twin parlors and carefully checked those room dimensions. Two of the bigger carpets would fit. The rugs were identical in pattern with only the background colors reversed. One had a dark cranberry background with gold and forest green accents. The other one was the same dark green with gold and cranberry accents. Both would perfectly complement the historical theme of the house. She checked her furniture diagram and was satisfied that all the furniture would sit on them properly. She hated it when a sofa or chair was positioned half on and half off a carpet. She always thought the designer or homeowner had measured incorrectly and refused to admit their mistake. She would upholster the sofas and chairs in corresponding colors and paint the room's chair rails to match the rug's primary background color. The more she thought about it, the better she liked the idea. It was a perfect solution.

Beautiful crystal chandeliers and wall sconces would complete the look and reflect their light onto the highly polished mahogany floors. Dawn took a moment, closed her eyes, and could almost smell the pungent scent of wood oak logs burning in the fireplaces. She imagined distinguished, beautifully dressed guests wandering around the house, admiring its décor, nibbling on delicious canapés, and sipping fine burgundy wine from antique stemmed glasses. Britt would look stunningly handsome standing in the doorway in a black tuxedo and his presence would command the room. She could hardly wait for him to call so she could talk to him about it.

But what about Charlotte? What was she to do about her?

CHAPTER 11

Four weeks passed. Dawn heard nothing from Britt, not a word.

The month of May arrived in DC with warmer temperatures and sunny blue skies. Multi-colored azaleas and bright yellow forsythia came to life in gardens and parks everywhere. The last of the late-blooming cherry blossoms still drew tourists and photography buffs throughout the city and to the Tidal Basin for one last look at their soft pink buds.

Charlotte continued to make a nuisance of herself and called Dawn at the office and on her cell phone, often leaving long, meandering messages. Dawn artfully dodged her and then left apologetic messages in return, promising to call her back soon. It was not like her to be dishonest with or ignore her clients. She prided herself on always being available to them. It was one of the reasons they paid so much for her services. But the Charlotte situation was perplexing. She could not dodge her forever. Britt had put her in an awkward position by insisting that she avoid Charlotte. How was that even going to be possible?

Finally, after Charlotte's fourth attempt of the day to reach her, Dawn became angry. She did not need this ridiculous stress in her life. Exasperated, she dialed Britt's number. Her call went straight to his voicemail. She left a terse message and then called the senator's office and spoke to his aide.

"When will Senator Holmes be back?" she asked impatiently. "Or better yet, can you ask him to call me right away. It's important – about his new house and a situation that's arisen."

"I'm sorry Ms. Sutton. The senator is currently unavailable. I have no way to reach him or any idea when he will return. He was in Delaware on business when the Speaker of the House asked him to join a bipartisan delegation and travel to the Middle East. The trip was top secret so he could not tell anyone that he was going. He was expected to return last week, but unfortunately his car was hit by rounds of shrapnel, and he was among those wounded. He was treated by military medics at the scene and is now being transferred to a safe hospital. For security reasons we have not announced the attack or his injuries to the press yet. So, please… consider this classified information until it becomes public knowledge. You must not say anything to anyone. He has no family so there is no one to notify about his injuries."

She was horrified. "Oh my God! Is he okay?" Her whole body suddenly felt limp, and she was dizzy, trying to absorb the shocking news. "Surely he'd want his fiancée to know he's been hurt."

"Oh, you mean his little southern friend with her frilly dresses and ridiculously expensive designer scarves." The aide's tone was condescending, and disrespectful. Dawn found herself inexplicably feeling protective of Charlotte.

"I still think she has a right to know. If you told me, why not her?"

"Because before the senator left," Owen continued stiffly, "he specifically instructed me that no one, especially Charlotte and her father, should be told about this trip. Of course, he never expected to be wounded. I'm only telling you because strangely, he did advise me that if anything happened to him, I should contact you, and only you. He also left you a note. I have it here on my desk, and as a matter of fact, I was just about to contact you and send it over to your office by messenger."

"Okay, thank you. But why would he only want you to notify me? I barely know the man." She was astonished. "Of all the people he knows in this world, why would he choose me?"

"I don't know ma'am. But that's precisely what he said. I'm just following orders."

"Oh my God." Dawn had to sit down. The room was spinning. She was full of so many questions. "Will he be alright? How bad are his injuries?"

"I don't know all the particulars but he's in critical condition," the aide answered solemnly. He sounded more compassionate than he had been when discussing Charlotte. "He's lost a lot of blood and might also lose his leg. As soon as he's stable, the medics will fly him to Landstuhl Regional Medical Center in Germany. It's the nearest secure US Army facility. Once he's there, he'll have to undergo a number of surgeries and recover from them before he can be transported back to the States. Then he'll go to the Walter Reed National Military Medical Center for his rehab. I haven't talked to his doctors directly but from what I've deduced, he'll be in the hospital in Germany for at least two months, maybe longer."

Dawn was overwhelmed and suddenly alarmed...for Britt, for Charlotte and, surprisingly, for herself. She did a quick calculation and realized that if Owen was correct, he would not return home until at least July. There would be hundreds of decisions she would have to make on his behalf in the meantime to meet his November deadline.

Unexpectedly Senator Holmes had appeared in her life, and instantly he had become an enormous part of it. And now, just a little over a month later, he was halfway across the world and might be dying or permanently maimed. *What should she do? Did she still have to honor Britt's ridiculous wish and not speak to Charlotte. The idea seemed insane now. How could she keep this life-shattering news from his fiancée?*

And why should she?

CHAPTER 12

Dawn hung up the phone and stared off into the distance. Her heart was racing, and her mind was a jumble...an accumulation of horrendous scenes she'd seen on the television's nightly news programs showing the Israeli and American hostages, the death and utter destruction in the region, the unbearable suffering and everything else that had happened since, the failed peace talks, the bombings and civilians starving and displaced. And now Britt was somewhere out there, in that chaos, wounded and alone.

It was hard to grasp that the dynamic potential candidate for President of the United States was hurt in that ravished land, fighting for his life or for the very least, his leg. *What was she supposed to do now?* She had no idea whether to cry or to scream in rage. Helpless and in unfamiliar personal and professional territory, she wanted to do anything and everything she could to help Britt. But what? *Would he even live to see P Street completed and under the tragic circumstances, would he even care?*

"You look like you've seen a ghost," Lolly stated bluntly when she saw Dawn's pained expression. "What's wrong? Did someone poach one of our clients or did pirates hijack a freighter with our furniture on board?"

"No, much worse." Dawn threw her hands up in the air in a gesture of frustration. "But I can't tell you. I swore not to say anything. Oh, my God, this is awful."

"Don't be ridiculous. You can tell me anything and always have? What's the problem?"

Dawn felt trapped, pinned to her chair. She'd been told that Britt's injury and trip were matters of National Security, and even though she trusted Lolly with her life, she could not betray her country or Britt by telling the truth. Determined to do what his aide asked of her, she hedged and kept the devastating news to herself. "Sorry, I can't say anything now. I'll tell you everything soon, I promise, but in the meantime, I'm expecting an envelope from Senator Holmes's office. Please let me know when it arrives."

"That's why I came looking for you." Lolly waved an envelope in front of her friend. "This just arrived."

Dawn grabbed it, as Lolly, looking bewildered, returned to her own office.

Dear Dawn,

I'm sorry to burden you. In my pursuit of financial support for my presidential candidacy, I've done some questionable things to try to guarantee my victory in the polls. Now these same people, whom I asked for help, are using me to attain their own agendas. They'll do anything to achieve them.

From the moment we met, I felt you were a woman I could depend upon. I'll have to rely on those instincts because there's much more going on with Charlotte and her family than is apparent and I can't explain to you now. Please, stay away from them!

In my absence, proceed with the P Street renovations. Spend as much money as you need. Make it the showplace we discussed. It's vitally important that this project moves along quickly and ends on time. I know I can count on you and that you won't let me down.

The enclosed key is to my safe deposit box #2047 at the Capitol Hill Bank on First Street, N.E. Please use it if anything happens to me but tell no one that you have it...not even Owen. It contains incriminating papers that you'll need to destroy. It's vital that no one else must ever see them. It's a matter of national security.

Britt

Dawn gingerly fingered the small key that she had nearly missed hidden at the bottom of the envelope. She placed it in the change purse of her wallet for safekeeping. Now she was more confused than ever. *What was all this about?* She had not signed up for any hush-hush business when she'd sought him out as a client. She had only wanted prestige for her company and the huge commission his job would bring. In retrospect, she should have kept her damn shoe on and not engineered a meeting with him. Now it seemed that she had innocently walked in her Louboutin stilettos right into the middle of some national conspiracy. From the little she knew about Britt, she liked him a lot, but she wanted no part of this drama. No matter what his aide said, she could not keep silent and needed to talk to Lolly and maybe to her lawyer about what was going on. She got her chance sooner than expected.

"Turn on the TV," Lolly sounded distressed as she spoke into the intercom. "It's about Senator Holmes."

Dawn ran for the remote and tuned into CNN in time to hear the reporter say, "Last night, Britt Holmes, the personable and popular Delaware senator was wounded while with a US delegation somewhere in the Middle East. He was last seen in Tel Aviv but then he and his group disappeared. We have since learned that his caravan was targeted, and his vehicle was bombed by a series of drones. The senator was thrown from his vehicle just before it exploded, and the car burst into flames. He is thought to be the only survivor of the attack and was severely injured. The names of the deceased who were accompanying him are being withheld until official notification to their families. This unprovoked attack might bring a tragic end to the senator's impressive public service career and his aspirations for the presidency. His fervent supporters and the entire country must pray for his recovery. More details as we get them. Now onto news of Putin and the Kremlin."

CHAPTER 13

Dawn poured over a variety of newspapers and listened to 24-7 news, but there was no more information about the attack on the American delegation or the status of Senator Holmes's wounds. She called his office, but they were as much in the dark as she was. Not knowing what else to do, she went over to P Street to supervise the demolition crew who were removing the old kitchen and expanding it into the enclosed garage bays. The job was dusty and loud, but the noise and humming activity distracted her from constant worry about Britt. She could think of little else.

For her sanity, she had to believe that he would recover and proceed with his plans for the presidency. She fought to maintain some semblance of a normal routine and met with her kitchen design people, approving the selection of flooring, backsplashes, and countertops. She ordered top-of-the-line appliances: two convection ovens, two Miele silent dishwashers, a large Sub Zero refrigerator-freezer, with an extra freezer to be kept in the garage for overflow items, a microwave, a floor-to-ceiling temperature-controlled wine refrigerator, and a commercial grade ice maker. There would also be a space for built-in coffee and espresso machines and two separate sinks with garbage disposals in the kitchen and another sink in the adjacent pantry and one more utility one in the laundry room.

She completely organized the items needed for the catering kitchen but held off on the appliances for the outside one, preferring to wait until the house was further along and the flagstone terrace completed in the back. She had no idea if Britt liked to barbecue himself or whether he left that to his household staff or his personal chef. It did not matter. That decision could wait until he returned.

Taking her cobb salad from Whole Foods and a bottle of flavored water, she slipped into the library to escape the confusion and concentrate on her choice of kitchen cabinets and hardware. The kitchen design called for a mix of open and closed shelving and some glass fronts to allow the display of special pieces of decorative China. She began studying and adjusting the layout for the cabinets and drawers. Her approval and signatures were necessary before the kitchen company would order the first screw. She could not afford to make a costly mistake. Custom millwork orders were not returnable.

Deep in concentration, she barely heard the persistent knock on the door. When she looked up, annoyed that she had been interrupted, Charlotte Randolph sashayed into the room, anger clearly visible on her face.

"What the hell's going on?" She spat the words out. "Why are there all those men tearing my kitchen apart?" She looked accusingly at Dawn. "And why haven't you returned any of my calls. It's been almost six weeks. No one's that busy! What's wrong with you?"

"Sit down, Charlotte," Dawn said evenly, taken aback by the woman's sudden appearance. She should have expected it and was feeling guilty for ignoring her for so long. A major confrontation of some sort between the two was bound to happen, but she was not prepared for it to happen today. Dawn slowly laid down the plans she'd been studying and chose her words carefully. "First, let me say how sorry I am that Senator Holmes had been wounded." She was curious to see Charlotte's reaction to the tragedy and to learn if Charlotte had heard from him. "How is he?"

"Okay, I guess," she answered tersely. "I haven't been able to speak to him. His staff's very protective and secretive. I'm told that his cell phone doesn't work over there, but don't try to distract me. Britt's injuries are not the issue here. I want to know what's going on with you. Why haven't I been consulted about anything? I'm the co-owner of this property. Britt bought it for me, in case that fact slipped your mind." She had lost her southern gentile charm and was sounding peevish. Dawn did not blame her. She would have felt the same way in Charlotte's shoes.

"To be fair, remember you said the idea of renovating bored you and that I should work with Britt." She needed to find something diplomatic to say to appease Charlotte without betraying Britt. She came up with a far-fetched excuse. "I've been working on your idea for a deluxe chicken coop." It was lame, she knew, but all she could think of at the moment. "It's going to be soundproof so your neighbors won't complain." *What a ridiculous notion. No one could soundproof an entire backyard.*

Charlotte did not respond. She stared at Dawn and waited for her to continue.

"You didn't seem interested in any of the specific details about the house, so I've proceeded without you." Dawn forged on. "At our one meeting, Britt told me to move as quickly as possible and make all the decisions for both of you if he was not available. I'm sure he did not anticipate being away for so long. I hope I didn't overstep." She tried to look and sound sincere and actually felt sorry for Charlotte. "I was only following his orders. The senator wants this home to be everything you could possibly want or dream about."

Charlotte stopped her ranting long enough to consider Dawn's words. "Did he really tell you that?" She was surprised because Britt had barely discussed the house with her before he left, and she had not heard a word from him since. She was concerned that her fiancée was not as enamored with her as he'd been when he proposed. Why else would he not have called her? She had tried to reach out to him through his office, but Owen Marshall always put her off, saying the senator was unavailable. It infuriated Charlotte and she was taking her anger out on Dawn. She had only learned of Britt's injuries from the television when the rest of the world was told about them.

"My Mama warned me that Britt might be getting cold feet about the wedding and that I need to use all my charms to keep him interested and committed to getting married. But how can I do that? I don't even know where he is, much less what hospital. Besides," she made a childish face of disgust. "I hate hospitals and sick people depress me."

"I think he wants to surprise you with the house when it's done and not tie you down with endless, boring details. It's actually very considerate and loving of him. Even I get bored deciding where to place all the electric outlets and picking out dozens of door handles and knobs, but... if you want to take that on, be my guest. I could really use your help."

Charlotte looked guiltily down at her lap and studied her nails, which needed polishing. "No, I guess you should keep doing all that tiresome stuff. But check in with me from time to time. I don't like being excluded. I still can't believe Britt bought this monstrosity of a place," she pouted, "and then he went off and almost got himself killed. She looked like she was about to throw a tantrum. "It was very inconsiderate of him."

"It's not as if he intended to get injured." Dawn fought to hold her temper. Charlotte was clueless, a selfish and spoiled child. She was caught up in her own small world and seemed to have little concern that her husband-to-be might be dying somewhere hurt and all alone while she worried about scheduling her next manicure.

"I'm glad you're here, Dawn, really. Thank you." Charlotte tried to sound contrite when she saw Dawn's troubled expression. "I must leave. I can't wait to get out of this dreary house. You can handle everything from now on. I won't interfere. I'm off to Pilates. Chao."

"Well, don't let me keep you." Dawn used her most polite, controlled voice. "Hopefully Britt will recover soon and come back to us in one piece."

"I hope so," Charlotte muttered. As she walked towards the door, she turned around and faced Dawn, placing her hands theatrically on her hips for emphasis. "And remember I want a huge hot tub...at least big enough for six people, and it must be Barbie pink...like in the movie."

CHAPTER 14

D awn took a few minutes to recover from Charlotte's outburst. The childlike woman, if she could be called a woman, was a picture-perfect caricature of a southern belle, complete with her sweet tea fetish and her over-perfected accent. *How could Britt have fallen for her? Was there a single genuine part in Charlotte's entire body?* Her false fingernails, her surgically enhanced breasts, her expertly applied hair extensions and even her bright blue contact lenses spoke to her artificial and superficial nature. Men could be such fools when they were sexually attracted. Britt, apparently, had been no exception. Maybe widowers were especially vulnerable to women on the prowl.

Dawn suddenly remembered Britt's cryptic note. Did his words imply that he had had an epiphany and seen Charlotte for the phony, immature person that she was, or was something else more nefarious going on? Time would tell...*but would he have the time?* The thought of his precarious situation and that his life, at least as he knew it, might be over brought hot tears to her eyes. She dialed the senator's office and asked once again for any word on Britt's condition.

"I can tell you this," Owen replied. "We learned early this morning, through a state department source, that Senator Holmes safely made the trip to Germany. He's undergoing the first of several operations to save his leg. Once he's in stable condition, he'll be able to make phone calls. I'm sure I'll hear from him then. When I speak with him, I'll ask him to contact you."

"Thank you," she mumbled gratefully. "This waiting is torture."

* *

Two more days passed by without any further news of Britt's condition. Dawn was so worried about him that she was barely able to function. She could not concentrate on her work or meet with clients effectively. She was too distracted. In an impulsive moment, very much unlike herself, she went online and bought a one-way airplane ticket to Ramstein, Germany – the nearest airport to the Landstuhl Medical Center. As she sat that night in her first-class seat, facing an eighteen-hour journey with two changes of planes and long layovers, she shook her head at her outlandish action and wondered what had possessed her to fly to the bedside of a man she barely knew…who might not even want to see her. It made no logical sense. She had never done anything so precipitous and rash before.

Once she got the idea in her head, Dawn had been in such a hurry to be with Britt that she had not taken the time to tell Lolly about her trip. She sent her a short text asking her to "hold down the fort" and that once she saw Britt, she'd be in touch. She also begged her not to tell anyone where she had gone, especially not Charlotte Randolph.

Deplaning at her final destination, Dawn looked around the vast airport and tried to make sense of the signs. Most were in German, but some were also in English…directions to the baggage claim area, the restrooms, and the taxi line. Once through security and the passport checkpoint, she dragged her overnight bag outside and stood in a long line for a taxi. She had not slept well on any of the long flights and was exhausted and disheveled.

The weather was much colder than she had anticipated, and she'd packed in such haste that she did not think to bring a coat, only a short leather jacket and a Washington Commanders burgundy and gold scarf. The taxi line seemed endless, and she was shivering and shaking by the time it was her turn. Many in the line looked tense and worried. Maybe they too were en route to visit loved ones with no idea what they would find at the hospital.

Dawn had not thought of a plan, which was extremely unusual for her, but for once she had operated strictly on emotions. She had no idea what to do or what to expect when she arrived at Landstuhl. After paying the taxi driver, she entered the sterile hospital lobby feeling slightly disoriented and a little foolish. Taking a deep breath, she forced herself to walk boldly up to the information desk. "I'm here to see Senator Holmes. He's had surgery and I believe he's in the ICU."

"Your name please. Are you a relative?" The receptionist asked.

"No. But I'm a good friend," Dawn answered, caught off guard. She should have known that only family would be allowed to visit a patient in the ICU. It was the same way in the States. "Please, I've flown all the way from the United States to see him. Please let me in."

"I'm sorry, Miss. But I don't have that authority. You'll have to take it up with the hospital's Commander of Medical operations." She impatiently looked at the line of people forming behind Dawn. "You'll have to move along now." Then she reverted back to speaking German. "Nächste in der Reihe." (Next in line.)

Dawn moved aside and watched as one person after another was given a paper badge admitting them to various patients' rooms. She was so tired and frustrated and at a complete loss as to what to do next. She looked around the lobby for anyone who looked American or seemed to be speaking English. Finally, she spotted someone and approached a middle-aged woman standing by herself in the corner of the lobby. "Excuse me, is there a hotel nearby?" she asked. "I just arrived and don't have a reservation anywhere."

"The Hotel Pfeffermuhle is walking distance from here. It's a bit down the road on your left. I'm staying there myself. It's clean and the food is decent."

"Thank you." Dawn smiled weakly. She was too tired to walk and drag her suitcase behind her, so she took a taxi and checked into the hotel fifteen minutes later. After showering and washing her hair, she lay down on the bed for a few minutes to rest but instantly fell into a deep sleep. Three hours later she awoke. Maybe the shift at the reception desk had changed, she thought, and she could try again. She dressed quickly and retraced her steps back to the hospital.

Passport in hand, she marched up to the reception desk, determined not to be turned away again. A young man wearing a nametag "Holgar Schmitt" stared intently into a computer screen and looked up as she approached him. "Ja?"

"Do you speak English?" she asked.

"Yes, Ma'am," he answered with a barely detectable accent. "How can I help you?"

"I'm here to see Senator Holmes. He was injured and flown here for surgery. I was told that he's in the ICU."

"And you are?"

"Dawn. I'm Dawn Sutter." Noticing the blasé expression on the man's face, she realized that she was about to be denied admission and turned away again. She could not let that happen. She was beyond frustrated and began to wonder why she had come at all. But she had, and now, nothing or no one was going to stop her from seeing Britt. In a moment of near panic, she had an inspiration and boldly blurted out, "I'm the senator's wife and I demand to see him right away."

"What is the patient's name again?" He sighed and looked at her suspiciously.

"Britt Holmes. Senator Britt Holmes." She was trying not to lose her patience or her temper, but she was shaking and close to becoming unhinged. *Why was he being so difficult?* "For Heaven's sake, what's the problem? Call your supervisor, if you must, but I need to see my husband right now! He's in critical condition."

Holgar nodded and studied his computer screen. "I don't see his name here on the patient registry. Oh, no, wait. Sorry. I've found it. Your husband's been moved from the ICU to the step-down orthopedic floor. He's in a V.I.P. suite, number 1062."

"Thank you," she said gratefully and started to move towards the elevators before he could ask her any more questions.

"Just a minute," He walked around the desk to confront her. "There are no names on his visitor's list. I'm afraid I can't let you in."

"But that's absurd," Dawn protested. "He's been gravely wounded, and I need to be with him. His recovery is not at all certain. I've flown all the way from the US," and she thought – *What can I say to get this guy to let me in?* Tears of frustration formed in her eyes. She swiped them away. This was not the time to show vulnerability. She would tell as many lies as necessary to convince this man that she needed to get to the tenth floor.

"Again, I'm sorry, Mrs. Holmes, is it?" He noticed the discrepancy in her last name with that of the senator, but many Americans did not assume their husband's last names when they married. He thought it was an odd practice and appallingly disrespectful to men, but it was none of his business.

"Britt was flown here in critical condition. There was no time for him to make a visitor's list," she improvised, biting her tongue. "He was probably unconscious, for God's sake. Please, we're wasting precious time. He could die at any minute." Then she had an inspiration. "His doctors say he's lost his will to live. I have news that I know will give him a reason to fight for his life. He's going to be a father." She gave him a shy half-smile, patting her belly gently. "We've always wanted a family and now it's going to happen. Please, I must tell him." *Maybe Lolly had been right, and she should have been an actress.*

The young man was torn between his duty and his sentimentality. In the end, the sight of the distraught woman won him over. "All right, I'll make an exception but just for today. But you must ask your husband to put your name on the visitor's list immediately or Gerta, she's the day shift lady, will turn you away tomorrow without a second thought. She's a stickler – is that how you say it – for rules and regulations."

"I will, I will. I promise." Dawn was so relieved she finally let her tears fall. "Thank you. You've been very kind."

Holgar handed her a tissue. She was a beautiful American woman, one of the prettiest he had ever seen, and he hoped for her sake and her baby's that her husband would recover. "Take the elevator on the right to the tenth floor. Good luck and remember about that visitor's list. Gerta can be a terror."

CHAPTER 15

As soon as she got off the elevator a young doctor in a white lab coat approached her.

"Mrs. Holmes?" Dawn did not respond and kept walking. She was not used to answering to that name. "Mrs. Holmes," he asked again, this time standing directly in front of her. "May I speak to you for a minute about your husband's condition?"

She nodded and looked embarrassed. "Of course. I'm so worried and distracted."

"I understand," he said in perfect English. "Holgar, the chap at the reception desk, paged me and said you were on your way up here. Your husband is in pretty rough shape but doing amazingly well for what he's been through. I thought I should explain his condition and tell you what you can expect before you see him. I don't want you to faint at the sight of him."

"Thank you," she said gratefully. "Does he look that bad?"

"I'm afraid so," he said compassionately as he led her to a little waiting room off to the side. They sat and he began to explain. "My name is Dr. Frank Baringer. I'm the physician in charge of the senator's case. As you know, he was critically injured in a car explosion that nearly blew off his right leg. Shrapnel and jagged pieces of the car's frame and windshield glass penetrated his body, damaging his spleen and the lower quadrant of his left lung. He also sustained facial burns and a severe concussion. A team of specialists has been monitoring him closely in the ICU for several days, running tests, scans, and MRIs. They waited for his vitals to improve enough that they felt he could survive anesthesia and the first in a series of necessary surgical procedures."

"It all sounds horrible," Dawn gasped. "Were you able to save his leg? Is he in a lot of pain?"

"Yes, he's in pain, but we're trying to keep him as comfortable as possible, and he's not totally coherent or awake. He keeps drifting in and out of consciousness. That's normal after such extensive surgery. The best things for him now are doses of heavy-duty intravenous antibiotics and plenty of rest. As to his leg, we're hopeful it can be saved but it will take a few weeks to know for sure."

"Will Britt know I'm here?" She suddenly felt guilty for lying to the people who saved his life and hopefully his leg. She was a fraud and had no right to hear this private medical information. Tempted to turn and bolt from the hospital, she made herself take deep breaths and try to remain calm.

"He'll feel your presence, and hear your voice, even if he can't see you clearly. His face is heavily bandaged, so his vision is compromised."

"May I go see him now?"

"Yes, of course. But I wanted to prepare you. He's a strong man in otherwise good health and if the leg operations are successful, he'll be in for many months of strenuous and painful rehabilitation. If he recovers as well as we hope, he'll be transported to the Walter Reed Hospital outside of Washington, DC. There, he'll undergo very rigorous in-house and eventually outpatient physical therapy. This is the beginning of a very long process and he'll need your support and Maggie's."

"Maggie?" *Who the hell is Maggie?*

"I'm sure you're extremely grateful to her. She flew here the day he was admitted and has rarely left his side. The floor nurses are so happy for her help. She's been a true angel."

Dawn was confused but did not want to raise any red flags by asking more about Maggie. That could wait. "If my husband's leg reattaches successfully, will he be able to walk normally again?" The thought just occurred to her, and she felt panicky. His master bedroom in the P Street home was on the second floor. Would she need to add an elevator? "Will he be able to go up and down stairs?" *How could I be thinking of such mundane details at a time like this?* she wondered. The mind worked in strange ways when under stress, and hers was in overdrive.

"The answer to both questions is 'yes' but he may have a slight limp. The walking will come back first and then eventually the ability to do stairs as he strengthens his quad muscles to compensate for his compromised calf."

"Thank you, Doctor Baringer. You've been very helpful and kind. I'm sure I'll have some more questions later. But I'm really anxious to see my husband now." It was amazing how easily those words came off her tongue.

"Of course, but if you have any needs or questions, don't hesitate to ask a nurse to page me...or Maggie. I'm almost always somewhere in the hospital...and before you go into his room, please put this on." He handed her a mask. "Infection is the greatest enemy of post-surgical patients."

CHAPTER 16

Dawn stood outside the door to room 1062, retouched her lipstick and ran a brush quickly through her hair. She'd been in such a hurry to get to Britt when she awoke from her unintended nap, she had not taken the time to style it or apply makeup. He would have to see her "au naturelle."

Taking a deep breath, she knocked softly on the door and entered the room. What she saw was shocking. Britt was lying on the bed looking like a mummy, his face and neck wrapped almost entirely in white gauze, with his damaged leg heavily bandaged and elevated at about sixty degrees above the sheets. Wires and tubes were coming out of him from everywhere. A machine that measured his heart beats and blood pressure beeps incessantly. Approaching his bed cautiously, she whispered. "Britt, it's Dawn. I'm here and the doctors say that you're going to be okay." She reached for his hand but there was no place to touch it. Wires ran from his veins to yet other machines or bags hanging from the bed. His eyes were closed, and he did not appear to be aware that she was there. "Can you hear me?" she whispered gently, willing him to respond. He remained motionless.

"I'm afraid he's still not fully awake," a strikingly beautiful, tall Asian woman said as she came into the room. She began fussing with one of the monitors and changed a bag of liquid hanging from a pole that was dripping into Britt's arm. "I'm Maggie, the senator's private nurse. Holgar sent word that the senator's wife was on her way up here." Maggie sized her up and said acidly, "we both know you're not Mrs. Holmes, may she rest in peace. Who are you and what are you doing here? Do I need to call security?"

"News travels fast." Dawn was stunned. Who was this brazen woman to speak so rudely and confront her? "You certainly have quite a gossip grapevine here. You'd think you all had better things to do with your time."

Maggie was not interested in Dawn's assessment of the hospital gossip mill. "I repeat," she said harshly. "Who the hell are you and what are you doing here?"

Dawn did not know what to say or why she had to explain anything to this stranger. However, it was clear that Maggie somehow knew Britt was not married. If she confessed and told her the truth, and Maggie told the authorities, she would surely be unceremoniously escorted out of the hospital and banned from returning. She was hemmed in by her own lies and had no choice but to tell the truth and hope for the best.

"My name is Dawn Sutter," she explained. "I work for the senator back in DC as his interior designer. I know he had no family, so when his office told me about his injuries, I made a spontaneous decision to come here. It was precipitous, I know, but for some reason I felt compelled to be at his side. And you…Maggie, is it? Who are you and why are you here?" Dawn was more than curious.

"I was Britt's wife's hospice nurse. I lived with him and Taylor for six months until she passed. After she died, Britt seemed lost and at loose ends. He hated being alone and asked me to stay on and help him dispose of her personal things, clean out her closets, distribute her jewelry to her friends as per her will, and do things like that. One thing led to another, and I never left. I moved to DC and have been his personal assistant ever since. Actually, I'm happy to meet you. He planned to introduce us, but then this," she pointed to his hospital bed, "happened. I'm sure he never expected to be here or that we'd meet under these circumstances. I'm sorry I was rude. I thought you were another nosy reporter trying to get a scoop. Ever since rumors of his run for the presidency surfaced, they have not given him a moment's peace. I guess I'm a little overprotective. Sorry."

"Apology accepted. And truthfully, I have no idea why I'm here either. I came on a sudden whim thinking I might be able to help in some way, but looking at him lying there, I don't see what I can do. I'll just stay long enough to say hello and tell him a little of what's happening at the house and then I'll head back to DC. It was stupid of me to have come at all."

Maggie made no comment and busied herself by checking one of the monitors again. She looked tenderly down at Britt. "God willing, if he survives this ordeal and things go back to normal, which in Britt's case, with the presidency in his future, will be nothing less than complete chaos, he'll need both of us. Hopefully we can work together and be friends."

Dawn was perplexed. If Britt and Maggie were so close, why hadn't he given *her* his safe deposit box key and put *her* in charge of paying for the house restoration costs? She was surprised that he had never mentioned having a personal assistant and Maggie in particular. And she wondered if Owen Marshall and the senate office staff knew about Maggie and that she was here in Germany with Britt. Owen had never mentioned her either. The more questions that came to her mind, the more confused she became.

"Britt has raved about you and your company and how creative you are. He's really excited about what you're doing at the house. I'm sure he'll be pleased that you're here."

"How is he, really?" Dawn worried. He had not moved, even twitched a muscle since she'd come into the room.

"He's had a very difficult few days and last night was terrible. He needed more morphine. It really knocked him out, but he's doing a little better now. Over the next few days, the doctors will slowly wean him off the pain meds. Then he'll be able to talk to you. Right now, he sleeps most of the time, but that's nature's way of helping him heal. Maybe if you come back later this afternoon or perhaps tomorrow, he'll be a little more alert."

"All right." Dawn was reluctant to go after just arriving, but he clearly was not aware she was there, and she could do nothing to help him while he slept. "I'll leave him in your capable hands. I'm staying at the Hotel Pfeffermuhle down the street. If there's any change, please call me." She handed Maggie her business card and wrote her cell phone number on it.

"Yes, I will, don't worry, Dawn. I'll take good care of him. I always do."

"Thank you," Dawn smiled at the nurse and spontaneously reached over to kiss the gauze covering Britt's forehead. "I'll be back," she whispered to him and quietly moved away. From the doorway, she looked back at his bedside and saw Maggie tenderly tucking a sheet around Britt's good leg and taking a seat in the chair next to him. Apparently, she was prepared to spend the rest of the day there.

In the hallway, Dawn leaned heavily against the nearest wall for support and gave into her emotion with tumultuous sobs. She had been shocked by Britt's ghost-like appearance. If she had not known it was him in the bed, she would never have recognized the vibrant senator. How was it possible that such a rich and powerful man, with a brilliant future before him, could end up like this? She kicked the wall in anger and frustration and winced.

Life was definitely not fair.

CHAPTER 17

Leaving the hospital, she waved to Holgar on her way out. He smiled and gave her the thumbs up signal. She was happy that she would not have to avoid Gerta in the morning. Holgar, with his loose tongue, would have informed her that Dawn Sutter was Senator Holmes's pregnant wife and probably everyone else in the hospital too.

Lost in thought, with the harrowing image of Britt lying helplessly in the hospital bed, she walked slowly back to the hotel, silently praying for his recovery. The fresh air was brisk and being outside made her feel alive and energized. Britt's room had been stifling and the whole hospital smelled of unpleasant disinfectants and chemicals. She had a fleeting memory of Charlotte saying that she hated hospitals and sick people. Dawn felt almost the same way at the moment. Seeing Britt in his helpless condition had shaken her to her core. In her mind she could still hear the beeping machines and see the endless intravenous drips invading Britt's body. She shook her head, trying to physically rid her mind of those frightening images. Her stomach growled and she realized that it had been many hours since she'd eaten a hard roll and coffee on the plane. She decided to try the hotel food and get some lunch before returning to Britt's bedside.

When she walked into the dining room, she asked for a table for one. "Eine person," she said using one of the few expressions she knew in the German language. The hostess smiled. She appreciated it when foreigners tried to speak her language. So many visitors arrogantly used their native languages as if there were no others in the universe and they shouted their words, as if the sheer volume of their voice would make them better understood.

Before the hostess could seat her, Dawn spotted the lady who she had talked to earlier in the hospital lobby – the one who had recommended this hotel. The lady waved at her with a friendly gesture from a nearby table. "Please join me. I could use the company," she said graciously.

Dawn started to decline. She was not in a chatty mood, but she had no excuse not to be sociable. It would be rude. Putting on a forced smile, she sat and took the menu from the hostess. "I'm Dawn."

"Elenor Blaine," the English woman said. "My brother's been in the hospital for almost a week. He was working on a construction job and fell off the scaffolding. They need to fix his shoulder. I'm the only family he has, so here I am. Why are you here, if you don't mind telling me? My friends say I'm too nosy for my own good." She could see that the American lady was stressed.

Damn, Dawn thought. *Here I go again…lie or tell the truth?* If she admitted her deception to Elenor, she risked being kicked out of the hospital. She was not willing to take the chance, so she continued the fake marriage narrative. It was her only option now, and solely her fault.

"My husband," she began, surprised by how nice the words sounded, "was on a fact-finding mission with some US Senators in the Middle East when his convoy was struck by enemy drones. The car he was riding in took a direct hit and was blown to smithereens. He was badly hurt."

"Oh my, how awful," the woman emphasized. "I'm so sorry, dear. How is he now?"

"Not great." Dawn answered honestly. "He's sedated after serious surgery. I don't think he knows that I'm here. After lunch I'm going back and plan to stay with him until he wakes up. It's terrible seeing him lying there. It makes me feel so helpless." Her voice began to tremble. Maybe it was a delayed reaction to seeing Britt so incapacitated.

"I understand, dear." She reached out and patted Dawn's arm. "Let's have a nice lunch together and then I'll walk back to the hospital with you. My brother's so crabby that I need to take a break from his constant complaining. He's mad at the world and worried about how soon he can get back to work. He lives paycheck to paycheck. I'll help him as much as I can, but I live on my dead husband's pension and the few pounds I earn from my artwork."

"What kind of artwork?" Dawn was happy to change the subject. Elenor did not look like a starving artist. As a matter of fact, she looked exceedingly well fed.

"I do charcoal pictures of the local children and landscapes on commission. I don't make much, but people seem to like my work and it keeps me busy. Being a widow is lonely. There are too many hours in the day, so I try to fill them by drawing, and I love to read. I practically live at our local library."

"I like to read too," Dawn answered with a smile. "But I don't have much time to do it these days." The two women continued to chat and enjoyed a nice lunch together. The food was surprisingly tasteful, and Dawn felt much better after the meal. Then the two strolled leisurely back to the hospital.

"I usually eat dinner at the hotel around 7:00 and breakfast at 8:00," Elenor said warmly. "The hospital won't let visitors in until after the doctors finish their morning rounds at 10:00, so there's no need to rush over there in the mornings. If you want company, you know where I'll be. Join me anytime, please."

"Thanks," Dawn answered sincerely. She liked the Englishwoman and if she found herself alone at mealtimes, it would be nice to have someone to talk to. She doubted Maggie would leave Britt's bedside long enough to eat with her, even in the hospital cafeteria. She had seemed very committed to being by his side and almost afraid to leave him alone. *Was it out of medical concern or might she be worried that he'd say or do something in his drugged state that he'd regret?* It was an interesting premise and one she needed to think about some more. She knew so little about Britt and even less about Maggie.

After she and Elenor put on their visitor badges, they went their separate ways with a promise to meet up again later. Holgar was still at the desk and said "welcome back" as she passed by him on the way to the elevators. Her lies had given her an advantage. She would not have to sneak by the desk and Gerta ever again.

"Good afternoon." Maggie cheerfully greeted Dawn when she entered Britt's room. "He's more alert. You should be able to talk with him soon." She quickly moved her hand away from his to make room for Dawn at the bedside.

"Thanks, I plan to stay for as long as they'll let me," she answered, taking a seat. "I came prepared." She pulled a thick paperback from her purse. "Peggy Chernow's latest romance novel."

Maggie nodded. "I love her books. She's one of my favorites. I'll give you some privacy, but I'll be right outside at the nurse's station. I'll come in every thirty minutes or so to check on him. Buzz if you need anything." She pointed to a red button attached to the top of the bed, "and the doctor will be in to change or remove the facial dressings, depending on how Britt's face is healing. Once that's off, it will be easier for him to talk and maybe he'll begin to look more like himself."

"That's reassuring," Dawn said gratefully. "Thank you, Maggie."

Dawn stared at Britt, but with all the bandages and equipment attached to him, there was little she could recognize. She noticed that one of the IVs had been removed. His hand was bruised and swollen from where it had been inserted, but she saw a patch of his skin and gently stroked it. "Britt, it's Dawn," she said softly. "I'm here whenever you feel like talking." There was no response. She tried to read, and chatted briefly with Maggie every time she came in to check on Britt. She was impressed and pleased that the nurse was unusually attentive. Dawn was happy that Britt was getting such good care.

In the first few hours that she was there Dawn saw no change in Britt's alertness, but by early evening his eyelids began to flutter, and he seemed to be struggling to make his mouth work. She fed him ice chips, which he greedily swallowed whether consciously or by instinct, but at least she felt she was being useful and maybe helping in some small way. Maggie watched from the sidelines; her mouth drawn in a tight smile.

Dawn put her book away and decided to start a steady stream of conversation...maybe Britt would hear her voice or understand some of her words. She knew it was silly that a man in such pain would be interested in hearing her driveling on and on about her ideas for his house, but she began anyway, meticulously describing every detail she could recall about each room, one by one, even down to the color and placement of the wall switches and the number of the electric outlets on the kitchen counter. She described the two oriental rugs for his parlors and how well they would fit in with his presidential history theme. She knew she was being long-winded and boring, but she continued to talk, to keep her mind occupied and wile away the time.

She watched him closely for some kind of a reaction and was disappointed when he remained completely still. The machines seemed to be making more and more noise, so she spoke louder to ensure that she could be heard above their constant chirping. "And," she added, desperate for a response, "I've designed a ridiculous two-story chicken coop at Charlotte's request. It's a mini replica of the White House, complete with columns and a portico. When you move in, you can supply your neighbors with fresh eggs every day. You'll be very popular, and it might even win you a few votes." She chuckled and thought she heard him try to laugh. It was probably her imagination.

"Mrs. Holmes, it's nice to see you again," Dr. Baringer said as he came into the room. "I'm going to remove the facial bandages now and we'll see what's going on underneath. I'm afraid I must ask you to step out of the room for that. You can come back when I'm done. Maggie will help me and then the night nurse Caitlin will be here until morning. Although," he said thoughtfully, "Maggie never seems far away. I think she sleeps in here," and pointed to a sofa against the wall. "She's so devoted. A true credit to the nursing profession. I wish we had more like her."

"She does seem excessively devoted," Dawn thought. *Maybe too devoted.* "I'll go down to the cafeteria for a bite. Then I'll wait outside his door until you come to get me."

Dr. Baringer appeared later looking pleased. "The burns are going to heal nicely. I don't think there'll be much facial scarring, certainly nothing that a good plastic surgeon can't fix, if need be. But removing the gauze was painful for him so I gave your husband a shot. He'll sleep through the night, so you might as well go back to the hotel and get some rest yourself. When you come back in the morning. I think you'll see quite a change in him. I've also ordered a reduction in his pain meds, and his Foley catheter removed, so he'll be much more comfortable. The nurses plan to get him up and put him into a chair for a few minutes tomorrow. We need to stimulate his circulation."

"That all sounds positive." Dawn said wearily. Her neck and back ached from her long bedside vigil. She started to leave. "Dr. Baringer, do you think that he knows that I've been here?"

"I think so, on some level," he smiled kindly. "I'm not sure if he really understands his situation or where he is, but he muttered the oddest thing to me before I left his bedside."

"Oh? What was that?" *Had any of her words gotten through to him?*

"I couldn't quite understand but I think he said something about chickens." The doctor looked puzzled.

A broad smile spread across Dawn's weary face, and she felt the tension in her shoulders finally begin to ease.

"Yes, he heard me, Dr. Baringer. He definitely heard me." Tears of gratitude glistened in her eyes.

CHAPTER 18

Dawn went back to the hotel. She was too tired to face Elenor, so she ordered a glass of wine and a cheese platter from room service. While she waited for the food delivery, she called Lolly.

"I know it's practically the middle of the night there," she announced. "Sorry for waking you, but this is the only time I could get away to call you."

"That's all right," Lolly yawned. "How is Senator Holmes and was he surprised to see you?"

"I'm not sure he knows I'm here yet. He's been heavily sedated and not fully conscious. I've been sitting in his room for hours, keeping up a one-sided conversation in the hopes he'd respond, but so far nothing. His doctor thinks he heard him say something, but he wasn't really sure. The staff are all wonderful though. They predict I'll notice a big improvement in his mental status tomorrow, so I'm hoping for the best. And I was completely surprised. It seems Britt has a private nurse, Maggie, who's worked for him for years and she's here with him now."

"That's interesting. Has he ever mentioned her to you?"

"No, and I think that's really strange. I'll ask him about her when he wakes up."

"How long do you plan to stay there? Your clients are getting restless and asking about you. I told them you had a family emergency and would be back soon. Charlotte is making a pest of herself and demanding to know where you are. I get reports that she pops into the P Street house several times a day. Carlos tells her that you haven't been there in a few days and are out of town, but she doesn't seem to believe him. I've told her repeatedly that you'll be in touch when you return, but she doesn't believe me either. What's wrong with her? Do you suppose she suspects you're with Britt?"

"I have no idea. She's an enigma. One minute she wants nothing to do with the house and calls it a monstrosity, and the next she is dropping by all the time. You know the expression 'the elevator doesn't get to the top floor,' I think that might describe her. We should probably consider keeping the front door locked. However, with all the trades coming and going, it would be a full-time job to man it. Besides, I don't put it past her to climb the fence and break in through a window if she thinks I'm in there with Britt. Maybe she doesn't believe he was really wounded and thinks he's run off with me somewhere." Dawn chuckled but what she said held a grain of truth.

"Let's not worry about her. I want to know about you. Are you sorry you went there, and when you can finally talk to the senator, what do you plan to say? Won't he think it ridiculous that you flew all the way to Germany to see him? You can't say it's to get his approval on a design." Lolly tried to lighten the mood.

"I don't honestly know," Dawn answered wearily. "And to top it off, I had to lie and pretend to be his wife in order to get into the hospital. They have strict 'family only rules.' Everyone calls me Mrs. Holmes. It's funny but a little disconcerting."

"Well let's hope some hot shot investigative reporter doesn't hear that information. Can you imagine Charlotte's reaction if she thinks that her fiancée has gone off and married you while she's still wearing his ring. All hell will break loose, and the tabloids will have a field day. I can see the scandalous headlines now."

"Oh God. Don't go there." Dawn chided her. "One problem at a time. I'll call you tomorrow after I've talked to Britt. I'll know more about what to do then and when I'll be coming home. I know you think I'm crazy, but I'm here because I feel such a strong attraction and connection to him, and I think he feels the same way. But it's hard to get a reaction from a sedated, almost comatose man."

"Or from someone who hardly knows you." Lolly was sarcastic. She could not pretend that she approved of what Dawn had done. She thought her best friend was crazy.

* *

The next morning at 10 a.m., Dawn walked into Britt's room feeling well- rested and optimistic. To her delight, he was propped up in bed, his leg elevated only on two large pillows. His army-issued hospital gown had been replaced by a pair of green silk pajamas that Maggie had brought him. He did not look like a man who had been at death's door only a few hours earlier, but he did not look at the peak of health either. His hair badly needed washing and was matted down from all the bandages. His complexion was sallow, and his eyes were watery. She sucked in her breath at the sight of him but even in his rumpled, disheveled state, he looked handsome to her.

He glanced up as soon as he heard the door open and was thrilled to see her standing there like an angel in a white silk blouse and white slacks, with her long wavy brown hair loosely dusting her shoulders. She was a vision…maybe a dream. He shook his head gently to be sure he was seeing correctly. His eyes seemed to clear and become brighter, and they twinkled with recognition. "Am I hallucinating? Is it really you?" He tried to smile, although the tender skin around his lips was tight and hindered the effort distorting the shape of his mouth. "I heard a rumor that you were here. But I did not believe it. Maggie told me the most amazing story – that you and I got married when I was comatose," he winked, looked at her curiously and waited for her reply. "Well, did you take advantage of me?"

She chuckled. "Is nothing sacred around here? Holgar, the guy at the front desk, apparently had nothing else to do with his time but talk about me. It's a long story. I had to pretend to be your wife to get in here. There's a 'relatives only' rule for visitors. Then one thing led to another, one tiny white lie followed the next, and here I am, Mrs. Britt Holmes in the flesh."

"And looking beautiful, I might add. And pregnant too?" he said playfully. "Am I to understand that you're the second immaculate conception in the history of the world?" He started to laugh but moaned in pain and grabbed his sore ribs. "I can't begin to understand why you're here, but I'm damn glad you are." The effort of speaking seemed to tire him. He lay back and closed his eyes. Talking took tremendous effort and he was suddenly so tired.

She let out a sigh of relief when she heard his voice and realized he still had his full mental capacities. His injuries and his concussion had not affected his brain. She had been worried about that. "I wasn't sure how you'd feel about my coming. I was afraid you'd be furious. But, when I learned how gravely you'd been injured, I knew I had no choice. I had to come. It's very presumptuous of me, I know, but I was never conventional or one to follow rules."

She began nervously fidgeting. "I suppose I owe you an explanation." Sitting beside him, she braced herself for a lecture. She waited for what seemed like an eternity for him to speak, but he said nothing. The only sound she heard was the incessant beeping from the one remaining machine recording his vitals. Curious at his silence, she took a closer look at him, prepared to justify, and defend her actions, but his eyes were closed, his face was relaxed and his breathing steady. He had drifted off to sleep, more exhausted than either of them had realized.

"I'll get some coffee and be back when you're awake," she whispered, happy that she had a reprieve before she had to confess her foolishness. If she was a sensible person, she would have gone back to the hotel, packed her bag, and taken a plane back home. He was obviously on the mend and Maggie was taking exquisite care of him. She was not needed after all. But when it came to Britt Holmes, she was most definitely not sensible.

CHAPTER 19

Elenor was drinking coffee when Dawn walked into the cafeteria. "My brother's being discharged today," she said gratefully when Dawn pulled up a chair. "He's getting his follow-up home care instructions now. He'll need rehab on his shoulder but should be back at work in two months, but he'll have to have physical therapy even then and wear a sling for a while. It could have been so much worse. I've had nightmares that he'd have to move in with me permanently and that I'd have to support him for the rest of his life." She rolled her eyes. "I love him, the good Lord knows that I do, but I like my privacy and I'm not well-off. Supporting him would have put me on the dole, and I'm not one for handouts. I'm very independent." She sipped her coffee and looked at Dawn with concern. "How about you, dear? What's the word on your husband? Will he keep his leg?"

"I think so, but I haven't spoken to his doctors today. His private nurse, Maggie, told me that the blood flow to the leg is good, and the muscles are attaching properly. Healing will take a long time though and he'll need at least two more operations. Then after a lot of PT, it should function pretty normally. He might have a slight limp but in contrast to wearing a prosthesis, that's a tradeoff that I'm sure he'll willingly accept. Today, I'll ask Dr. Baringer when he thinks Britt can leave," she sighed.

"I'm afraid it could be at least another two months and I can't stay here much longer. My clients will stage a revolt. I've never spent so many days away from my business before."

"I'm sure they know you're worth waiting for." Elenor stood up. "It's been nice getting to know you, Dawn. I have a little gift for you." She handed her a small box. "It's plain ginger. It's the best homeopathic cure for morning sickness, calms the 'queazes,' as I call it. You haven't mentioned feeling nauseous, but sadly it can happen at any time, so now you'll be prepared." She smiled warmly. "If I don't see you again, take good care of yourself and your little one. I hope she's a darling little girl as beautiful as yourself."

Dawn gasped. "So, you heard I'm pregnant. Holgar, I presume?"

Elenor laughed. "Yes, Holgar. He's a regular motormouth. I'm surprised he hasn't organized a baby shower for you yet."

Damn him, Dawn thought angrily. "He's such a gossip."

"He means well." Elenor could see that Dawn was upset. "His life must be so boring that he lives vicariously through all the people that he meets here. It's kind of sad when you think about it. Anyway, congratulations again and if you and your little family ever find yourselves in the Cotswolds, look me up. I'm the only Blaine in the village of Chedworth. Everyone there knows me. I'm easy to find." She hugged Dawn briefly and left her alone to finish her breakfast.

* *

Dawn returned to Britt's room and crept quietly to his bedside in case he was still sleeping. "Hello Sunshine," he greeted her sleepily. "Sit down please. I have a few questions for you."

"Only a few?" She tensed, expecting an inquisition. "And I have some questions of my own for you."

"Let's start with how and when we got married. "His voice was even and revealed nothing about what he was thinking. "And also, we apparently have a baby on the way?" He shifted his position ever so carefully so that he could look directly into her eyes. "Have we discussed names yet?

She blushed bright red. "Of course not. We aren't married and there's no baby. It all just kind of happened and before I knew it, then my lies spun out of control."

"I know how that can happen." He sounded very serious. "Lies can take on a life of their own and be very dangerous if discovered by the wrong people."

She took his hand and explained about being turned away at the information desk after her first attempt to visit him, and that when she returned that afternoon, she had lied to Holgar and then by necessity to the doctors, the nurses, and even to Elenor Blaine, claiming to be Mrs. Holmes. "Once I started, there was no way to untangle the mess I'd made without the risk of being sent away. I couldn't take the chance."

"Well, thank you for that, but I'm beginning to question your moral fiber," his eyes twinkled, and his mouth formed a boyish wide grin. "But I'm glad you had the gumption to come here and do whatever was necessary to stay. And frankly, being married to you isn't such a bad idea, but I'm not sure about a baby. I'm not the fatherly type, and certainly not at my age."

She grinned. He had not lost his sense of humor. "So, you're not upset at me? I was afraid you'd think I was some crazy groupie or worse yet, a deranged stalker."

"If I had a stalker," he teased, "I'd be happy for her to be you. But I still have to wonder why you're here?"

"You're not going to let me off the hook, are you?" she said churlishly. "So, okay I'll come right out and say it. I felt...no, I feel an intense connection to you, and I didn't want you to die without my telling you."

"Don't put me in the grave so soon," he baited her, but chuckled. "To be perfectly clear, I feel connected to you too. Why else would I have entrusted you with so much money and my safe deposit box key, and revealed my innermost concerns about Charlotte?"

"I haven't figured that out." She looked at him intently. "And that brings up what I've wanted to ask you. Why not give Maggie your money and your key? You two seem pretty tight? Surely, as your personal assistant, you trust her above everyone else. And, by the way, why didn't you ever mention her to me?"

"It just didn't come up," he said evasively and looked away, not wanting to meet her inquisitive eyes.

She studied him skeptically. "And then there's the fact that you hinted in your note that there was enough time to change things with Charlotte and warned me to avoid her. What was that all about?"

"I guess I was a little too cryptic." He admitted.

"You think?" She grinned. "But whatever the case, Charlotte hasn't gotten the message that there's anything amiss between you two. I spoke to Lolly yesterday and she informed me that Charlotte is making a nuisance of herself, showing up at the house at all hours, bothering my construction foreman, Carlos, ostensibly looking for me. I think she suspects we've run off somewhere together. Did you ever give her reason to think that, to doubt your loyalty?"

"No, never. Charlotte has a jealous nature and a vivid imagination. She's completely controlled by her father and does very little, if any, original thinking on her own. He dictates everything in her life, and she obeys him faithfully in return for a huge monthly allowance and a very comfortable lifestyle."

He reached for the water glass by the bed. Dawn grabbed it and handed it to him carefully. When her hand accidentally brushed his lips, she quivered and quickly moved her hand away. "These meds make me so thirsty," he said, trying to ignore the physical sensation he too had felt at her touch. "What I meant," he continued, knowing he had to be honest, "is that I've been having second thoughts about Charlotte and this whole marriage thing for a while. She and I are such different people. My friends have pointed out and now I agree – she hates politics and is too immature to be a senator's wife, much less the country's first lady if it should come to that...which it will," he said definitively. "I will be our next president or die trying."

Dawn was surprised by Britt's intensity. Maybe it was the drugs talking. "She does seem naïve," Dawn offered warily, not wanting to disparage Charlotte. "I can't see her running the First Lady's side of the White House or being the country's official hostess."

"No, you're right. When I met you," he confessed in a husky voice, suddenly everything about my lunacy with my proposal to her crystalized. I came to my senses and knew that marriage to her would be a disaster, but before I could tell you or Charlotte, I had to leave town." He paused and looked at Dawn earnestly, reaching for her hand. "I don't know if there can be anything serious between you and me, but I want to give us a chance. I simply can't spend my life with Charlotte, although extricating myself from her, and thus her father's ferocious grip on me will be very tricky. It could, in the end, possibly cost me the presidential nomination. Ralph will be furious." Britt looked more frightened than devastated.

"Oh my God. I can't be responsible for anything like that. If there's to be anything between us, and I have no idea if you and I could ever be a couple, you must break it off with her first." She had already questioned his choice of a life companion and now it was time for him to make a decision about her.

"My wife, Taylor, had been dead only a few months and I was still deeply mourning her and totally devastated by her loss," he explained. "The Randolph family and their many influential friends had been large donors and big supporters of mine for years. They'd backed my two senate races in Delaware and pledged to stand by me if I ran for the presidency. Anyway, one thing led to another, and Ralph introduced me to his daughter. Then a few months later, he took me aside and rather forcefully twisted my arm and suggested that if I married her, he and his friends would guarantee me the presidency. I should have been alarmed and backed away then. But I felt so strongly that my policies could change the government and the country for the better, and I never expected to fall in love again, so it seemed that marrying Charlotte was a reasonable thing to do. But it was selfish and shortsighted. I see now that it was a poor decision fraught with terrible consequences."

"How so?" Dawn stood up, stretched, and began to pace the floor. "That's quite a confession. Tell me all about it and I'm curious, did you ever love her?"

"No, I don't think so, but I do like her. She's attractive, sexy, and funny and I knew that I needed to have an attractive wife to win the presidency. Most voters in the US still want to see a happily married man as their leader, not a bachelor who brings a different plus-one to every official State dinner."

Dawn noticed Britt's eyes blinking heavily. "I can see that you're tired. Get some rest now, but we really need to talk some more later. I have so many questions."

"You'll stay?"

"Yes, I'll stay," she whispered. "We have a lot more to iron out, but you should sleep now. I'll be here when you wake up."

It was only after he fell asleep, and she replayed their conversation in her mind, that she realized he had never answered her question about Maggie.

Why would he dodge that? And, what were the terrible consequences that would come from not marrying Charlotte?

She had so many questions and not one single answer.

CHAPTER 20

Dawn remained in Landstuhl for five more days, consulting with Britt's doctors and spending precious time with him. She rarely left his side, much to Maggie's undisguised displeasure. She ate all her meals in his room, and she only left to shower and sleep back at the hotel.

They talked endlessly. She tried to learn as much about him as she could. He reaffirmed his commitment to run for the presidency and they discussed his timetable for announcing his candidacy officially. He explained in detail his thoughts about how he envisioned organizing his campaign and concentrating on the central themes of fiscal responsibility and strengthening the military. He was an excellent debater and was looking forward to that part of the race.

Even though Ralph Randolph had assured him a victory when he was planning to marry Charlotte, he could not count on that going forward. He told her that his plan was to travel to every state at least once in pursuit of delegates to the convention. Dawn asked him about his strategies for participating in the caucus and primaries and which states he thought he could win outright, and which would require more in-person campaigning and some arm-twisting of major players or labor unions in those states. His eyes lit up as he talked and his old fervor seemed to return, until he tired, and had to nap. So far in advance, Dawn did not know how he could possibly be so positive about his chances of winning. She found out much later.

Once he awoke, they resumed their conversations and discussed the pros and cons of his two major competitors…although Britt did not seem seriously concerned about either. One was the young and dynamic Governor of Florida and the other, the prominent and much-admired LA prosecutor. Both had been semi-campaigning for months, playing a cat and mouse game…each waiting for the other to declare.

Britt told her that he and Owen had begun building a whiteboard showing all the states and how many delegates they thought Britt had in the bag already. Then his injury occurred, and all the planning stopped. His future had been too uncertain. However, now – after talking extensively with his doctors – he was optimistic about his chances of a full recovery. He had to face at least one more operation and more hospital and rehab time, but his mind was sharp and his ambitions strong. He was prepared to go forward, and this time without Ralph Randolph's support. His office was about to begin a massive fundraising effort, with promotional videos shot from his bedside. "My bandages may even get me some sympathy votes," he joked, but was half serious. "I might as well take advantage of these injuries." He was not ashamed to exploit the situation. To the contrary, a well-placed limp or an occasional wince or moan from pain might get him the attention that he craved.

Dawn wanted desperately to convince him not to play that card, but if she did, it would be so hypocritical. After staging her own ankle injury in order to meet him and secure him as a client, she could hardly criticize him for doing the same things to get delegates. His injuries, unlike hers, were real.

"Sometimes it takes a little creativity and ingenuity to achieve one's goals." She did not know if he suspected that her accidental tripping in front of him had been planned and rehearsed, but she did not want to bring it up.

"If the end result is important and worth fighting for, then go after it with all you've got." He smiled. "Risk versus reward."

Isn't that the truth, she thought to herself.

Curiosity finally got the best of her, and she asked him about Maggie again. She could see by his physical reaction that it made him uncomfortable and was a topic he preferred not to discuss. He sighed deeply and explained that her job was to look after him, as he had done since Taylor's death. "She'll do my personal shopping and run my Delaware and DC homes. She's my work-wife, with none of the special benefits. Can we leave it at that?"

Dawn was still suspicious. What was it about Maggie that Britt did not want her to know? "What does Charlotte think about her being so involved in your personal life and in running your homes? I can't imagine any woman willingly tolerating such an arrangement. I know I wouldn't, not for a nano second. Too many cooks spoil the broth," she said with conviction.

"What Charlotte thinks won't matter much longer. I intend to break off our engagement as soon as I return to the States, but I need to do it in person after I speak with her father. If you and I are together, and you still want Maggie gone, so be it. But I'll need her for the duration of my campaign. After that, she can go back to her own life. But for now, and until after the election, I need her with me."

Dawn wasn't happy with his response but at least she had a timeframe and an answer. When later that day, she was ready to fly home, she felt very comfortable with Britt but still troubled by nagging concerns about how he had been so sure of his presidential victory and how uncaring he had been about Charlotte's emotions by stringing her along when he knew he did not love her. They needed to talk about that more if anything meaningful was to happen between them. But the hospital was not the place to do it, and especially with Maggie always hovering and eavesdropping on their every conversation.

"I hate for you to leave but I know duty calls." He was aware that she had to get back to her business. "Your clients need you and I'm anxious to see pictures of my house."

"Lolly says it's right on schedule but there's nothing like having the boss on site to make things happen faster. I'll deliver it to you on time as promised."

His simple smile caused her heart to beat faster and her stomach to knot. "I'm going to miss you. Take care of yourself."

"It'll only be for a while longer. The next operation is scheduled for a week from Monday. Hopefully that will be the last one. Then I'll fly back to Walter Reed. That's only a thirty-minute drive from Georgetown and your office. I can't wait to get home. The doctors and nurses have all been wonderful here. They saved my life and my leg, but what I wouldn't give to be in my own place watching Netflix with an authentic Big Mac and some skinny fries on my plate."

"I promise to bring you some McDonalds when I see you at home."

"That's a deal. And remember, not a word to anyone about where you've been or about my condition. When you're safely home, Owen will make an announcement about my injuries. Charlotte must never know that you've been here. She'd go ballistic and her father would literally shoot me. I'm a big boy and prepared to endure Mr. Randolph's fury. It's a small price to pay to avoid a calamitous marriage." He looked at her as if trying to memorize her face and his eyes filled with longing. He took her face in his hands and kissed her deeply.

His warm breath seemed to fill every corner of her body with white heat. Immersed in the unexpected passion of the moment, she clung to him tightly and kissed him back.

"This is just the beginning. When I can fully function again," he pointed to his still-bandaged leg that kept him from moving properly and then at his already stiff and engorged penis. "You'll be helplessly under my spell and beg for mercy."

"You're so conceited, but I can't wait," she giggled, and threw up her hands in frustration. She knew she would need all her strength to get through the next few weeks without him, but she had no choice. There was nothing more she could do for him now except complete his house on time. And she was desperately needed back at Sutter Interiors.

Maggie watched their goodbyes intensely from behind a partially closed door, and barged in when it looked like they would kiss her again.

"Dawn, the car's downstairs," she spoke in a harsh, stilted tone. "It's time to be on your way."

Britt shot Maggie a stern disapproving look and redirected his attention to Dawn. "We can talk all the time. Thank God for Facetime. I know it won't be the same, but it's all we have at the moment." He grimaced as he tried to readjust his position.

Maggie literally nudged Dawn out of the way and made a grand show of straightening the bed covers and fluffing Britt's pillow.

Dawn leaned over the bed and whispered so Maggie could not hear. "I'll be thinking of you every minute we're apart."

"Me too." He took her face gently in his hands and kissed her passionately. The memory of the sweet taste of his lips on hers would have to last until they could be together again. She kissed him again once more.

Turning to leave the room, she nodded curtly to Maggie. As soon as Dawn was gone, she marched up to Britt's bedside and let out a stream of expletives. Her angry shouts could be heard up and down the hospital corridors.

He turned his head away from her vitriol with a frustrated expression on his face. He knew that he had brought this havoc on himself and now he had to fix it.

CHAPTER 21

Dawn walked into her showroom, weary from her long journey and jet lagged. She was greeted by Lolly, stacks of phone messages, and piles of paperwork.

"Before you get buried under all of this," she pointed to the pile, "fill me in on Britt."

"He's much better and the surgical team was able to save his leg. The plan is for him to stay in Germany for a while longer and have one more surgery. He'll then need time for his leg to heal. They removed his spleen, and his lung was damaged, so they have to continue monitoring him. Then, when the doctors feel he's strong enough, he'll be flown to Walter Reed for the rest of his recovery. Right now, he's pretty much bedridden with an occasional wheelchair but he should advance to a walker by the time he returns stateside, and then in time, he'll be able to walk on his own. However, I'm afraid his skiing and bungee jumping days are over." She smiled weakly. "It could have been so much worse."

"I'm happy to hear that he's doing well physically, but I mean, what about you and Britt." She looked anxiously at her friend. "If you're together as a couple, that could make things very complicated with Charlotte. She continues to drop by here and the P Street house pestering everyone for information. I told her I know nothing about the senator except what I've read in the papers and that you are away on a family emergency."

"I'm sorry you've had to put up with her and continue to lie for me. Britt feels strongly that he wants to wait until he's home before he tells her it's over between them. He owes her a face-to-face explanation. Their breakup is not about me at all. He realized that she was a mistake and if they married, they would both be miserable."

"Easy for him to say, but I'm pretty sure Charlotte won't feel the same way. She'll be looking for someone to blame and you'll be a convenient target…and a woman scorned, etcetera."

"I expect you're right, and I'll face her when the time comes. In the meantime, I need to get back to work." She looked at the huge pile on her desk. "But where to start?"

"You didn't answer my question. Are you and Britt together?"

"No. I feel guilty enough about going to Germany without telling Charlotte. If the situation were reversed, I'd be furious and so hurt…but I'm very attracted to him, I admit, and we did share a kiss…or two…but nothing more, and we've made no plans or promises to each other."

Six hours later, Dawn had returned most of her phone messages and gone through a stack of bills with new and old requisitions. Thanks to Lolly, her ongoing projects and two new ones were on target to finish on time, as promised. Even with lingering supply chain issues and labor problems, her clients would get the services they had come to expect, and she was sure that they would be more than satisfied with the results.

Later Lolly stopped by her desk. "You haven't taken a break. Did you eat any lunch?" She was worried. "You can't do two weeks' worth of work in one day."

"I know, but I can try," Dawn answered glumly. "It seems the more I do, the more I find I need to do." She rubbed her tired eyes and rolled her head around, trying to release the tension in her neck. "The time change is catching up with me. I need a good night's sleep, but first I want to run by P Street so I can report the progress and send Britt some pictures when we talk. Will you lock up here, please?"

"Sure, but can't all that wait till tomorrow? It's the middle of the night in Germany. The house will still be there in the morning."

"I know, but if he wakes up and calls, I want to give him good news. I'll just do a brief walkthrough and head home, I promise."

"Stubborn is your middle name." Lolly shrugged. "See you in the morning."

CHAPTER 22

Dawn pulled into the P Street driveway. The construction workers and their trucks had all left for the day and the house looked deserted. She pulled the key out of her purse and headed to the front door. A red Porsche came out of nowhere, careened around the corner at breakneck speed, and pulled to an abrupt stop, directly at her feet.

"What the..." Dawn spun around as a familiar figure leapt from behind the driver's seat and ran menacingly towards her. Charlotte's eyes were glazed, and her face burned bright red with fury. She waved her hands wildly in the air and screamed, "Where do you think you're going? Give me back my key. It's my house. You're done here, bitch!"

"Charlotte, I don't understand." Dawn stood her ground but was shaking. Charlotte looked deranged. "What on earth is the matter with you? I've been away for a few days and need to check on the house."

"Away, where? Were you with him? Were you two screwing like bunnies on some Tahitian Island laughing at me, poor clueless Charlotte? He always liked a good lay and bragged about how good he was in bed. Did you please him? Do unspeakable things to him that I wouldn't?" The veins on her slim neck stood out and pulsated with every hateful word. She began inching towards Dawn and came so close that she could smell Charlotte's bourbon-laced breath.

Dawn attempted to move past her and escape into the safety of the house. *If I can get inside and lock her out, I'll call the police,* she thought in a panic. "Calm down, please," she urged, feeling a sharp jab of fear grip her spine. She could see that Charlotte had snapped and was out of control. "Please calm down. Let's meet tomorrow." She forced herself to think on her feet. "I'll show you the plans for the chicken coop and the Barbie hot tub. They're just what you wanted."

"Sorry, but you're not conning me. Mama always warned me about conniving Yankee women. I knew from the first minute I saw you that you were a witch. You tripped at the Wise Owl on purpose to get Britt's attention, didn't you? Did you think I didn't see you undo your strap at the restaurant? What kind of a fool do you think I am? You've been after my man since before you even met him and lady, it's not going to happen!"

Dawn sighed. Charlotte was partially right – about the tripping part anyway, but not the rest. She had never slept with Britt, but this was not the time to make her case. Charlotte was too distraught to listen. An explanation would only stir her up more. "Charlotte, please. I swear on a stack of bibles that I have *not* slept with Britt. Think about it. How could he physically do anything that strenuous? He's wounded and stuck in a hospital bed, and I've been away on a family emergency."

"What kind of family emergency," Charlotte hissed in her exaggerated southern drawl. "I looked you up on Google and you have no siblings, and your parents are dead. You have no family. You were with him; I just know it."

Dawn tried to reason with her, but it was useless. Charlotte was not buying her explanation. Dawn looked around the yard and realized that she could not get away unless she somehow distracted Charlotte. That's when it happened, as if by God's intervention. "Look," she shouted and pointed behind Charlotte. "You didn't put your car in gear. It's rolling down the driveway towards the street."

Charlotte spun around, her sunglasses shattering as they hit the driveway. Her wildly colored Hermes neck scarf flew off as she ran to catch up with her runaway car. In her haste to confront Dawn, she had not turned off the engine. The Porsche was rolling backward down the incline of the driveway, gaining speed. She ran up to the driver's side window and tried to reach inside to grab the emergency brake.

Dawn used that moment to sprint into the house and slammed it shut, falling heavily against it in relief. She heard the sound of grinding metal when Charlotte's car hit something on the street and then came to a crashing halt. She frantically searched for her phone and dialed 911.

CHAPTER 23

The Washington Post headline read, "Senator Holmes's Fiancée Involved in Bizarre Car Accident...DUI Charges pending." Dawn put the paper down and called Britt immediately.

"Hi. How are things going there? Do you feel any better?" She began not wanting to blurt the bad news out at first.

"Same old, same old," he grunted. "Hospitals don't change their routines much. You've only been gone a few days, so not much else is new, but I did manage to hobble down the hall a couple of times on crutches. It felt so good to get out of this room on my own power and not in a wheelchair."

"I bet. That's great news." She stalled, dreading telling him her news.

"I had hoped you'd call last night," he said petulantly, "but the phone never rang. There's not another man in your life so soon, is there?" He pretended to be jealous. "But seriously, is everything okay?" He thought he detected a strain in her voice.

"Everything's okay on the decorating end, and your house is moving along nicely. However, there's been a significant glitch here...one that will definitely affect you."

She had made him curious. "In what way?"

"Yesterday, after I finished work, I went by P Street to check on everything. As soon as I got there, Charlotte arrived in a frenzy and accused you and me of, and I quote, 'screwing like bunnies.' I tried to reason with her, even tried to change the subject by bringing up the stupid chicken coop, but she would have no part of it. She called me a conniving bitch, and more. Anyway, that's not important now, but she was threatening, and I admit, I was afraid."

He swallowed hard. "I'm so sorry. I should not have let this drag on so long. "I'll have to talk to her from here. Are you alright? Did she hurt you?"

"No, but I think she would have liked to. She didn't get the chance. She had jumped out of her car so quickly to confront me that she forgot to shut off the engine. The car started to roll back down the driveway towards the street and crashed into an oncoming Tesla. The police came and someone must have contacted a reporter because the story is headline news in *The Washington Post* today and it's on all the local news channels here. There was a woman and a small child in the car. They were badly shaken but not hurt. At least not that the paper's mentioned. They did arrest Charlotte though. They made her take a breathalyzer test and she was definitely very drunk."

"But why all the attention for a fender bender? I'm sure she has plenty of insurance. It was a stupid accident, from what you're telling me, but surely not particularly newsworthy."

"Anything is newsworthy when it's related to you, I'm afraid. And Charlotte did not take kindly to being arrested."

"How so?" Britt sat up taller in his bed and was becoming increasingly alarmed. He was well aware that Charlotte had a bad temper and could become unreasonable when agitated. *What had she done now?*

132

"She went on a full-blown tirade, shouting to everyone in earshot, that she was engaged to Senator Britt Holmes and how you'd been unfaithful to her with another woman, and that woman was me. She accused me of being your mistress, for God's sake. My name and picture are plastered all over social media as the other woman in your sordid love triangle. I can weather that personally, but it's the damage to your reputation and my career that worries me. Just when you're about to make a presidential run, accusations like this can ruin your chances and create hell for you."

"I'm so sorry, Dawn." His voice sounded like a hollow semblance of itself. "I'll take care of it. Please don't give any interviews to the press or talk about this matter with anyone. I'll handle Charlotte and Ralph and try to put out the fires from here. In the meantime, lay low and I think it's best that you don't call me until this mess settles down. I don't want some genius computer hack or enterprising reporter doing a deep dive and linking us together personally. I'll erase my call history on my cell, and you should do the same. Please just act as if it's business as usual and keep working on the house. You have my permission to do anything you want there. Pretend it's your home and make it the way you'd like, down to the last detail. I'll be in touch as soon as I can. Stay strong. We'll get through this."

"But…" She heard him angrily mumble something to Maggie who must have been, as usual, attached to his hip. She could not make out what Britt said or what Maggie replied.

"But Britt…"

The line went dead.

CHAPTER 24

Dawn stared at the phone. He had hung up on her. There was so much more they needed to discuss. She wanted to know what to do next and what if Charlotte came after her again? Should she get a restraining order?

Dawn was upset and needed to talk with Lolly. As she made her way through the showroom, she passed by the front door and was horrified to see a small crowd gathering there. Some of the people were obviously reporters armed with cameras and microphones and others appeared to be curious spectators. A few carried hand-painted signs: "Dawn's a HomeWrecker" and another, "Boycott Sutter Interiors." *How could this have happened so quickly?* Dawn felt bile rise up in her throat and she ran to the bathroom gagging.

"Have you seen what's going on out front?" she called out angrily.

"Yes," Lolly answered. "I could barely get through those crazy people when I came into work this morning. They're blocking the doorway and demanding to talk to you. We need to hire a security guard until this madness passes. Who knows what they might do next. I don't think we're safe here by ourselves."

Dawn rang her hands together nervously. "How could Charlotte stir up so much trouble?"

"I doubt she did. Someone had to make up those hideous signs and I don't think it was her."

"But who then? And why?" She looked at Lolly askance. "I bet it's Charlotte's father. I know he's been an advisor and a big financial supporter of Britt's and strong-armed him into proposing to his daughter. He must believe Charlotte's nasty accusations about me are true and sees his daughter as a wronged woman, a victim who's been publicly humiliated by a philandering politician. He's reacting as an angry father, probably more to embarrass Britt than to defend Charlotte's honor."

"Well, you know the media. They like nothing better than a juicy story. Remember Monica and Stormy. The press is like a rabid dog with a bone when they think they have found something scandalous and won't let up until the next hot story comes along."

"I spoke with Britt earlier, and he told me not to talk to anyone and to lay low. He's going to try to fix this from his end, but I don't see how he can."

"I guess you'll have to trust him. Politicians have ways of spinning things and making the bad stuff go away. Look how beloved Bill Clinton is today, even after his famous, 'I did not sleep with that woman' lie on national TV."

"But wouldn't it be better to just tell the truth? We did nothing wrong. I went on my own to Germany. He didn't know I was coming, and he never dishonored Charlotte. We never slept together. He was planning to break his engagement as soon as he returned home, but he wanted to do the honorable thing and tell her in person. I had nothing to do with that decision. He had made up his mind to do that before I arrived at the hospital. Now his political career may be ruined and it's all my fault."

"Sit down," Lolly ordered. "We have to think this through logically. It's not only Britt's career that may suffer, but yours...ours. Did you see the signs out there about boycotting us? We can't afford that kind of bad publicity and our clients aren't going to fight through an angry mob to get in here. They'll take their business elsewhere."

"It isn't exactly a mob," Dawn bristled, "but I get your point. I won't allow Charlotte and her wild accusations to damage our business. It's not going to happen. But...I wonder why Charlotte is so determined to blame me. She must know in her heart that her relationship with Britt is not working, and she needs someone to blame. And also," she paused long enough to gather her thoughts. "There's no way she could know that I spent time with him in Germany unless someone told her. But who would do that? No one but you knew."

"I guess we'll have to wait and see, but in the meantime, what's the plan?"

"I don't know. I haven't had a minute to think about what's next. I wish I could speak to Britt, but he emphatically told me not to call him. He's afraid someone might trace our calls and that would only stir things up more. For the moment I'm on my own."

"No one knows you went to Germany, right?"

"Just you." Dawn tried to make light of the situation. "And I trust you didn't tell Charlotte. She can't make her accusations stick and the press will eventually see her for what she is, a confused, spoiled brat having a very public temper tantrum. Maybe she should take a hint from Taylor Swift and write a breakup song about it instead of making threats."

"I guess, under the circumstances, that we'll have to ride this out. You can work from home and avoid the mess out front. I'll reschedule your appointments, so clients don't have to come here for a few days until this blows over. I'll interview some security companies also. How does that sound?"

"I suppose it's the best we can do for now. Is anyone around in the back?"

"No, I don't think so."

"Good, I'll leave here by that door and take an Uber home. If the crowd sees my car parked in the lot across the street, they'll assume I'm still here working, and I can make a clean getaway. But what about you?" She worried for her friends' safety also. She could hear the crowd getting more restless and shouting for her.

"I won't leave until I've hired a security guard to stand in the front. When it's time to leave he can escort me out. Those crazy people don't have any interest in me. It's you they want to hound."

"Thank you." She hugged Lolly. "I'll call you when I get home. Let me collect the files I'll need for the next few days, and I'll slip out the back. Maybe you could open the front door just a little and make a show of asking them to leave. That will distract them long enough for me to escape."

"Flick the showroom lights when you're ready to leave and I'll take care of the diversion. "I feel little I'm watching a spy movie," she snickered. "But without the popcorn."

"Well, since neither one of us are CIA affiliated, let's hope our amateurish ploy works. I'm so sorry to have put you and the business in this predicament. I still think I should speak to Charlotte face-to-face and try to straighten this out...get her to retract her accusations. I'm pretty good at convincing people."

"It's too late for that. The horse is already out of the barn."

"And galloping towards Capitol Hill." Dawn said ruefully. "What a mess!"

CHAPTER 25

D awn made her escape from the showroom but had been naïve enough to think she could put something over on the Washington press corp. They were used to devious tactics when covering stories. When her Uber pulled in front of her home, the entrance was blocked by another gaggle of reporters and news trucks lined the street.

"I don't know how I'll get inside," she groaned to the driver as she nervously looked up and down the street. Her stomach tightened and her palms began to sweat. "I think I'm trapped in your car. There's no alley behind my house or any other way to get inside except through my front or garage door."

"Don't worry," the driver said calmly after looking over the situation. "I've driven a lot of celebrities around this town and also have worked as a security guard at the Bank of America and for Wells Fargo. I'll make sure you get inside safely. Stick close behind me. Hold onto my arm so no one can separate us. We'll make a run for it. Have your house key in your hand. Let me know when you're ready."

He parked the car at the curb further down the block and jumped out. No one paid any attention to him. Opening the rear door, he helped her out, took the armful of files she'd been carrying, and walked her slowly down the sidewalk. As they approached her house, someone recognized her, and the crowd moved as one towards her. Eager reporters began shoving microphones and cameras in her face, shouting questions: "How long has your affair with Senator Holmes been going on? When were you planning on telling his fiancée? Don't you have a guilty conscience for betraying such a sweet young woman?"

"Enough! Get out of my way." The Uber driver shouted, pushing his way by brute force through the throng with Dawn in tow. "Leave the lady alone." Flash bulbs went off as the two forced their way to her front door. Dawn nervously fumbled with the lock, and once it opened, they quickly slipped inside. She secured the door firmly behind them. The driver put her papers on the nearest table and gazed at her with curiosity. "That was something. You'd think you were Taylor Swift or Katy Perry. Who the hell are you?"

"No one special. My name is Dawn Sutter. But apparently, I'm the newest scandal in town…the one with a metaphorical scarlet letter pinned to my chest like Hester Prynne."

"Ahh, as in Hawthorne's classic novel," he chuckled. "I'm a literary buff myself and from pictures I remember seeing of her, you're much prettier, if that's any consolation. I'm pleased to meet you, Dawn. I'm Don Hamilton…at your service."

Dawn smiled. "I don't know how to thank you," she said gratefully. "I wasn't expecting to be ambushed like that. The press were congregating outside my interior design business on M Street, but I never thought they'd be waiting for me here too. This is all new and very disconcerting. I've no idea how to handle this attention or how to get rid of them. And frankly, I've done nothing to generate such interest in me."

"If I may be so bold…I can protect you until whatever this is blows over. But first, could I have some water, please. I worked up quite a thirst."

"You and I both," she laughed, in spite of the precarious situation. "Come into the kitchen, Don. Let's talk."

CHAPTER 26

awn found Don Hamilton fascinating. From their lengthy conversation she learned quite a bit about his past and was impressed with the man and his credentials.

Don was forty, never married, and an ex-Navy Seal. He had worked security details for the pentagon and escorted many visiting dignitaries to ensure their safety while in DC. He occasionally lent himself out to celebrities making appearances at The Kennedy Center or other concert venues. He drove an Uber as a distraction between jobs and as a lark because he did not like the confines of office walls.

"Many important people, even Supreme Court Justices and the White House Chief of Staff, use Ubers nowadays in favor of limos. They project the wrong signal – the image of extravagance and privilege. Their long, black cars are like red flags to a bull, and bring out negative reactions from the public about government extravagance and overspending."

"I hadn't realized," she said thoughtfully. "But I think you're right. By the way," she asked, "with all your qualifications, why don't you stick to one job, like becoming head of security for just one person or one company?"

He shifted uncomfortably in the chair. "I have some commitment issues," he stated honestly. "It started after my Navy Seal experience. I lost someone very close to me and I've been reluctant to get too attached to anyone since, so I move around before that can happen. At least that's what my shrink says."

"I see," Dawn said, surprised by his candor, but she really didn't understand. Don was an attractive, Yale-educated man with a nice personality and muscles of steel. She could see no reason that he should remain afraid of his feelings and stay single. He would be a catch by anyone's standards. She supposed that he simply had not met the right woman. Maybe, if she was subtle, she could play matchmaker and do something about that. However, she had other things on her mind at the moment. It was an intriguing thought, and she had a certain someone in mind for him.

"How about giving up Uber driving for a while and staying on to protect me and my assistant, Lolly. We'll both need to be able to come and go from our homes and the showroom and visit our clients in their homes without fear of a mob attack. What do you charge? Whatever it is, I'm sure we can work something out. We really need help as you can see from the outside. Will you try it for a week? Hopefully this will all blow over by then."

"What exactly is 'this?'" He was curious. She had said nothing about why the local press was camped out on her front lawn and news vans from CNN, FOX, MSNBC, and the Entertainment Channel were parked at the curb. "What did you do?"

"Nothing," she defended herself, "at least not intentionally." She told the whole story about meeting Britt, and his subsequent injury. "I can't explain why, but I felt compelled to see for myself that he was going to survive. He was all alone, in pain, with no family and confined to a hospital bed. His bride-to-be thinks something's going on between us. She has no proof because there is none. Honestly, we have just become friends. All we did was talk, until the last day, when we kissed goodbye. But I swear that was all there was to it. Nothing else happened. The poor man can't walk, and he's confined to his bed or to a wheelchair. His fiancée's name is Charlotte, and she went to the press with her accusations. Thus," she pointed to her door, "this atrocity."

"Adultery can be a mental thing too," Don interjected, as if speaking from personal experience. "Infidelity comes in all shapes and sizes and is always hurtful to someone."

"Well, this is not adultery," she said, gritting her teeth. "Britt and Charlotte are only engaged, not married. And I can't help it if he's having second thoughts about her. If you met her, you'd see that they're not well-suited for each other and she's frankly a royal pain in the butt."

"How do you really feel about her? he chuckled. "Hell, hath no fury like… etcetera, etcetera."

"I guess I do sound a little bitchy. It's just that her ridiculous outburst is all over the news. Britt has serious political aspirations, and Charlotte's childish behavior may have ruined that for him. She could have taken the modern-day equivalent of a John F. Kennedy down before he had a chance to shine and create his own *Camelot*."

"Take my word for it. When the dust settles more people will know his name now than ever before, and they'll be curious about him. They'll want to know what kind of a man he really is, and what he stands for. In my experience, there's no such thing as bad publicity, especially in politics."

"I hope you're right," she sighed heavily. "But for now, I have to find a way to be able to work, to move about freely. Will you stay with me for a while? And if so, can you find a way to get me in and out of here and my office without the press on my tail 24-7? I won't allow myself to be a prisoner in my own home."

He thought for a moment, considering her offer, and then answered. "Yes, I'll accept the job…for a while. Nothing gets my juices flowing more than a damsel in distress. But seriously, I have a plan that's worked in the past for Beyonce. I think I used it to help Katy Perry out once too."

Dawn was impressed and felt a sense of hope. "Tell me, please. I'm intrigued and all ears."

"It'll require the help of a girlfriend, one who's about your size, coloring, and height. Do you know anyone like that?"

"Yes, sure. Lolly. She's my best friend and my assistant at Sutter. But she's blond."

"That's what wigs are for. Go online and buy a brunette one that looks like your own hair. Be sure it's available and in stock. Amazon's amazing. They'll deliver it here later today or by tomorrow morning at the latest. They have a huge distribution center nearby in Virginia."

"Okay." She pulled out her phone and Googled "wigs." After a minute, she found one that would work, showed him the picture of it and when he nodded his approval, she ordered it. "I know Lolly will help me. What will she need to do?"

"It's really quite simple and so far, it's worked every time. We dress your friend up in your clothes with a hoodie, baseball cap, or a scarf, something to hide most of her face. She pretends to be you. I leave your showroom or your house with her and be sure we're seen publicly pushing our way through the crowd. The press will believe that you've left for work or for home, so they'll temporarily disperse. But they'll be back later. We'll have to keep up this hoax until a hotter story comes along or they lose interest in you. In the interim, you'll be free to move about undetected. After they've all gone, you can call a taxi or an Uber or better yet, use my car and go wherever you please. We'll stay in touch throughout the day and pull the reverse switch when you want to come home. If your friend would agree to spend a few nights here with you, it would be much easier."

"I'm sure Lolly will do anything to help me. I'll call her now. Should she come right over?"

"Yes, if possible. The press won't harass her. They're only after you and the senator. For the moment he's out of their reach in Germany, but when he shows up at Walter Reed, he'll need to beef up his own security."

Dawn nodded. What an awful mess she had made by going to Landstuhl. Her spontaneity had caused terrible repercussions. "Make yourself at home, Don. I'll call Lolly."

"Ask her to bring several changes of clothes. But tell her to put them in a grocery bag or two and place food conspicuously on the top to hide them. The press won't be suspicious of someone bringing you groceries. However, if she arrives with a suitcase, it would pique their curiosity."

"Consider it done." Dawn smiled. "And what are the sleeping arrangements? Will you be spending nights here?" she asked, fascinated by how clever he was and how detail-oriented. He seemed totally confident that he could pull off the switch with Lolly. "I'm not sure how this security stuff works."

"Yes. It's better if I stay here. I'll slip out later and pick up a few things. If you have a guest room that'll be ideal, otherwise I'll take the sofa. I've slept on much worse."

"My guest room's the second door on your right and it has its own bathroom. You can stay there for as long as you need to. It also has a view of the street so you'll need to close the blinds so the paparazzi can't see in there. Lolly can stay upstairs in the room next to mine."

"That'll work." He smiled playfully. "Are you ready to have some fun? To turn lemons into lemonade, so to speak. I really get a kick out of outsmarting the press seeing their embarrassed faces when they realize they've been tricked."

"To each his own," Dawn snickered. "Let the games begin."

CHAPTER 27

Lolly rushed through Dawn's door, carrying two heavy grocery bags and her overstuffed briefcase. "Wow, it's a zoo out there." She plopped the bags on the kitchen table and noticed a handsome stranger rummaging through the refrigerator. "And who are you?" She looked at him sideways, smiled, and waited for him to say something.

"Don Hamilton, your new security guard. I assume you're Lolly."

"I am." She looked puzzled. "Where's Dawn?"

"She's upstairs changing. When she comes back down, she'll explain everything," He studied Lolly carefully and was pleased with what he saw. She was very pretty, a little younger than he guessed, and she looked very sexy wearing gray yoga pants and an oversized bright pink tee shirt with a matching pink headband. It held her long blond hair off her face. With a brunette wig and in Dawn's clothes, she could easily pass for her friend in the switch to fool the press.

"Oh, I see you've met," Dawn said jauntily as she entered the kitchen. "How about I make us all a sandwich and we can talk. I'd like to go to the P Street house tomorrow and spend the day there, if possible." She looked at the handsome ex-Navy seal imploringly. "Can you make that happen?"

"Only if the wig comes."

"What wig?" Lolly was baffled. "Please, someone tell me what's going on and why I had to bring my clothes here in a grocery bag."

Dawn fixed the sandwiches and began to explain Don's switch plan.

"I'm happy to help," Lolly said without hesitation. "This is going to be fun."

"I think it'll work, at least for a few days until we can figure out what to do next. I wish I could call Britt and explain what's going on, but he specifically asked me not to contact him." Dawn explained.

"Why don't you call his office instead and see if his aide can get a message to him," Lolly suggested. "He was helpful to you once before. I'm sure Britt would want to know the hell that Charlotte's shenanigans have caused and what we have to resort to."

"Good idea, and while you're at it, have his office line up extra guards for him when he comes to Walter Reed. The Secret Service should take care of that. If you think there's a mob at your office and outside of here now, you haven't seen anything yet. A scandal involving a US Senator who's also a presidential hopeful can start a feeding frenzy, like sharks circling in bloody waters. The longer these rumors go unaddressed, the worse the speculation becomes." Don sounded deadly serious. "I know you both think this is fun, and in a way, it can be, but it's also deadly serious. People have been hurt and killed by over-zealous paparazzi – remember Princess Diana.

"That's a sobering thought." Dawn looked pensive.

"And remember the commotion when Buckingham Palace kept Kate's cancer diagnosis hidden. There were scurrilous rumors and even speculations that William had been having an affair with his neighbor and that Kate had found out and left him," Don said soberly.

Lolly was an anglophile and a devout follower of the monarchy and loved tales of the royals, so she knew exactly what he was talking about.

His lips tightened into a tense line. "The cover-up is often worse than the crime, aka Nixon and Watergate."

"Hold on." Dawn was slow to anger but Don was testing her patience. "There was *no* crime here, certainly not by me, and absolutely *no* cover-up. How many times do I have to say that? I am simply, at Britt's urging, not answering ridiculous rumors fabricated by an unstable woman. He says if we ignore this insanity, it'll go away on its own."

"That's how you see it," Don answered and looked at Lolly and Dawn skeptically. "But that's not necessarily how the rest of the world will. Telling the truth is always better and less hurtful in the end. Talk to the senator and see if you can convince him that his silence makes you both look guilty and ask him to make a statement refuting Charlotte's idiotic claims. He owes you that much as your friend. From what you've told me, he has no right to pull you into his personal problems and damage your reputation and your design business." Don liked Dawn and could see that she was uneasy in the position the senator had left her in and now she was dragging Lolly into his mess as well.

Dawn suddenly lost her appetite and tossed her sandwich in the disposal. She called Britt's office.

"Senator Holmes's office," a pleasant voice answered. "May I help you?"

"This is Dawn Sutter, a friend of the senators. I need to speak to his aide, Owen. It's urgent."

"I'm afraid Owen is unavailable today, but I'll be happy to take a message."

Dawn hesitated, not sure what to do. "I was hoping that he could send a message to Landstuhl and ask the senator to call me. It's a very important personal matter. He has my number."

"I'll see that Owen gets the message. Have a good day." She hung up.

"Well, that was no help," Dawn said in a huff. "I'm tempted to call Britt myself."

"If I may," Don jumped in. "I'm sure the senator had valid reasons for asking you not to contact him. I believe you should respect his wishes."

"I agree," Lolly smiled at Don. He smiled back. "Let's plan Dawn's escape to P Street tomorrow..." Before she could finish her sentence, there was a knock on the door.

Dawn ran to a window and peeked out behind the closed drapes. The press were still milling around in her front yard and the news vans were parked haphazardly on the street. An Amazon Prime truck was pulling away. "The wig must be here," she said gleefully. "But I'm afraid to open the door to pick it up."

"I'll handle that," Don volunteered. "It's time the press sees me anyway. They have to learn that they have to get past me to get to you." He opened the door just wide enough to retrieve the package.

A reporter shoved a microphone in his face, shouting, "We want to interview Ms. Sutter. She can't hide in there forever. The American public deserves to know what's going on between her and Senator Holmes."

Don grabbed the microphone and threw it on the ground behind the reporter. It landed with a thud on the sidewalk. "Ms. Sutter is unavailable to the press and will not be making any statements. Refer all your questions to the senator's office in the future...and please leave. This is private property. I'll call the police if her front yard is not cleared in fifteen minutes." He slammed the door closed.

Lolly could not help but chuckle. "You're my hero."

"Mine too," Dawn grinned. "Give Lolly the wig. I want her to try it on."

CHAPTER 28

The next morning Don and Lolly made their way through the gaggle of reporters and photographers to Dawn's silver Mercedes, which was parked in the driveway. Lolly was wearing Dawn's favorite red *St.* Johns power suit and sported a bright red head scarf and dark Tom Ford sunglasses. She had mastered the mysterious Greta Garbo look perfectly. Don was impressed and told her that she looked sexy as hell. She blushed appropriately and added extra swagger and a little hip action to her steps.

The crowd spontaneously pushed forward, shouting a myriad of intrusive questions. Don paid no attention. He cleared a path with his outstretched arms and escorted Lolly to the safety of Dawn's car. Only seconds later he drove it onto the street heading to Sutter Interiors. The reporters ran to their cars to follow in pursuit.

"I think they really believe I'm Dawn," Lolly laughed. "The switch worked perfectly."

"That was the idea." He winked. It was hard not to keep staring at her. She looked exceptionally beautiful in red, and the short suit skirt showed off her legs to perfection. Her long limbs were distracting, and he lost his focus momentarily, swerving to avoid an oncoming car. "I'll drive right up into the showroom parking lot, and we'll go inside through the front door. I don't think the press has figured out that there's a rear entrance.

Let's keep it that way. We may need to sneak in or out through it from time to time."

"Okay, sure. I just hope Dawn can get to P Street safely without being harassed. She's been away almost three weeks and that's an eternity in the construction business."

"She'll be fine. Once we're inside the showroom, there's no reason for any more reporters to hang out at her house. I'll have you walk by the office street windows every hour or so. That way they'll see you inside and think you're working. Dawn will have all the time she needs. Once she's safely back inside her own house, we'll call it a day here and make a big show of leaving."

"It's all deliciously exciting," Lolly grinned, looking behind her at the line of cars in pursuit. "I only wish this wasn't necessary. How long do you think it will last?"

"As I told you and Dawn yesterday, at least until the senator makes a plausible statement and possibly even after that. But he can make this much easier on Dawn by drawing the attention off her and onto himself, where it rightly belongs." He privately thought Britt was being cowardly and extremely selfish by forcing Dawn to tackle all the repercussions from his misguided, angry fiancée. "I guess we'll have to wait and see what happens. I hope he calls her today."

"Me too."

A few minutes later, Don parked Dawn's car in the showroom's lot, and he and Lolly made their way towards the front door. There were more reporters and some curious spectators blocking the entrance. But they allowed them to pass. He put his arm protectively around Lolly and guided her gently forward. "Don't let them rattle you. Look straight ahead. They're just a bunch of bored jerks looking for some excitement. It's only a few more feet to the door."

He squeezed her shoulders reassuringly. Lolly nodded, but he could feel that she was shaking under her clothing. The crowd grew bolder and more aggressive. They began hurling obscenities…slut, whore, home-wrecker. Before Don could prevent it, someone threw a cup of hot coffee directly at Lolly's face. She screamed in pain when the scalding liquid hit her cheek and lips, narrowly missing her eyes. "Tramp, Tramp!" The protesters yelled in unison. "You deserve that and much more."

Don grabbed the guilty party in a choke hold and forced her to the ground. "Call the police. Someone, call the police!" he shouted angrily as he saw the telltale red blisters forming on Lolly's skin. He knew she had suffered a bad burn, but he did not want to let the woman get away. Tossing Lolly the showroom key, he ordered her to go inside and wait for him. "Once the police get here, I'll send the paramedics in to take care of your face."

Some of the crowd was shocked into silence by the sudden outbreak of violence. They began backing away as photographers shot videos and snapped still pictures of the scene. Bystanders pulled out their phones, took their own candid pictures and several dialed 911.

In less than five minutes, three squad cars and a fire truck arrived with screaming sirens and flashing lights. A policeman approached Don who explained what had happened with the coffee. They handcuffed the woman and informed her that she was being arrested for assault and disorderly conduct. The paramedics ran inside to take care of Lolly's burn.

CHAPTER 29

Dawn sat with the newspaper, enjoying a peaceful moment alone after Lolly and Don's departure. She walked to the front window and snuck a peek outside. The front yard was empty, and the news trucks had gone. She went back to the kitchen, finished her coffee, and waited fifteen minutes more. Then she rechecked the front to be certain that the reporters and photographers had left.

Pulling her black hoodie over her head, she grabbed two satchels of floorplans, tile samples, and other paperwork before sprinting out the door to Don's car. Following his advice, she drove a circuitous route to the P Street house, drove around the block there twice to be sure she wasn't being followed, and pulled into the attached garage. She used her remote to close its heavy door quickly before exiting the car and entering the house through the new mudroom.

"Well look who's here," Carlos, her job site supervisor, welcomed her. "I was beginning to think you'd abandoned us."

"No such luck." She put her satchels on the makeshift counter in the center of the kitchen and looked around. "I see the drywall is finished. You've made remarkable progress in my absence. Can you walk me through everything so I can catch up and see what's gone on while I was away, please?"

"Sure thing, boss. And it looks like you've become a celebrity since you were last here."

"You mean a notorious cheater," she said testily. "Do you mind if we don't go there? I need to concentrate on finishing this project, and nothing else."

"Your call," he rolled her eyes. "But some time you're going to have to address the elephant in the room. Everyone's talking about you and the senator. You're a hot topic today."

"I did nothing wrong. Tell them that." She looked at him scathingly. "I – and we all – have a job to do. We're on a schedule with a definite deadline. Gossip about me and the owner of this house has no part in this. Capice?"

"Capice," he answered, somewhat ashamed. He had always admired Dawn Sutter and had worked well with her for several years, but the scurrilous rumors about her were a distraction and a constant topic among his crew. He had to constantly order them to put down their phones and concentrate on doing their jobs.

* *

Dawn walked through every room with Carlos, inspecting the electrical and plumbing work that was in progress and the new ceiling beams that were being installed in the two front parlors and in the library. She approved the tile and brick faces for all the fireplaces and finalized the selection of the stain for the newly installed hardwood floors throughout the first and second floors. She had hoped to keep the original floors to save money but discovered they were termite ridden and had to be replaced. It had been an expense that she had not counted on, but Britt had not objected and told her to do whatever she needed to do. When she finished the tour, she took Carlos back into the library – it still was the only room with any furniture and a place where they could sit and talk privately.

"I said I didn't want to talk about the senator but there are a few things I must share with you."

He watched her closely and noticed that she had developed a nervous tick. Her left eye twitches frequently. He attributed it to the stress she was under. "What can I do to help? You know I am on your side."

"Thank you," she smiled gratefully. "Senator Holmes was badly injured while on a secret senate fact-finding mission in the Middle East. He's been in an army hospital in Germany recovering from the removal of his spleen and other internal injuries, and he almost lost his leg. The surgeons were able to reattach it so that in time he'll be able to walk again. He is in a wheelchair now but recently was able to move about with the help of crutches and a walker."

"Oh, I had no idea," Carlos said with genuine concern. He had never met Senator Holmes, but he very much admired the man's political beliefs.

"Very few people know, and for a while, he wants to keep it that way. I'm sure that you've heard he plans to run for president. He wants to keep the specifics about his injuries under wraps until he's completely recovered."

"That's admirable, I guess. And I'm very sorry to hear about this, but what does any of this have to do with me?"

"Now, you and I have to figure out a way to redo the first floor here to make it handicapped accessible without the crew or the press, or anyone else for that matter, realizing why. When the senator is able to come home, he wants to move in here to finish his rehab and run his campaign from this house. The upstairs will have to wait. We must concentrate all our efforts to make completing this first floor our priority. We have to put 'a rush' on it and try to finish it in a few weeks. We also need to revise the plans for his office here. I need you to change the half bath into a handicapped one with easy access from a wheelchair in case he still needs to use one from time to time. It must have a no-lip shower with several grab bars inside, a handicapped toilet with side handles, and you'll need to build a Murphy bed into one of the bedroom walls. He'll stay in there and use it as his bedroom until he's able to do stairs. We need to find space to install an elevator also. That's imperative under the circumstances."

"It'll be very tight, if not impossible to finish up that soon. Our men have to sleep."

"I understand that, and I don't expect heroics from them. The solution is for you to hire an additional crew and a supervisor of your choice. They'll work nights. I want this place humming 24-7 with two twelve-hour shifts, six days a week. If you complete the first floor in four weeks, there'll be a big bonus in it for everyone. Can you do that for me – for him?"

"I'll make it happen, Boss. But," he said looking at her curiously, "there must be some truth to the rumors that you're involved with him. I've never seen you so committed to a renovation before."

"My lips are sealed," she said nervously. "I stand by what I told you previously. Just get the job done. But also remember, we've never worked for a future President of the United States before either. That demands extra effort, don't you think?"

"Yes, you've got me there and," he said thoughtfully. "I think I should build a ramp from the garage into the new mudroom so he can come in and out if he still has to use a wheelchair occasionally and maybe widen the doorways."

"Go ahead. Do whatever you have to do to make him comfortable. Money is no object. I trust you, but time is of the essence."

CHAPTER 30

"Luckily, it's only a superficial burn," the young paramedic assured Lolly as he applied a cool damp cloth to her face. "If it still hurts in an hour, you should see your doctor to get a prescription for pain. In the meantime, take ibuprofen now and I'll apply a thin coat of petroleum jelly to your face. You should do it a couple of times for the next few days. Try not scrub or scratch your face or use ointments unless prescribed by your physician. They can cause an infection. We treat these kinds of burns as we would a bad sunburn. It will heal itself in time."

"Will my face be scarred?" she asked apprehensively.

"I don't think so, but again it's best to check with your own doctor."

"All right, she will," Don stepped in. "Thank you for coming so quickly and for your help. Do you know what happened to the deranged woman who threw the coffee? It all happened so fast that I never got a good look at her."

"I saw the police cuff and take her away. Whether she's actually charged with any crime is anyone's guess these days. Under a dumb new policy, criminals are often released only hours after being arrested with the no-cash-bail rule."

"I know," Don commiserated. "It's a problem. Thanks again for your help." He opened the door for the paramedic and was relieved that most of the angry crowd had left.

"Should I call my doctor?" Lolly asked, reaching for a mirror to check out her face.

"If you'll feel better seeing him, then yes, of course. But under the circumstances, you'd better ask him to make a house call here at the showroom or to come to Dawn's. I don't want you facing another attack."

"I think I'll be alright. My face feels hot, just as the EMT said. It's like I have a bad wind or sunburn. Let's see how it feels after we get back to Dawn's later. I'd better get to work now, and I'll walk by the window from time to time like you suggested, in case some nut's still out there gunning for Dawn. Will you be close by?" She reached for his hand, her eyes begging him to stay. She was not as brave and unrattled as she pretended.

"I'll be right here for anything you need," he answered softly. "I'm so sorry I couldn't stop that crazy lady from hurting you."

"It wasn't your fault," she took his hand and squeezed it gently. "Let's hope that's the last we see of her."

CHAPTER 31

Dawn's cell phone rang as she was heading out of the library. "Yes," she answered, looking at the caller ID but not recognizing the number. Thinking it was a member of the press, she was about to hang up. "Dawn, it's Britt." She recognized his voice although he was whispering.

"Oh my God! I'm so happy to hear from you." She ran back into the library and closed the door. "There's so much going on here, but I want to hear about you first. Are you okay?"

"I can't talk for long," he warned. "The doctors are hovering around, still constantly poking and prodding me, and that's when they're not busy taking blood or pushing my body through one contraption or another. I'm scheduled for an additional MRI of my leg in a few minutes, so I'll have to be brief." His voice warmed her heart. She realized how much she missed him.

"They've taken wonderful care of me," he continued, "and I expect to be released ahead of schedule, maybe in two weeks. They'll fly me to Walter Reed where they think I'll need to stay for a few weeks going through intense rehab, but then I can go home. That's what I want to talk to you about…our timeline for P Street. It called for completion by the end of November, but I want to go there directly from the hospital. My staff can pack up my old place. I'll only bring my clothes and a few personal items. The rest they can donate to charity. I'll sell my condo completely furnished, so there's no need to worry about that. I know the whole P Street house can't be ready in time, but can you finish a few rooms so I can move in?" He took a deep breath. Talking was still an effort for him. She could hear him wheeze through the phone.

"I'm already way ahead of you," she said proudly. "The first floor will be ready by the time you are. I'm doubling up on the crews and am really on top of everything. But – about you – are your lungs any better?" Her initial excitement at hearing from him turned into concern. He was still not a well man.

"Yes, they're functioning reasonably well and I'm trying to strengthen them by blowing into a stupid plastic tube several times an hour. My lungs are the least of my problems, so let's not waste time talking about my health. How are you? I miss you."

"I miss you too," she said with conviction. "More than you can know."

"Charlotte hasn't bothered you again, has she? I had a heated talk with her father by phone. I didn't tell him that I plan to break up with his daughter, but I did say that we were not as compatible as I originally thought and that we needed to talk and figure out where to go from here. I said her recent behavior and arrest for a DWI were unacceptable."

"How did he take that?"

"Not well. He blamed me and claimed that I drove her to drink. He threatened me again by saying that if I didn't go through with the wedding, he'd cut off his funding to my campaign and would use all his influence to blackball my nomination. I persuaded him to do nothing until we could talk in person, but he was relentless in his verbal attack, accusing me of one horrendous thing after another. He lambasted me for taking the senate trip and putting myself in danger. He claimed that caused Charlotte to spiral out of control and to drink excessively. That's pure nonsense, of course. She did not know about the secret mission or the seriousness of my injuries until long after the fact. Anyway, he was defensive and completely unreasonable."

"I'm so sorry." She repeated.

"I assured him that you and I were not lovers…that you are not my mistress, and I swore that the rumors of sex between us were ridiculous and started by Charlotte herself from her own insecurity. I pointed out that I was in Germany, and you were in D.C. Remember, he has no way of knowing otherwise. He hung up angrily and told me to think long and hard before I broke his daughter's heart. It was a not too well-veiled threat."

"Oh, how awful for you." She was upset for him and for herself. He had done nothing to deserve this vicious attack. He had been honorable and had not crossed the line with her. If there was an aggressor between the two of them, it was herself. She's the one who bought the ticket and flew to his side with no encouragement from him. "I'm so sorry. All of this fiasco is my fault."

He groaned when he inadvertently changed the position of his injured leg. "I told him repeatedly that you and I have never slept together and we're only in communication because you're my interior designer. Believe me, it was not a pleasant or friendly talk; I expect his full wrath when I break it off with Charlotte." She could almost see him wincing, more from the imagined pain of that expected confrontation than from the actual pain in his leg.

"I'm so sorry. I should never have come to Germany."

"Never regret coming. It was kind and unselfish. I'm so glad you did but no one, especially Charlotte or her father, must ever know. That's our secret to take to our graves. I'm realizing that the Randolph's are an unhinged, narcissist family and I'll be glad to be rid of them – even if it costs me millions in financial backing. But I will not let him take the presidency from me...no matter what I have to do."

"Let's not waste another second talking about Charlotte and her father. There's so much more we need to discuss. And by the way, how did you manage to get hold of a safe phone?"

"I borrowed Maggie's."

Naturally, dear old Maggie to the rescue once again, she thought irritably but held her tongue.

"No one will think to tap it. Mine's been swept clean if anyone should check. If you need to reach me, call this number. She'll either answer it herself or give me your message. She'll be coming to live with me at the house. I told you that before, didn't I?"

"No, you definitely did not," she answered testily, "but there's plenty of room." Once again, she resented how ever-present Maggie was in Britt's world. She thought quickly about where she could put her temporarily and noted that she now would need to buy extra furniture for that room too.

"Won't you be able to manage on your own by then?" Dawn could not stand the thought of angelic Maggie hovering around Britt and always being underfoot.

"Yes, but Maggie's indispensable to me," he answered defensively. "And she's agreed to stay with me until at least the election. She's thrilled for the chance to be in DC because she has a sister and two nephews who live in Northern Virginia, so it's a perfect situation for her."

"How nice." Dawn almost choked on her words, thinking that Maggie could live with her sister and commute to work like normal people. She did not have to move in with her boss. She squeezed her eyes shut and felt like screaming in frustration, but since she had only a few minutes to talk to Britt, she did not want to spend them quarreling. When he moved into P Street, she would make her case and hopefully convince him to let go of Maggie's stranglehold on him. In the meantime, she would be sweet, agreeable, and bite her tongue.

"There's been a lot of interest in me and my relationship with you," she began sarcastically. "Actually, it's quite disconcerting and becoming very difficult to handle. The press are…"

"Sorry Dawn," he cut her off. "They're here to take me for my MRI. I'll call you tomorrow." The line went dead.

Dawn shook her head angrily in frustration and then pulled out her notebook containing dimensions, pictures, and delivery dates for all the furniture she had ordered for Britt. She would now need to buy floor samples from Rooms to Go or City Furniture…some place with plenty of furniture stock on hand and able to deliver it in a day or two. It was the only way to furnish the house quickly enough for Britt and now Maggie to move in. Most components of her design scheme, including the oriental rugs and furniture from France and Italy, were still months from their promised delivery date. With the Baltimore port hampered by the collapse of the Key Bridge, receiving goods could now take weeks to months longer than anticipated. That tragic bridge accident had wreaked havoc on so many businesses, hers included.

Sighing deeply, she forced her attention away from Maggie and made a careful first-floor, room-by-room list of what she would need to purchase immediately – including towels, blankets, sheets, a desk, a printer, table lamps, and a few sturdy chairs with arms so Britt could sit and pull himself up easily. She and Lolly would also need to find a decent sofa for at least one of the parlors and a daybed for the library where he could sleep until the Murphy bed was installed. Britt could then function until the rest of the rooms were finished. Maggie would have to make do with the maid's room off the kitchen until the upstairs guest rooms were completed. This new move-in date would necessitate a quick trip to Crate & Barrel, Target, and Best Buy. Then she and Lolly would have to fully stock the kitchen. It was a daunting and unexpected task, but she could, and would, do it...for Britt. She also needed to update Carlos and beg him to finish the maid's bedroom and bath for Maggie by the new schedule. Britt was not making her life easy.

By 4:00 p.m., Dawn was exhausted but felt confident she had thought of everything, even down to padded clothes hangers and toothpaste. Her design training had taught her to be thorough, and organization was her middle name. Carlos's crew had packed up their tools and left for the day. The house was finally quiet. The newly hired night crew was due to start in another hour and Carlos was coming back to orient them.

Wearily, she dialed Don. "I'm done here for today. I'll leave now and meet you at the house."

"Okay. Call me back when you're safely inside it and then we'll leave the showroom. Don't stop anywhere. Did everything go well today?"

"Yep. But Britt threw me another curveball, about Maggie. I'll tell you later." Her voice reflected how tired she was. "The house is coming along nicely, but there's still so much to do. Lolly and I have huge tasks to perform in a very short time, but we'll manage. Although, I'll need for you to work your magic and sneak us into a few stores this week or the beginning of the next...unexpected shopping," she explained ruefully.

"No problem. See you soon." The news about the hot coffee and Lolly's burn could wait until they were all together. Dawn did not sound like she was in the mood for more upsetting news.

He strolled confidently across the showroom into Lolly's office. His sudden appearance startled her, but she was glad to see his handsome face and greeted him with a warm smile. She had been absorbed in designing an open floor plan loft on N Street. "I've heard from Dawn," he said casually. "She's on her way home, so we'll give her half an hour to get there and then head out ourselves. How's your beautiful face?" He was still concerned about her burn and blamed himself for her injury. He should have been more alert, and she had suffered because he had not been. He could not forgive himself.

"I'm sure my face will be fine." She touched it gently. "But it still stings a little and feels warm. I'll put on more Vaseline before we leave. I've been concentrating on this design layout so intently that I forgot all about it."

He looked at her bright red face and grinned. "I'm sure Dawn will have a few questions when she sees you. She'll think you snuck off to the beach or at least to a tanning salon."

"I wish," she chuckled, scratching her head. "I can't wait to take off this damn wig. It itches like hell."

CHAPTER 32

Dawn left P Street via the garage and headed directly home, careful to adhere to the speed limit and not draw attention to herself. She pulled her hoodie lower over her forehead and kept her eyes on the road until she pulled Don's car into her garage. In a short while, she was sipping iced tea in the kitchen when she heard a ruckus out front.

Lolly and Don pushed their way through a new crowd of rude, arrogant reporters who had just arrived and were calling out scripted lines. "Did that coffee teach you a lesson, little lady?" "Do you feel the anger from Charlotte's friends and family?" "What do you have to say for yourself, slut?"

He put his arm protectively around Lolly and led her to the front door, shielding her body with his. The obnoxious shouting continued. "You won't always have a bodyguard," someone bellowed. "You'll have to talk sometime," another shrieked. "Where's the illustrious senator from Delaware? Is he hiding under your bed?" Still another yelled. "He's a bloody coward."

Lolly was frightened. She sensed real hatred in the air and clung firmly to Don. She had never experienced anything like this before. When they were safely inside, she let go of his arm and slid like a limp noodle to the floor. Dawn came running over. "What's happened? Lolly, honey, are you all right."

Lolly looked up at her with hot tears streaming down her very red face. "I've had better days," she sniffled. "Much better."

They went up to Dawn's bedroom where in the good light from her dressing table, she studied Lolly's face carefully. "I think the paramedic gave you good advice. You look like you've been sunbathing on a Caribbean beach all day with baby oil and iodine on your face. It will probably peel a bit, but it doesn't look too serious."

Lolly looked at her aghast. "Is that all you're going to say? I could have been blinded or worse today. You've got to make Britt do something about this craziness. It has to stop!"

"I know, I know," she mumbled, feeling horrible for what Lolly had experienced because of Charlotte. "I feel so terrible, so guilty. I had no idea things would get so out of hand."

"So, what do we do now?" Lolly asked, staring at her image in the mirror. "You – we can't hide forever. There has to be a way to end this."

They both looked at Don for answers.

"Celebrities deal with scrutiny issues all the time, but they also have teams of security people to protect them. I'm only one man and I can't be with each of you all the time. I can bring in more people, but the real solution is for Senator Holmes to make a statement, take the heat off Dawn and put it on himself where it belongs. What kind of a man is so self-centered that he puts others in danger because of his own political aspirations. Does he even know what his silence is costing you, Dawn?"

"No," she said in a subdued voice. "He called me earlier today, but I didn't get the chance to tell him about it. He had to cut the conversation short because of an MRI. He said he'd call tomorrow, but at least I have a way to reach him now – on Maggie's cell."

"Ok, then. Let's give him a chance. Fill him in tomorrow, but if he won't speak up after that, I think Dawn should issue a statement herself. That's the only way the press will leave her alone. This situation is only going to get worse, and Lolly could be really hurt the next time. We can't take that risk."

"There won't be a next time," Dawn steamed. "Not if I have anything to say about it. I'm not going to wait until tomorrow. I'll give Britt another hour to finish his MRI and then I'll call him back." She was determined to make this right and put Lolly and herself out of danger.

"Anyone for a glass of wine and some dinner? I make a great Caesar salad and I personally vouch that Dawn makes a terrific cheese omelet." Lolly attempted to change the subject. "We all have to lighten up and try to relax."

"Good idea," Don smiled and took Lolly's hand gently in his, affectionately kissing her palm. "And just in case, let's work together on a brief statement that Dawn can read to the press if the senator insists on remaining silent. "We'll give him a chance to be a gentleman. I know he doesn't want to hurt Charlotte, or rile up her father, but she must be made, along with the rest of the country, to know the truth. There will be a wedding to Charlotte and there is no affair going on between him and Dawn."

"Thank you," Dawn smiled gratefully at Don and suddenly was struck with an unsettling thought. *What if Britt was indeed having an affair – obviously not with her – but with his precious Maggie? Was it possible?*

CHAPTER 33

Dawn put aside her suspicions, attributing them to her exhaustion, and repeatedly called Maggie's number throughout the evening, but her phone only rang and rang and never went to voicemail. It was annoying that she was not able to leave a message. "I'll try again in the morning," she promised herself in exasperation.

She and Lolly decided to put off in-store shopping for another day and work from home. Neither felt up to coping with the press and the strain of switching their identities again. Lolly's face was a little less red but felt tight. It was greasy from all the coats of Vaseline, and she did not want to be seen in public. Dawn was out of sorts and moody at not being able to reach Britt, and she still harbored lingering suspicions about Maggie.

She and Lolly spent hours huddled over the computer, exploring and comparing shopping websites, and they began ordering items for the P Street house. They went room by room. It turned out to be fun, and they got a little giddy and added a few whimsical items for themselves like a bright red popcorn popper and a hotdog shaped vibrator that played "Don't Worry, Be Happy." By the time they finished, they were both laughing and in much better moods. They had narrowed the list of needed items and were left with only major pieces of furniture to purchase in person.

"I never realized that almost everything one could ever need can be bought online with the click of a finger," Dawn shook her head in amazement. "It's awesome…anything from soup bowls to dental floss. Why would anyone go to a real store when they can shop from the comfort of their homes? It's awesome."

"Let's hope our clients don't realize how easy it is to find furniture and accessories that way," Lolly added. "It could make our business obsolete."

"Never," Don chimed in. "Good taste can't be found on a website or delivered by Amazon."

"That's right." Dawn finished crossing products off her list after numbering and assigning them to specific rooms. "Anyone can shop on Wayfair, Ikea, or Pottery Barn, but they have to have the knowledge to coordinate styles, colors, fabrics, and such. But I must admit, this was fun today."

"I think we're down to the basics of needing chairs, sofas, and a few tables. We should be able to find those tomorrow." Lolly double-checked the list and put it on the counter. With a grin, she challenged the others. "Anyone want to take a break and play a game of gin rummy?"

"Sounds like fun," Don grinned, "but there's something I want to do first. Hopefully it will get rid of the bloodhounds out front for a day or two."

Dawn looked at him with interest. "Want to share?"

"No, just stay back from the door, out of sight, and listen."

He walked resolutely to the front door, opened it, and stood under the portico. "Ladies and gentlemen, I have a brief announcement and will take no questions." He watched and waited as the crowd drew closer.

"Miss Sutter is ill. She has a fever, nasal congestion, and is showing the classic symptoms of COVID-19. She'll be testing herself regularly. Regardless of the results, she has elected to self-quarantine for five days as a precaution. I urge you all to leave here now as there will be no further opportunities for taking pictures or to speak with her this week." He looked up towards the ominous sky. "And it's about to pour." A clap of thunder startled the crowd and proved his point. "I suggest you all leave and try to stay dry. Thank you." He turned and reentered the house.

"Wow. That was very inventive." Dawn smiled and congratulated him. "You probably should have done that before. Will they believe you?"

"I think so. The mere mention of Covid still scares the shit out of people, excuse my words. Let's watch and see." He moved to the living room and shifted the curtains enough to take a peek through them. "The large majority of people were leaving. Only a few stragglers seem determined to stay behind. They're huddle together on the sidewalk under big umbrellas." With the next loud clap of thunder, accompanied by a bright streak of lightning that lit up the sky, they too ran for cover.

"I think your little speech combined with Mother Nature worked," Dawn said. "Thank you."

"Yes, thank you." Lolly threw herself exuberantly into his arms and gave him a warm hug. "How did I ever manage without you?"

He smiled playfully at her, enjoying the sensation of her warm body so close to his. "If I'd known I get such great reactions from a little speech, I'd have made one much sooner."

"But when the storm is over, do you think they'll come back?" Dawn was still skeptical.

"Maybe, but I hope not. Let's enjoy the moment. He went to the refrigerator. "Anyone want a beer?"

"It's five o'clock somewhere," Dawn smiled. "Sure, I'll have one, please.
Lolly echoed her. "Me too."

They took the beers into the family room, got out a deck of cards, and
turned on the news. "How did that happen so fast?" Dawn looked amazed
when she saw the screen. The commentator was showing the video of
Don speaking out front. "It hasn't even been ten minutes."

"Modern technology," he grinned. "Most of the time it's a hassle but
in this case, it worked for us."

Dawn looked at her watch. "I've been so busy today that I forgot Britt
was supposed to call me. Now it's already past midnight there." She was
tempted to call Maggie's phone anyway. "He couldn't have been having
tests all day long." *Was he ignoring her?* The thought made her anxious.
"I don't want to wake him in the middle of the night, so I'll wait until
morning."

Lolly rolled her eyes and wished Dawn would spend more time
protecting herself and less time worrying about Britt and his precious
sleep. Waking him up in the middle of the night did not seem so egre-
gious. It would not cause a major health setback. It was well past time
for him to take responsibility for his actions, or in this case, his inac-
tions. Both she and Don were running out of patience with him and
with Dawn's lame excuses for his thoughtless behavior. Annoyed, she
excused herself to go to bed, but she had trouble sleeping. She kept
thinking about Don and the unexpected intense attraction she felt for
him. He was so strong and masculine, so kind and protective…and
feeling his body so close to hers when they hugged, had awakened
feelings she had not experienced in a very long time. She thought he
might feel the same way because she had felt his hard erection when she
pulled away. She smiled to herself before finally drifting off, wishing

the vibrator she had ordered earlier as a joke was in her hand now, or better yet, Don himself.

Don lay in bed speculating about Senator Holmes. His reluctance to take the spotlight off Dawn was worrisome. *If he really cared about her, why was he subjecting her to so much angst? Was there something more going on?* When he stopped fixating on Britt, his thoughts went to Lolly, her soft skin, her beautiful eyes, and her genuine warmth. He could not remember another time when he felt so protective or cared about a woman as much…not even when his first love cheated on him and slept with his best friend. That had hurt and disillusioned him so much that he had avoided entanglements ever since, but somehow, he knew Lolly was different. This might be the time to take a risk and love again. Tossing and turning alone in the bed, he wished she was snuggled next to him, lying in his arms. He was tired of being emotionally walled-off, and all of his raging male hormones were telling him that it was time to do something about it.

CHAPTER 34

Dawn awoke early and immediately reached for her phone. She had so much to tell Britt – about the swarming press, about needing to hire Don Hamilton for security, and about the hot coffee thrown in Lolly's face. He was so insulated in Germany that he had no idea what was going on at home or the recent havoc in her life, and she had not been able to tell him. It was maddening and could all change in an instant if he issued a simple clarifying statement. All he had to do was say that the rumors concerning his relationship with Dawn Sutter, his interior designer, were vicious lies. She was renovating his new house for his bride-to-be and himself. *That was still true…at least for the moment… unless he'd spoken to Charlotte overnight.*

She dialed Maggie's number and waited impatiently for her to answer. At this hour, she should be at Britt's bedside and could simply check her caller ID and hand him the phone. After ten seemingly interminable, unanswered rings, she hung up irritated and ready to scream in frustration. There had been no answering machine again, no way to leave a voicemail, which was odd. Britt had assured her that calling Maggie was the best and safest way to reach him. Grumbling to herself, she showered and tried Maggie once again. No answer.

Lolly and Don were engrossed in deep conversation when she walked into the kitchen. "So, I'm not the only one up with the roosters," she grinned.

"Nope." Don poured everyone some orange juice. "I guess none of us are sleeping very well these days."

"I kept jumping out of bed checking to see if the press had come back." Lolly admitted sadly. "I'm pretty jumpy."

"No need to be," Don went over and put his arm reassuringly around her shoulders. "Lolly, I promise, I won't let anything happen to you…or to Dawn. And I'm damn well going to put a stop to this nonsense, even if I have to go to Capitol Hill and ruffle some feathers in the senator's office myself."

"That won't be necessary. I'm sure once Britt hears how bad things are here, he'll make a statement. Let me try him right now." Dawn picked up her phone and pushed the redial button. Again, no answer. "Maybe he and Maggie are at PT." She did not even believe what she was saying. There was no excuse for Maggie ignoring her. She knew she could see it was her from the phone's caller ID. Something was going on, and she needed to find out exactly what it was.

"If you don't reach him soon, I'll find a way to do it myself. He's put you two in an untenable situation." Don's serious voice and stern demeanor reassured Lolly but worried Dawn. She wanted less confrontation and strife in her life, not more. She worried that he was turning against Britt, and that could signal trouble.

After repeated attempts throughout the morning and into the late afternoon, Dawn had to accept that Britt, for whatever reason, had no intention of talking to her. He was ghosting her. *But why?* And Maggie could have easily answered her phone at any time but had not. *Did they know what was going on and chose to ignore it?* She wondered. *Surely his office would have told him about the confrontations with the press and the terrible rumors floating around. How could he leave her hanging and exposed like this?*

Don and Lolly spent the day talking and flirting with each other. They disappeared into his room from time to time and returned looking sly and disheveled. Dawn pretended not to notice and paced nervously around the house, becoming more and more agitated and repeatedly calling Maggie's number. At this point, she had lost her patience and did not care if she was becoming a nag. She was angry and worried. "I'm going stir crazy," she finally declared, throwing a tea towel angrily in the sink. "Don, can you take me to P Street? At least there I might be able to do something productive."

"I'd like to go with you. I haven't been there in a while." Lolly suggested. "Can we all go together?"

"I guess so," he answered cautiously. "Because of the rain and the threat of COVID, the reporters have apparently backed off. We should be okay. Let me make a phone call first and then we'll leave."

"No wig?" Lolly joked.

"No wig." He winked and disappeared with his phone.

Twenty minutes later, Dawn and Lolly, with Don standing guard between them, opened the front door and made their way to Don's car. They felt safe and saw no one lurking about. No members of the press were there to stop or harass them. Or so they thought.

"How are you feeling, Dawn?" Someone shouted, suddenly appearing from behind a large forsythia bush.

"So do you have COVID or not?" another called out, jumping down from a limb of a tree by the sidewalk.

"Does the senator know you're spreading a lethal virus around town? What happened to isolating?" A woman shrieked coming out from her hiding place behind a parked car.

Shocked, but trying to ignore the clamor, the three quickly entered Don's car. He floored the gas pedal and drove away. As expected, several members of the press ran and jumped into their own vehicles that they'd parked further down the street, out of sight from Dawn's home. They began a pursuit.

Don, having suspected something like this might happen, smiled mischievously, deliberately driving way below the speed limit and using his turn signals so the tailing cars could not possibly lose him. He steered around the same three blocks, excruciatingly slowly, four times. Horns honked and he saw raised fists and a few fingers directed at him in the rearview mirror. Chuckling, he finally made a sharp turn into a short driveway. A high wall hid the elegant older building from the street and a gatehouse stood guard over the entrance. Greeting the familiar man inside the booth, he was immediately allowed inside, but the media, much to their consternation, were stopped in their tracks.

Don parked the car in the "members only" parking lot and the three scurried into the private club. He stopped to briefly chat with a few members he saw en route to the back terrace. Dawn and Lolly followed him through a lovely courtyard with tables set for outdoor dining and into the back alley. Before either of the girls could question him, they were met by Don's friend Larry and told to jump into his black SUV.

"Where to?" Larry asked with a grin.

Don introduced them and gave him the address of the P Street house. Dawn figured out what was happening. She reached over from the back seat and handed Larry the P Street garage clicker. "Pull right in and close the door quickly, please," she said conspiratorially. "We don't want any-one to see your van."

"It's a wonder no one has figured out where Britt's house is yet and that you would surely go there frequently." Lolly was amused at the cloak and dagger adventure. "Real estate transactions are in the public records. Anyone could find the address easily, unless..." She looked at Dawn curiously. "Britt bought the house under a different name, so no one has made the connection."

"I've no idea. I never had a reason to see his sales contract." Dawn looked perplexed. "But I'll check into it. Many wealthy people put real estate as well as their stocks and bonds in corporate names or LLCs to avoid taxes or hide their ownership, like in the case of a pending lawsuit or a cantankerous divorce."

"I guess that's possible." Lolly sat up straight and screamed. "Look, look," pointing straight ahead.

There were three fire trucks and an ambulance parked in front of Britt's house. Flames and black smoke poured out of the first floor, and when she rolled down the car window, she heard loud popping noises coming from inside as windows blew out, one by one, sending pieces of shattered glass darts everywhere.

Without thinking, Dawn jumped out of the car and ran up to the first fireman she saw. "This is my job site. What's happened? How bad is the fire?" She panicked when she saw a man on a stretcher being carried out of the front door. "Who's that? Has someone been hurt?" She screamed loudly at the firefighter to make herself heard over the noise and more approaching police sirens.

"He's one of the construction crew," the fireman answered. "He tried to put out the fire himself and inhaled too much smoke. We think everyone else got out unharmed, but lady, you can't come any closer. Stand back out of the way."

When Don and Lolly joined her, they huddled together watching in horror as the angry flames continued to leap out of the windows, licking the front of the building with black soot. Six firemen, laden with heavy hoses, stormed through the front door. Curious neighbors began to form a concerned group on the opposite sidewalk and talked nervously amongst themselves, watching the frenzied activity.

"Oh my God," Dawn moaned. "I think that's Carlos on the stretcher and," she looked back at the house in alarm, "the inside's going to be completely ruined. How can this be happening?" She stared at the house in shock and began to shake.

"You two stay here," Don ordered. "I'll see what I can find out and where they're taking your foreman." He ran over to the ambulance that was loading the stretcher. "What's the name of the patient and where are you taking him?"

CHAPTER 35

"They're taking Carlos to G.W. Hospital," Don announced gloomily when he returned. "He'll be fine, but they're treating him for smoke inhalation. At the hospital they'll check for a tracheal burn. He's experiencing eye, nose and throat irritation, which is to be expected, and he's wearing an oxygen mask. He's already called his wife. She's going to meet the ambulance at the emergency room."

"Were you able to talk to him?" Dawn asked with concern. "Was he lucid? Was he burned?"

"No burns that I could see. I only spoke with him briefly. He expects to be sent home after the doctors check him out. He asked that you not come to the hospital. He'll call you in the morning. There's nothing you can do for him now."

Dawn was very worried about Carlos and the house. "I guess I should call our insurance agent and arrange for a restoration company to come over and assess the damage. They'll need to give me an estimate for debris removal and repairs. God, what a mess! How long before I can get inside the house?"

"I don't know." He answered. "First the police have to declare it safe to enter, and then you and a restoration company can go inside. All your drawings, floor plans, etcetera were in there, weren't they? You'll have to begin everything all over again."

"Actually, Carlos has copies of all his plans in his home office and I brought most of my paperwork home with me when I realized we were going to have to push up Britt's move-in date. Oh," she wailed, "Britt. I have to tell him about the fire. There's no way he can move in now as planned."

"Poor man, he may have to camp out in a suite at *The Four Seasons*. Such a hardship." Don muttered under his breath. "Let's get out of here. There's nothing we can do, and I, for one, can't face the hassle of going back through the Center Club again. The hell with the press. Let's have Larry drive us home and I'll get someone to bring my car over to your house in the morning."

"I suppose that's okay," Dawn said wearily. "But I'd really like to check out Carlos for myself."

"I understand, but the doctors probably won't let you in to see him until after they've finished their examinations. That could take hours," Lolly said kindly. Carlos was invaluable and she knew how critical he was to Dawn's work. "We should go home and then call his wife. It's Maria, isn't it?"

"Yes." Dawn was overwhelmed. "I'll reach out to her in a few hours when she knows more about his condition. In the meantime, let's pray that he'll be fine. He has four little kids to support."

The three made their way slowly back to Larry and his SUV. "Will you drop us off at Dawn's house?" Don looked at his friend. "And arrange for someone to bring me my car from the club in the morning?"

"Sure thing." Larry answered solemnly and started the engine. As they drove along the congested street, they saw that the crowd of curious neighbors was dispersing, and the firemen were reloading their hoses and equipment, preparing to leave the scene. The police were busy cordoning off the perimeter of the property with yellow tape and hanging "no trespassing" signs.

Dawn looked out the window in a daze back at the house and then she thought she saw Charlotte Randolph cowering by the hedge on a neighbor's yard. Were her eyes deceiving her or was it her overwrought imagination playing tricks on her? "Did you see her? Did you see Charlotte?" she asked breathlessly. What would she be doing here?"

"No. Where?" He looked where Dawn pointed, but there was no one there. "Carlos told me that he overheard a fireman talking inside."

"And?" Dawn looked at him, puzzled.

"And he said that he suspects the fire was deliberately set…that it did not start on its own."

"Arson?" Dawn barely croaked out the word. "They think someone intentionally set the house on fire?"

"Yes. That's his first reading of the situation."

Dawn could not make herself believe that Charlotte would have done such a thing. No one spoke on the ride home. They were each upset and lost in their own private thoughts. Dawn was the most distraught of the three and planned to call the central number of the hospital at Landstuhl as soon as she got home. She would demand to be put through to Britt's room. She was not fooling around any longer. It did not matter about the time or Maggie's availability to her phone. Enough was enough.

Don had a different idea. He planned to barge into the elusive senator's office the next day, confront his aide, and demand to be put in touch with Britt. He could see the toll his silence was taking on Dawn, and therefore on Lolly. It was inexcusable and had to stop. He felt protective of his two new friends and was determined to see them through this crisis.

CHAPTER 36

As soon as Dawn returned home, she dug in her purse for her phone. It was not there. She momentarily panicked until she saw it sitting on the kitchen table. In her haste to get to P Street earlier, she had forgotten to take it with her.

When she checked it, she saw seven voice mails from the same number – Maggie's. Pushing "play," she turned up the volume and listened intently. All of the messages said pretty much the same thing. Britt had fallen and underwent emergency surgery. He was out of recovery and had been moved to another private room, but he was still groggy from the anesthesia.

Dawn frantically dialed Maggie's number. Emergency surgery, that explained Britt's seemingly thoughtless silence. She felt guilty that she had doubted him. He had not, as she surmised, ghosted her. His medical condition explained his lack of communication. Waves of relief washed over her but were coupled with equally powerful swells of worry about what kind of medical emergency might be next. His body was weak after all the injuries and now it had endured yet again another surgery. She held her breath as she waited for Maggie to answer.

"Hello." It wasn't Maggie who answered. She recognized his familiar voice, but it sounded far off, thready, and weak. "Dawn?"

"Yes. It's me. I've been so stressed when I didn't hear from you, and now I'm beside myself worried about your latest operation. What happened?"

"I stood up and felt lightheaded. Then I passed out and landed hard on my bad leg, tearing the incision open. I also sprained my wrist trying to break the fall. The doctor had to go back in and suture my old wound again. And unfortunately, there wasn't enough good tissue to use, so he had to perform a skin graft from my hip. I won't look so sexy in a Speedo anymore."

"Oh no! Now that really is a tragedy." She tried to joke. "But seriously, are you alright?"

"I'll be fine in time, but it's going to be pretty rough and a prolonged recovery. For now, they have to keep me propped on my good side so the graft and the leg can heal. I can't even sit up to eat or drink so they're feeding me through a gastric tube. It's very painful. I guess my hope of moving into the P Street house anytime soon will have to wait." His voice began to fade. "Sorry, I'm struggling to stay awake. So many drugs. Can you call me back later?"

"Sure. I have so much to tell you that I can't wait." She was extremely agitated. "It's really important. Can I talk to Maggie please?"

He did not answer but Maggie came on the line. "Hi Dawn. Britt has had a bad time, and with all the meds they have in him, his attention span is very limited."

"I wish I could be there to help care for him, but I've had a few emergencies of my own here. I need to tell Britt what's been happening and find out what he wants me to do."

"Do you feel comfortable telling me the problems?" she asked, trying hard to be pleasant. "If so, I can relay the information as soon as he wakes up and get back to you with some answers. It'll be a good three days or maybe longer before he's off the opioids and can really concentrate long enough to have a decent conversation with you. His leg is a mess, and the doctors are worried about infection. He also suffered a slight concussion when he fell."

"Oh, my word. I'm so sorry. I guess you as a go-between will have to do." Dawn sighed heavily and began to relay in chronological order the facts about the press hounding her, someone throwing coffee on Lolly, and her hope that he would make a statement to clear her name and reputation. Then she described the ridiculous clandestine way she was forced to go in and out of her house and the office – the switch. She finished by describing the horrific house fire but omitted the part that the fire department thought the blaze might have been set intentionally. She did not want to worry Britt any more than she had to. There was only so much bad news a man in his frail condition could take. Besides, it was only conjecture. She'd wait until, and only if, she had proof. She ended the conversation by saying, "I'll call the insurance company and a restoration company, but I need his permission to file a claim and initiate the repairs. I assume his insurance will eventually pay for the repairs, but until they do, it will cost Britt a lot out of pocket."

"I can only imagine," Maggie answered quietly. "But you can sign everything. Britt gave you his power of attorney, so use it. He can't be bothered with any details now. I can't imagine any one house having so many problems. It's as if it's jinxed."

"Maybe it is." She remembered Charlotte thinking a ghost lived there. "But there's something else," Dawn added. "With all these problems, does Britt want me to continue with the renovation and decorating or would he rather cut his losses now and put the house on the market…let someone else modernize it? It would be easier, and he could find another place to live. Please ask him."

Dawn was upset that she had to go through Maggie and could not speak directly with Britt. That had not been part of her original arrangement with him, and she did not trust Maggie.

"I imagine with this setback it might be another couple of weeks before he has the strength to make the trip home. I'll keep you posted and call you about the other issue as soon as I can," Maggie said in an icy voice.

Dawn stared out the kitchen window. *How could so much have gone wrong all at once? What had started out as a dream job – the most thrilling and industrious project of her career – had turned into an incredible nightmare.*

"Did you speak to him?" Lolly asked as she and Don came into the room. They had been holding hands but broke apart. This was not the time to flaunt their newfound passion for each other, not when Dawn was so clearly and justifiably upset.

"Yes, I spoke to him briefly, and I'll fill you both in. But first, will one of you pour us some wine? There's cheese in the fridge and crackers in one of the upper cabinets. I think it's going to be a long night while I wait for Maggie to get back to me. Doesn't it seem like I'm forever waiting for her or Britt to call me?"

CHAPTER 37

Dawn was emotionally exhausted after witnessing the fire and learning about Britt's critical condition. She could not keep her eyes open and fell asleep on the living room sofa. Lolly and Don had gone to bed. This time they did not bother to hide that they were together.

At 3:30 a.m. Maggie's call jarred Dawn awake. She sat upright.

"Britt wanted to talk to you, but the transport team came in and whisked him away for some reason, so you're stuck with me."

"That's okay." After his fall, she had not expected to talk to him anyway. "What does he want to do – about the fire? And the house?"

"He was very clear. The house renovation is a 'must' for him, and he wants you to continue with it as planned. Hire a restoration company. You're to pay whatever is necessary to repair the damage and order any replacements for things ruined by it. I must say, I was impressed. He seems to know a lot about house fires and asked that you pay special attention to the electrical system and install top-of-the-line smoke detectors to protect the house in the future. He's asked me to arrange to send you more money for the costs. Owen will have it messengered to you later today."

"Alright. I'll proceed as Britt wishes, but there's *no* need to send extra money. I have more than enough." She picked up a pen and began making notes. "I'll get on everything first thing in the morning."

"And one more thing," Maggie added. "He wants me to remind you that he does not want any paper trail of these transactions. When he announces his run for the presidency, he wants to appeal to the average, middle-class voter – the farmer, the schoolteacher, the clergy, the owner of the local hardware store – you know – to everyday Americans. He does not want to be seen as super wealthy or extravagant, living in a mega mansion. The country had enough of those gaudy images with Donald Trump, and his yachts, golf courses, and private planes. Britt wants to be a man of the people."

"Yes, of course, I understand that, but people aren't stupid. When they see pictures of his house, even from the outside, they'll know it's a mansion."

"I can't speak to that, but it doesn't matter. My instructions are to reiterate to you that there must be no paper trails, period…nothing in writing to tie him to the house." She continued speaking matter-of-factly. "And Owen will continue to send you money. Simply deposit it in your business account and write your own checks for expenses as you've been doing."

Dawn was bewildered. "As I just told you, I don't need or want any more money. Please. He's already sent me way too much." Britt's compulsion to pay for everything in cash was bizarre and made her feel squeamish. *Why was Maggie so adamant about it?* "I would prefer we handle paying the bills in a more conventional way."

"This is not a conventional time." Maggie's voice suddenly sounded tense. "Have you ever worked for a future President of the United States? I don't think so." Her tone was condescending. "You can't be so naïve, Dawn. Things are done differently in that realm. Everything in politics is about spinning the truth and optics. Britt is a good, decent man with lofty ideals, but he can't achieve his goals for the country if he's not elected. You either do this his way, or he'll be forced to find someone who will. I'm sorry to be so blunt, but he does not have the strength and is not in any condition to argue with you. Please, I know you care about him. This is the one thing you can do now to make his life easier. I'm doing what I can at this end; you have to step up there. The poor man has so much on his plate. It's overwhelming, and I'm simply trying to ease his burden and carry out his wishes."

Dawn was speechless. She had used all her arguments and they had fallen on unhearing ears. Maggie tuned her out, but there was a ring of truth in what she said. Britt could not change the country if he was defeated at the polls. And logically, how could he possibly read and sign contracts and mail off checks from his hospital bed when he could not even sit up?

"I guess I have no choice. Of course, I want to do everything to help Britt get elected, but more importantly, I don't want to make demands on him that might hinder his recovery. Tell him I'll do things his way, at least for now, until he's stateside and we can talk face-to-face."

"Excellent. I'll let him know."

"But Maggie, what about issuing a statement? As soon as he's able, Britt needs to make one declaring that he and I are not together, and that Charlotte's accusations are false and unfounded."

"I understand." She sounded impatient, as if she was mollifying a child. "I'll ask his office to release something to that effect. He's too weak." Maggie abruptly disconnected, leaving Dawn feeling more bewildered and uneasy than ever.

What was she going to do with the extra cash? The bank manager was already suspicious, and with every deposit she made, he called her into his office and asked where the money was coming from. So far, she had been able to convince him with the lie that the funds were proceeds from several offshore oil investments. She had seen Tom Cruise use that same tactic in a recent movie and it had worked for him. The banker seemed momentarily appeased, but she was really pushing it by resuming the large deposits again. There had to be a better alternative. If he insisted on sending more money, she needed to find a safe place to put it until she could give it back to him. But where…certainly not in her house or in her showroom.

In the middle of the night, she woke up and remembered Britt giving her the key to his safe deposit box at the Capitol Hill Bank. When the next payment came, she would stash it there – in his own box. What better place? She suddenly felt better with a sense of relief. Now she had a plan, one that made perfect sense. The problem was temporarily solved. With her fears allayed, she fell back asleep for the rest of the night.

CHAPTER 38

Dawn awoke feeling refreshed and energized. She wandered into the kitchen to make coffee, hoping Lolly might be there and they could share a little "girl time." Since Don had moved in, they had little time together and were rarely alone. She took her cup and knocked softly on Lolly's bedroom door, opening it a crack.

She was not surprised when she saw Don and Dawn lying entwined in each other's arms, soundly sleeping. Grinning, she eased the door closed. After showering and dressing, she returned to the kitchen to wait for the two lovers to emerge from their cocoon of love. An hour later, Lolly strolled casually into the kitchen. "Good morning," she beamed. "Did Maggie call you back last night?"

"Yes, she did." Dawn could not help smiling at her friend. "By the way, you and Don don't have to play games with me anymore. I know you're together – and I couldn't be happier. He's a great guy."

Lolly blushed and hugged Dawn. "I'm so happy you approve." She called out in a loud voice. "Don, the jig's up. We've been caught. Come on down and face the music." She giggled like a schoolgirl. "I love him, Dawn. I really do. It's magical and I never expected to feel like this at my age. Finding him has opened a whole new world of possibilities for me – for us both."

A moment later, Don emerged in his bathrobe looking sheepish. "Sorry Dawn. We didn't intend to go behind your back. It's just that you have so much going on that we…"

"Say no more. I understand and I'm truly happy for you both." She blew him a kiss.

"Did you speak to Britt or Maggie last night?" He set aside his embarrassment at being found out and changed the subject.

"Yes, to Maggie. She told me to go ahead with hiring a restoration company and to continue the renovations. God knows why, but Britt's determined to keep the house. She also said that his office will issue a statement today, like we've asked them to. Let's keep the news on so we don't miss it."

She purposefully did not mention the new payments Maggie had said were on the way or her idea of where to keep the cash when it arrived. Don was already suspicious enough of Britt. She did not want to give him more reasons to question his character. And besides, she was still a little embarrassed and squeamish about accepting the cash deposit and the subsequent payments. She should have insisted on a check or credit card. Whenever she thought about it, she'd feel a prickle of unease and then it turned into a sharp stab. In her heart, she knew that what Britt was doing was not right, but she did not want to admit it to anyone, least of all to herself. She decided it would be smart to call her lawyer and seek his advice.

Dawn never kept anything from Lolly, but this time, she knew that her best friend would share Don's concerns about the cash. They were in the early stages of their romance, a time when it was a badge of honor for couples to share absolutely everything with each other…keeping no secrets in the precious name of new love. She did not want to burden Lolly with her concerns about Britt, so she remained silent.

Don switched back and forth between *Good Morning America* and *The Today Show*, but there was no announcement from the senator's office. Disappointed, Dawn and Lolly turned the sound down on the TV and concentrated on arranging to get estimates from restoration companies. They called Carlos to check on him and ask when he would be ready to return to work. Although his voice was hoarse, and he had a dry cough, he claimed to be fine and said he was ready to work whenever he was permitted back on site.

Don called Larry and arranged for his car to be brought over from the club. He then called the fire department to ask when work could resume in the house. He was told that there was an active arson investigation underway, based on initial reports of unknown ignitable liquids found at the scene that Carlos had not recognized and never ordered. But no definitive conclusions had been made.

During the investigation process, neighbors would be interviewed and asked if they had seen anything or anyone suspicious on the P Street property within the last forty-eight hours. Then, once any physical evidence was tagged and removed, and a structural engineer certified its structural soundness, the house could be reentered. The procedure was expected to take three to five days. Don had also been informed that arson was very hard to prove and that most cases were never resolved. The investigation would probably go nowhere.

"I guess, based on what Don found out, that we won't be able to do any work at the house for at least a week. We should all fly to the Caribbean and idle our time with piña coladas on the beach." Lolly laughed.

"That sounds like wistful thinking," Dawn lamented, "but not possible. And are you kidding with your red face? I don't think so. But on a serious note, do either of you have any idea who or why someone would want to burn the house down?"

"Charlotte, perhaps?" Don conjectured. "You did say you thought you saw her at the sight. She's the only person I can come up with, and I think she's a certified nut case."

"She hates the house and calls it a monstrosity, but even she's not that crazy." Dawn surprised herself by defending Britt's fiancée, but in the back of her mind, she did think it might be a possibility. "If the house is deemed unlivable, Charlotte would have a great excuse not to move in. That would be a perfect scenario for her."

"Look," Lolly pointed to the TV. There was a picture of Britt on the screen. She turned up the volume. The commentator switched to a live news feed from the Senate Office Building. Owen Marshall, Senator Holmes's chief aide, stood primly at a podium looking officious and read a prepared statement.

"I am here to announce that Senator Holmes was gravely injured on a humanitarian mission to the Middle East several weeks ago and has been hospitalized in Europe ever since. The doctors expect him to make a full recovery, and he is anxious to get back to work for his constituents in Delaware and for all the people of the United States. In the interest of privacy, his office will make no further comments about his medical condition except to assure you that he is on the mend, and you will see him working in the Senate again soon." He paused momentarily to let his message sink in. The surprised reporters began to shout questions.

"I will take no questions," Owen announced primly, "but," he waited for the crowd to be silent. "The senator does want everyone to know that he is engaged to marry the lovely Charlotte Randolph and that any and all rumors about him having an interest in or an affair with any other woman are total fabrications. It's all fake news and very hurtful to his fiancée. He asks you to respect his privacy and Charlotte's. Thank you for your time." He turned and walked away from the microphone.

The three friends looked at the television and then back at each other, stupefied.

"That's all he's going to say." Lolly was outraged. "What about me and the coffee thrown in my face? I could have been disfigured for life."

"And he didn't mention my name or defend me at all," Dawn declared angrily. "And damn Charlotte's stupid privacy. What about mine?" She was furious. That statement was pathetic and not at all what I'd hoped for."

"It was very deliberately generic," Don conceded. "I had certainly expected a much more specific mention and strenuous defense of you, Dawn."

"Me too." Dawn wiped away hot tears of frustration. He..." The doorbell rang and interrupted her. She was close to exploding in rage. "If it's a reporter, don't answer it."

Don stood up, left the room, and returned a minute later with a large manila envelope addressed to Dawn.

Forcing herself to temporarily suppress her anger, she grabbed the package. "I've been expecting this," she muttered. "I'll take it into my office because I need a little time to cool down and digest what just happened on TV...or more to the point – what didn't."

"Sure," Lolly said sympathetically. "We'll be here if you need anything." She was seething at Britt herself. *What a jerk!*

Dawn took the envelope and locked herself in her room. She angrily turned the package upside down and watched as packets of one-hundred-dollar bills fell out onto her desk. Taking a long, deep breath, she slowly began to count them...over three-hundred-thousand-dollars this time. She scooped the bills up and shoved them into her wall safe. Then she picked up her phone to call her friend and trusted lawyer, Andrew Hawkins.

"Andrew, it's Dawn. I need to talk to you as soon as possible. Could you come to my house sometime today?"

"Unfortunately, I'm stuck in Philadelphia at a deposition. I'll be home later tonight. I can be there first thing tomorrow morning. Is that okay?"

"I guess it will have to be." She was disappointed, but waiting another day would not kill her. "See you tomorrow."

CHAPTER 39

At 8:00 a.m. sharp, Dawn ran to the door and greeted Andrew. "Thanks for coming. I really need your help." Before he had a chance to take a seat, she began to ramble on about everything that had happened.

"Calm down." He could see that she was clearly upset.

"Sorry," she nervously smoothed her hair with her fingers and took a seat. "I'm being rude. Would you like some coffee or juice?"

"Not now." He sat down next to her. "Maybe later. Just start at the beginning, one step at a time. Tell me what's going on? What's happened, Dawn?"

She forced herself to focus. "Let me start by explaining how I met Britt Holmes and what's happened since." She began by telling him about reading in the newspaper that Britt had bought a huge home for his fiancée, Charlotte Randolph, and what she had done to try to secure them as clients. She admitted deliberately planning to run into them at the Wise Owl restaurant. She even confessed to her silly broken shoe ploy and went on to explain how he had asked her to design and renovate his new house.

"I met with Charlotte alone first to discuss the plans, but she was so bored that she announced that decorating was not her thing and that we should proceed without her. So, we did. I found that Britt and I have similar tastes and ideas about how his house should look in the end and what it should represent… a dignified presidential retreat. All Charlotte wanted was a southern-style screened-in porch, a chicken coop, and a Barbie hot tub."

Owen shook his head and chuckled. "So, am I to understand that if the illustrious senator becomes our next president, he will sell fresh eggs to his neighbors as a sideline and hold his press conferences in the pink tub? Surely, she was joking."

"I'd like to think so, but I'm not sure." Dawn rolled her eyes. "Charlotte's really quite childlike and anyway, that's not important. Let me get back on track. After our initial meeting, Britt hired me on the spot and handed me a briefcase full of cash and his power of attorney. He instructed me to use my discretion in decorating his house and that in the future, money would not be a problem."

It was an interesting story, but Andrew wondered why Dawn was so concerned. "I did hear Owen Marshall's comments on TV this morning," he said. "I was sorry about the senator's injuries. My wife and I are big fans of his and especially agree with his philosophy on balancing the budget and paying down the national debt. Our country needs more fiscally responsible people at the top. But in regard to your situation, I, along with most of the town, have heard the salacious rumors about you and your relationship with Senator Holmes. Owen's statement failed to clarify the situation in that regard and did nothing to quell the speculation about you in particular."

"Yes, and that's why I'm so upset. Britt promised to handle it, but he actually did nothing. For the record," she was more agitated. "We have never been intimate! And I would never allow myself to become romantically involved with him as long as he's engaged to another woman."

"I understand perfectly, so why am I here? Dawn, what is it that you expect me to do?"

"Well, since Britt didn't make a statement in my defense, I think that I should. My reputation and that of my business are going to be torn to shreds if this continues. I need to clear my name and get the paparazzi bloodhounds off my back. I'm not a writer, so I'd like your help to draft a succinct statement for me, and also," she paused for a moment and looked him directly in his eyes. "Will you promise that everything I say to you is confidential?"

"Of course. All conversations between a client and her attorney are privileged. I assure you that what you tell me will go no further."

"Okay then. I have to admit that I'm honestly concerned about the cash Britt's been sending me. He claims he doesn't want a paper trail that could lead back to him...that he'll be running on a platform of middle-class values, and his lifestyle can't appear to be too extravagant. He can't flaunt his wealth. But I'm very uncomfortable receiving such vast amounts of his cash. When I show up at the bank to make a deposit, the manager always looks at me oddly and questions me about where the money came from. So far, I think I've appeased him, but I'm not convinced that he totally accepts my explanation. I'm worried he might question me further and worse, that I'll get in trouble. I'm pretty sure there are some banking rules about how much money one can deposit at a single time or withdraw without prompting attention from the regulators."

Andrew nodded. "Exactly. Your bank is obligated to alert the FDIC about deposits above a certain amount and withdrawals exceeding $10,000. The manager has probably already reported your deposits. It's the usual procedure. I don't want to worry you unnecessarily, but the FBI may already have a file on you, charting these unusually large deposits. They probably don't suspect you of anything in particular, but they'll be keeping an eye on you, looking for a pattern. Drug deals are usually done in cash, so the Feds are always on the lookout for things that might suggest you're involved in something like that. From what you've described, you've done nothing illegal – but I'm sure you're on the radar now. You absolutely must not accept any more cash from the senator, not under any circumstances."

Dawn turned white as she grasped the serious implications of what Andrew had said, and she was very frightened. *Drugs?* She had never imagined that anyone would associate her with illegal substances, either by selling or using them. It was ludicrous. She hated the very idea and the whole concept was disgusting to her. She was so anti drug that she barely swallowed an aspirin. She never dreamed that depositing Britt's cash would cast suspicion on herself in that way. Dawn looked at her lawyer in horror. "Oh God, Andrew," she started to perspire. "What have I gotten myself into?"

"Hopefully nothing that I can't straighten out, but tell me exactly how much you've already deposited and how much more you'll need to finish the renovations."

"Quite a bit." She gave him a specific amount. "And, I don't have the final renovation numbers yet, but it won't be nearly as much as he's already sent me. Keep in mind that it's a large, old home and that I needed to upgrade everything, change out all the doors and windows, gut and modernize the kitchen, put on a new roof, and redo all the plumbing and electricity, and that's before I even ordered the first lamp or curtain. It's a mammoth project, and one I was really challenged by and looked forward to. I'm not so sure. Now I'm really spooked."

"If you complete the project, it should be a real feather in your cap and put you and your firm in the top echelon of design firms, not that you aren't well-known already. But if you want to stay out of jail, you must follow my instructions to the letter from here out."

"Yes, I understand." Her voice trembled. The thought of going to jail terrified her. "I think there's another problem too. I discovered that the house is not titled in Britt's or Charlotte's name. Its owner is an LLC. My contract is with Britt, not his tax dodging entity."

"An LLC is not unusual. You should remember that from your real estate days. It's perfectly legitimate and in most cases it's smart. I'll see what I can find out about the partners, where the LLC is registered, etcetera. But it shouldn't affect you one way or the other. Anything else?"

"Yes, there's more. Yesterday, the house mysteriously caught fire. I haven't been allowed inside to see the damage yet, but I know it's extensive. The fire department suspects arson and is investigating. They want to interview me, my contractor and his crew, Lolly, and the nearby P Street neighbors."

"That's standard procedure in suspicious circumstances. I wouldn't worry. But tell me, why do they suspect arson?"

"They haven't told me specifically." She looked more distressed than ever. "I know I'm rambling on and on and I hope for your sake that you charge me by the hour." She forced a smile.

"Not for you. Don't worry. We'll work out my fees later." He folded his hands together under his chin, deep in thought, and let her continue.

"I called Britt and told him about the fire and that fixing the damage would be very expensive. His nurse, Maggie, has become our go-between because he's a little out of it from all his medications and pain pills. Anyway, she insists on sending me more money. She says over and over that he doesn't want any nosey reporter tracing his personal checks and discovering the true cost of the house."

"I see." Owen stood up, clearly worried, and began to pace. "I guess I can somewhat understand his point. However, there are many other ways around that problem. In my experience, when something smells rotten, it usually is. I don't want you to accept any more cash from him under any circumstances. Refuse all future payments. Are we clear?"

"All right. But only yesterday, a courier from his office delivered another three-hundred-thousand-dollars in cash." She took a deep breath and shook her head in dismay. "That's over six million dollars that he's sent me since we began this project in April. It's preposterous. I'd have to install solid gold and diamond fixtures everywhere to come close to spending that much money."

"The whole business sounds a bit unorthodox," Owen admitted, "but so far, nothing appears to be illegal. Cash is still legal tender."

"I know, but honestly, I don't feel comfortable with the situation anymore. And I hate that the FBI might be looking into me. I put the money that came yesterday in my wall safe here in the house, but I want to take it to Britt's safe deposit box in his bank. I have the key."

"That sounds like a good plan for the moment, until we can figure everything out. But remember, accept no more cash under any circumstances."

"Okay. I'll go to his bank today – but there's one more thing. I worry that if, for instance, Britt and I have a falling out in the future and I've bought or installed something that he later decides he doesn't like, a sink or bathtub, he might get angry and sue me. We have no written agreement except for the standard employment contract between Sutter Interiors and himself. I'm listed as the interior designer in it, but it says nothing about my having the authority to buy whatever I want or how much I'm allowed to pay for it. He's given me verbal carte blanche to spend his money, but there's nothing in writing to prove it. I suppose he could always deny it. Where would that leave me? It makes me nervous and it's a hell of a responsibility, one that I never asked for."

"I agree. You'd be better off trying to get out of the contract, but if you decide to proceed, I should draft a waiver protecting you from any liability and/or any future lawsuits from him or his heirs. Since this arrangement was all his idea, he should have no objections to signing that."

"That addresses one problem, but I'm still so worried. Are you positive that paying his house expenses with cash is completely legal."

"Absolutely. It's odd but not against the law. The only danger is that the IRS or anyone else, like a nosy constituent or political foe, might question where you got the money. You'd say from Senator Holmes, and then it will be up to him to show his financial statements and explain, *not you.* Dawn." But Anthony warned her. "To protect yourself, you must keep impeccable records and write down every cash distribution you received and account for every dollar, actually every penny, you've spent."

"I'm already doing that," she answered despondently, "but as you saw when you tried to come inside here, it's not just the money. My life has been completely disrupted by these obnoxious reporters and photographs. They won't leave me alone. My friends and I have to play cat and mouse games, sneaking in and out of the house and the showroom like criminals. It makes living a normal life impossible. I think I should make a statement right now. This torture has to end. What do you think?"

"I suppose you could do that, but it might be better and more effective coming from me. And if I do it, you should stand by my side but not show any emotion. Keep your temper in check and don't answer any questions. I'll make a simple, very clear statement affirming that there is not now nor ever has been a personal relationship between you and Senator Holmes beyond normal work interactions, and I'll demand that the press's harassment cease immediately or will threaten to sue all the news organizations involved."

"Will that work?"

"Probably not," he answered honestly. "But it might slow them down a bit."

"Well, it can't make the situation any worse. When will you do it?"

"There's no time like the present. Go put on a simple plain blouse and a pair of jeans, not too tight. I want you to look innocent and vulnerable, like a distraught young woman suffering from the effects of untrue and vicious rumors. Remember, you're the victim here. Can you pull off that look?"

"I'll try," she said uneasily. "I'll do anything if you think it will help to clear my name."

"Good. I'll go out front now and alert the reporters that you'll be making a statement in about half an hour. That will give them time to get their news trucks and video cameras in place for full television and social media coverage. Then I'll speak for you."

CHAPTER 40

Andrew waited another fifteen minutes after the appointed time for Dawn's statement before he stepped outside and up to a mic. He wanted to generate excitement and ensure the largest possible coverage. This was his one chance to make Dawn's innocence known and attempt to restore her reputation.

"Ladies and Gentlemen, my name is Andrew Hawking, and I am Dawn Sutter's friend and her personal attorney. She has asked me to make a statement in response to the numerous rumors and fake news reports that have swirled around in regard to her alleged relationship with the senior senator from Delaware, Britt Holmes." He looked reassuringly at Dawn, who smiled shyly back at him.

"Ms. Sutter wants to make it perfectly clear that there is *no* relationship between Senator Holmes and herself other than the normal friendship that develops between designer and client. Some time ago, Senator Holmes hired Ms. Sutter to renovate and decorate a home he purchased as a wedding gift for his soon-to-be bride, Charlotte Randolph. In that capacity, Ms. Sutter has spent time in person and on the phone with her client discussing details about the project – everything from removing certain interior walls or whether to paint or wallpaper a powder room. Ms. Charlotte Randolph was always welcome at those sessions, but she

found them tedious and voluntarily decided to leave the decorating decisions to Ms. Sutter and the senator."

The crowd began to mumble, stir, and surge forward, edging closer
until they were practically on top of them. Someone shouted. "So, Ms.
Sutter is refuting Charlotte Randolph's sexual allegations?"

"Absolutely."

Dawn could not stand idly by and endure any more scrutiny from
the press. After everything that had happened, combined with Britt's
inability or unwillingness to defend her, she felt compelled to speak
for herself. Andrew was saying the right words but was not passionate
enough. Jumping in front of him, she grabbed the mic out of his hand.
"I want you all to understand that there most certainly has never been
a sexual relationship between Senator Holmes and me, not ever!" She
was indignant and her face turned bright red with anger. "I categorically
deny Charlotte's insanely jealous accusations. Her brave fiancée is gravely
wounded and lying in pain in a military hospital in Germany. I am working here in DC to ensure that he has a comfortable place to come home
to. Wouldn't you think that she, his supposedly loving fiancée, would be
by his side there? To comfort him? But no – instead she's preening before
you, the press, and grandstanding here like a damsel in distress. Why hav-
en't you seen through her attention-grabbing narcissistic act and harassed
and hounded her like you've been doing to me? As responsible journalists,
you need to demand proof of her allegations against me or back the hell
off. She's nothing but a pathetic, boldfaced liar…"

Andrew reacted quickly and grabbed the microphone back, interrupting Dawn's emotional tirade. "While, as you can see, my client's
obviously upset, her remarks are one hundred percent spot-on. Stop this
baseless harassment of an innocent person or she will be forced, upon my

recommendation, to take legal action against you for defamation of character among other charges." He turned abruptly, grabbed Dawn's clammy hand, and pushed her gently through the door, back into her house.

"Well, that went well," Lolly said sarcastically, winking at her friend. "But I think you made your point quite eloquently."

"Yes. Tell us how you really feel about Charlotte Randolph," Don laughed and hugged Dawn tightly. "I'm very proud of you and I just saw the fiercer side of Dawn Sutter come out. She's an awesome woman!"

Dawn calmed down and realized what she had done. "I'm so sorry." She looked at her attorney and apologized. "Did my outburst ruin everything? My temper sometimes gets the best of me, but Charlotte and her ridiculous charges make me so mad."

"Not at all," he grinned. "I think your emotional plea might have actually changed the tide in your favor. "Look," he pointed through the curtain to the street. "The crowd's breaking up. They seem to be leaving."

"Hopefully to confront Charlotte," Lolly snickered. "Let her handle them for a while. The lying witch deserves what she gets. And by the way, while you were out front sounding off, Captain Levy from the Georgetown fire station called and said that they are no longer pursuing their arson suspicions due to lack of sufficient evidence. They are, however, keeping the file open in case new information surfaces. The house has been cleared for reentry and you and a restoration company can begin to work. We can go in anytime now."

"That is good news." Dawn was relieved. "The day's certainly ending better than it began." She looked outside. To her relief, the sidewalk and yard were clear, and traffic was moving as usual down the street. "Anyone want to go out for breakfast."

"Sorry, but I have to get to work," Andrew grinned, but he looked at Dawn soberly. "You have an important appointment with a safe deposit box. Don't forget about that. But go out and celebrate your freedom first. I just hope it lasts."

"Do you see any reason why it shouldn't?" Dawn frowned, gritting her teeth nervously. "I thought this was over – the problem handled."

"It depends. Charlotte is apparently very volatile and unpredictable. We'll have to wait and see what she does, how she responds, but I'll be around if you need anything." The lawyer smiled.

"There's nothing more that Charlotte can say about you, is there?" Lolly asked, worry settling in her eyes. "She's given defaming you her best shot."

"I don't know, but I hope we're done with her." Dawn turned away and dialed a restoration company to arrange a meeting at the house for later in the day. "Let's put Charlotte out of our minds and go for breakfast before something else happens."

"Do you suppose I can go back home now?" Lolly asked in a playful voice. "It's not that I don't love you, Dawn, but I miss my own apartment. After your vocal rampage, I don't think you'll need me as a decoy anymore."

"Sure, you can go home," Dawn said gratefully. "You've been terrific, and I'll really miss you. Even under these stressful conditions, it's been fun having you as a roommate, just like in our college days at Duke."

"I'll miss you too." Don looked longingly at Lolly. There was more truth to his statement than even he realized. "But I should stay here with Dawn for a little while longer until we're sure everything's calmed down."

"I'd appreciate that." Dawn watched the flirtatious interplay between him and her best friend. "But Lolly might need protection too," she added mischievously. "Starting now, why don't you plan to divide your time – spend your days protecting me and your nights with her."

"Great idea. Sold!" He laughed and winked at Lolly. "Now how about those pancakes."

Andrew went to the door. "Have a good day and call me if you need anything more. I'll be most interested in Britt and Charlotte's reactions to our own little press conference. Stay in touch. And Dawn, don't delay. Go to the bank."

"Yes, Sir," she grinned and saluted him. "I promise."

"What's that about?" Lolly asked.

"I'll tell you over breakfast, but first I have to get an envelope out of my safe. I'll be ready to go in a minute." She started towards her bedroom and then realized she did not want to be sitting in a diner with three-hundred thousand dollars in cash in her purse. "Never mind. I'll get it later," she smiled. "I'm starved. Let's go eat."

CHAPTER 41

The next morning Lolly went to some furniture stores with her list and Don and Dawn went to the house on P Street. She was wary of what catastrophe she would find inside. Her fears met the sharp reality of the situation. There was a noxious smell of heavy smoke lingering everywhere and a layer of black soot coating everything. It reminded her of the ashes she'd seen on a college trip to Italy – to the archaeological site of the buried city of Pompeii. "It seems like we have our own Mt. Vesuvius here." She looked horrified and began to choke.

The two made their way, step-by-cautious-step through the ravished first floor, trying not to breathe in the soot too deeply. In the dining room, the magnificent six-inch crown molding was badly scorched, as were the matching original handcrafted chair railings. Seeing the debris everywhere made her stomach turn. Gingerly she reached down and felt the soaking wet floors where almost half an inch of water had accumulated. If not dried out quickly, the floorboards would buckle and cost thousands of dollars to replace. She gently ran her fingers over the charred and water-drenched drywall and picked up small chunks of ceiling material that had broken away, fallen down, and scattered indiscriminately all over. "Oh my God," she moaned. "This is even worse than I imagined."

Don tried to absorb the extent of the damage for himself. His eyes widened in dismay. The first floor, from what he could see, was in a deplorable shape. Carlos and his crew were probably going to have to start over, almost from scratch, once the debris was cleared away. It would be an expensive and time-consuming task. Scorched boxes containing new and very expensive Italian kitchen cabinetry and pieces of open shelving sat forlornly in puddles on the wet ceramic floor. Each box would have to be opened and the contents inspected to determine the extent of damage, and whether any could be salvaged or would need to be replaced. Dawn noticed a small, torn piece of orange and gold silk fabric stuck to the corner of one of the cartons. It stood out so obviously that it could have been planted there. Without giving it much thought, she picked it up and stuck it in her pocket. It must be one of the fabric samples for the kitchen stools, or the banquette, she thought absently, but could not remember ever picking it out. There was so much else on her mind.

Biting her lower lip, she fought back tears when she entered the library and saw that the only furniture that had been left in the house had been burned beyond recognition. Britt's desk and her drafting table with all her notes and drawings were nothing but a pile of black soot. "I can't believe this," she said gravely. "How can I ever describe this disaster to Britt? This fire will kill his timetable. There's no way he can move in here on time."

"Take pictures of every room and email them to him." Don suggested. "You'll need to document all the damage for the insurance company anyway." He grumbled under his breath but refrained from making a nasty comment to her about the senator. He did not give a hoot that Britt would be inconvenienced and that his moving plans would be temporarily thwarted. His concern was for Dawn...and for Lolly. All their hard work and hours of labor were for naught. The look of devastation on Dawn's face was heartbreaking, and he knew that Lolly would feel the same way. He walked over and hugged Dawn tightly. "I know this seems insurmountable, but you and Lolly can turn this around. And I promise that I'll help you. We're going to have to make sweet lemonade out of this sour lemon catastrophe…or something like that." He tried to put a positive spin on what they were seeing.

She nodded woodenly, grateful for his support. "Thank you." Her voice sounded as low and discouraged as she felt.

Their justifiable melancholy was interrupted by the sound of heavy boots slushing through water and stomping on the floor. "Hello. Is anyone here?" An unfamiliar male voice called out. "I'm from Calvary Restoration. Is Miss Sutter here?"

"In here," Dawn broke away from Don with a weak smile. "I'm in the library, second door on your right. Come in please."

Two hours later, Dawn held an estimate in her hand. It was for a complete cleanup of the property, the removal and disposal of all the debris, drying out the walls and the floors, and eliminating any mold. When that work was complete, Carlos and his crew would then have to repair the ceiling, replace any hardwood planks that were too damaged and redo the drywall throughout. Angus Todd, the man in charge of the restoration, explained that soot removal was the hardest part of his job because it ionized and stuck to all different types of surfaces and was incredibly difficult to remove. "But we're the experts. We charge a lot, but once we're done," he guaranteed, "you'll never know there was a fire here."

She and Don both felt confident in Angus's abilities, and with his company's good reputation, so she made a quick decision that it would not be necessary to secure more estimates just to maybe save a few hundred dollars. In the interest of time, and because Britt had repeatedly told her that money was not an object, she hired Angus.

"You've got the job. Where do I sign?" she said eagerly. "Can you begin today?"

"Yes. My trucks and men are on the street. We're ready to go, but you two will have to leave for a few days. There's a lot of chemicals and particles floating around in the air and by doing our job, we'll stir up more. Breathing in that stuff is terrible for your lungs. When I tell you it's safe to resume work here, plan to wear masks for a day or two, just as a precaution."

Dawn nodded and took one more walk through each of the rooms, hoping to find something to salvage, something that could be saved, but there was nothing. She absently fingered the fabric remnant in her pocket. It was the only thing she could take away from the scene, but it meant nothing to her. Maybe Lolly would recognize it.

"I guess we should go to the office, see what Lolly has bought and try to reconstruct this place on paper as best we can. I have duplicate drawings, fabric samples, and a catalog of the furniture we ordered. I'll need to meet with Carlos and ask him to bring in a new set of building supplies that he'll need. I wish Britt was here so I could run ideas by him. I hate having the sole responsibility for this with no feedback from him. It's a huge burden."

Don did not say anything, but he rolled his eyes. This job had become a nightmare of grand proportions, and he wished that she and Lolly had never taken on this job. Whatever they made from it would never be worth the aggravation and compensate them for the emotional toll. "I suppose you could run your ideas by Maggie. She seems pretty attuned to Britt's every thought and wish."

"Bite your tongue." She playfully kicked him on his shin. "Never."

"Ouch." He grabbed his leg, pretending to feel pain but grinned. "I think the local paparazzi have moved on to other targets," Don said as they drove through Georgetown to the Sutter showroom, relishing the normalcy of not being followed. *How quickly one can adapt to adversity and how freeing it seems when it's ended.*

"Maybe you two beautiful ladies can finally enjoy a peaceful, productive afternoon. I'll slip out and take care of a few personal errands and bring back some fresh clothes."

"Go ahead. You deserve to take some time off. Since you started working for me, you've been by my side 24-7. Go, enjoy yourself. I need to call Britt and believe it or not, I have a bunch of other clients who are probably wondering what's happened to me, and I need to focus on them too."

"Alright. I'll drop you off, but if you or Lolly need me, don't hesitate to call."

"No worries. We'll be fine, and look," she pointed to the showroom entrance, "not a photographer or reporter in sight."

CHAPTER 42

Dawn showed Lolly the pictures she'd taken inside the house, and they talked extensively about everything they'd need to do to get the project up and running again, including engaging a second crew, as before, to work around the clock. A three-month turnaround time was their goal, and maybe that was not realistic, but they had to try. Lolly pulled out her phone and showed her pictures of what furniture and accessories she'd bought that morning and assured Dawn that she had completed the list.

Dawn glanced at her watch. It was already past noon. "Let me look through my other cases quickly and make sure everything's going smoothly. I know there was a drapery issue on the Morris job and a box of missing bathroom tiles for the Sigals. I'll handle those problems and then call Britt and tell him the details of the contract I signed for the restoration and our new completion date. Will you please touch base with Carlos and ask him to give us a proposal for the new work as soon as possible. Although, I guess he can't be totally accurate until he checks the inside of the house for himself. I'll send him the pictures I took anyway."

Lolly looked thoughtful. "Okay, and I'll try to catch up on paperwork myself, so come get me if you need something. Where's Don?" she asked casually, noticing for the first time that Dawn had come into the showroom by herself. She missed seeing his face. He was normally always in sight.

"He's running some errands," Dawn answered. "And he went to pick up some more clothes. Is he planning on moving in with you?" she asked sheepishly. "Are you two getting serious?"

"I asked him to move in," she admitted happily. "He was pretty evasive and didn't answer me directly, but if he's gone to get more clothes, I guess that's my answer. Even with my red, peeling face, he tells me that I'm beautiful."

"Well, there you are. Love is blind. Congratulations. He said he'll be back in time to take me home and you back to your apartment. He believes the days of our having to dodge the paparazzi are over, but he wants to stay on here to help us until we finish P Street. He's such a nice guy."

"I know. You don't have to convince me," Lolly said wistfully. "I've grown accustomed to having him around. Who knew I could fall so hard for an ex-Navy Seal who carries a weapon. I've always been so against guns."

"I think it's called love," Dawn smiled. "Now scoot. We have work to do."

An hour later, Dawn had handled her clients' mini-crises and phoned Britt. She dreaded telling him about how long the renovation would be delayed, but she had no choice. He had messed up the timetable himself with his unfortunate fall, and now the fire and consequent repairs would further derail everything.

"Hello," she said, surprised when he answered Maggie's phone himself. "You must be feeling better."

"I am," he answered with a much stronger voice than in their last conversation. "All things considered, I feel pretty good."

"I'm so happy to hear that. I've been really worried. Maggie's account of your fall made it sound pretty harrowing. There's a lot going on here that I need to run by you."

"Here too," he said. She could hear a hint of relief in his voice. "I've finally talked to Charlotte. It was a rather civil conversation considering what could have happened, and as of last night, we are no longer engaged. I think on some level she was actually relieved. And incidentally I happened to catch your little impromptu speech to the press on the internet. It's what prompted me to pick up the phone and tell Charlotte that I did not love her and that we were done."

"So – does she blame me?"

"Surprisingly, no, your name never came up. I think she had some kind of an epiphany and realized that it was her father pulling her strings, manipulating her, and that he wanted her to marry me. She did not. By breaking up with her, it gave her a safe way out. He'll be furious at me for ruining his plans, but not at her. However, he saw his dream of an ambassadorship fly out the window. Charlotte will keep her comfy allowance and stay in her father's good graces. But not me. I'm waiting for his revenge, but what can he really do? I'm sure that I can find other donors to support my candidacy, and they won't demand that I marry their daughters in return."

"You're right. They'll be coming out of everywhere once you make an official announcement. I don't think you have to worry. My lawyer and even my construction supervisor have said that they'll vote for you. You're a popular choice."

"As soon as I get my strength back, I'll begin campaigning. In the meantime, I'll work behind the scenes, lining up party support and making plans to appear at various political functions." His voice softened. "It's early on in our relationship, but I have something I'd like you to consider." He paused, swallowed hard and then continued. "I'd like you by my side. Will you think about moving into the P Street home with me, make it your own and then, God willing, move into the White House as my wife and as the First Lady. Can you picture that – the two of us making a life together? It could be a hell of a fun ride."

"Oh, my goodness." She was staggered by his question. "I'm not remotely ready for that." She thought for a moment that he must be kidding. "We haven't even had a proper date and never said the three magic little words to each other…I love you. I'm sorry, but it's way too soon for that kind of commitment, although I'm flattered. We'll need to spend an awful lot more time together before I can give you an answer. This seems to be coming totally out of the blue."

She knew he was attracted to her. She vividly remembered his kiss goodbye in Germany. But men kiss women all the time without proposing marriage. Maybe he was high on his pain meds. That would explain his sudden, although less than amorous, proposal. Otherwise, it made no sense.

"I can't seriously consider your proposal now," she said honestly. "But I don't deny that the thought of being married to the President of the United States has a certain magical appeal and calling the White House my home is beyond my wildest dreams." She was speechless, but living in the presidential mansion, as intriguing as it was, was not enough reason to marry a practical stranger.

After an awkward moment of silence, Britt spoke again with more passion. "I can't do much about the dating part right now. I'm thousands of miles away, so that's a problem, but the other part is easy. Dawn Sutter, my beautiful angel, I love you."

"And I think that I could love you too…someday," she whispered in a silky voice. "But this had all happened so fast. We need to slow down."

"Slow is not in my vocabulary, but I'll wait for you for as long as it takes," he answered, swallowing hard. "I warn you, I'm not known for my patience."

"Can we get back to you and your health and the real reason I called," she begged. His proposal had completely discombobulated her. "You have totally distracted me with your insane marriage proposal. It's hard to think about anything else."

"You haven't seen any distractions yet," he joked. "But sure. Truthfully, I think Maggie and the doctors were filled with too much doom and gloom about my situation. They didn't take my determination and will power into account. I can sit up now and even take a few steps with the walker. PT comes in twice a day. And in between, with Maggie's help, I work out on my own. I'm regaining my balance and strength and learning to walk properly again. I'm also eating solid foods and even had a haircut this morning."

"That's wonderful." She was surprised but elated. "Have they given you a date to come back to the States?"

"If I continue to progress, it should be in three weeks. We're aiming for May first for me to check into Walter Reed and June first to move into P Street."

"About that," Dawn hesitated. "There's been a significant glitch at this end. As you know, there was a major fire a few nights ago and your house sustained severe damage from the combination of intense heat, the flames, and the water needed to put it out. At first the fire department suspected arson, but they have since thought it might have started with an electrical mishap. They don't really know but will continue to look into the cause.

I hired a restoration company and they have already begun work, but my best guess is that it will take at least three months to complete enough of the house so that you can live comfortably on the first floor. However, after that there will still be ongoing construction on the second and third floors for a few weeks."

Britt was shocked. "I had no idea it was that bad."

"I know. I took pictures and I'll forward them to you now by email. The restoration contract was for over a hundred fifty thousand dollars, and it could go higher if they find any real structural damage."

"I don't care about that," he reiterated. "But where am I going to live in the meantime? My lease is up, and the owners have sold the condo out from under me."

"I'll find you a place. Will you still be bringing Maggie with you." She held her breath – hoping the answer had changed to a "no."

"Yes, absolutely, as my nurse first, and after I'm fully recovered, I've asked her to stay on with me and work with Owen on the campaign."

Of course, she thought unhappily. If he was serious about his proposal and there was any chance of a real romance developing between Britt and herself, she needed time alone with him…with no Maggie standing guard. They continued talking for a while until Lolly appeared in the doorway and announced that Dawn had another phone call.

"Sorry. I have to hang up. Lolly and I have to duplicate all of our original designs for your house. It's going to be an awful lot of work."

"Just remember, P Street could be your home too, so that should give you an added incentive to finish it as soon as possible. Make it the way you want it. Add anything personal you'd like but," his voice became very serious, "given what just happened with Charlotte, let's keep our potential living arrangements to ourselves for now. There's no need to

THE HOUSE on P STREET

get the press or anyone else, particularly Ralph Randolph, all riled up again. Once I'm back in DC we'll make a point of going out in public and being seen together as a couple. Then we can make an engagement announcement. What do you think?"

"I think you're getting way ahead of yourself. I have definitely *not* agreed to marry you, although the idea is intriguing. If it's in the cards, everything will fall into place at the right time, but yes, I agree that we should keep whatever this is between us private. And," she was bold enough to state one of her many concerns. "I have no desire to share you or our house, if it comes to that, with Maggie. She's a big girl and can live on her own. That, Britt, is my real deal breaker."

She thought she heard him start to protest but then he said nothing and stifled a yawn.

"Get some sleep. We'll talk again tomorrow."

Lolly looked at her in astonishment from the doorway. "Did I hear you say you were going to share the P Street house with him?"

"Not exactly." She relayed the conversation. Lolly stared at her friend in amazement. "Why do you suppose he's so anxious to get married and proposed to you only a few hours after breaking his engagement to Charlotte? It's very troubling or maybe shows that he's excessively needy. His wife died, and he replaced her with Maggie, then Charlotte, and now he wants you. Don't you see a pattern of a man who's afraid to be alone?"

"I don't think it's that. He believes a president should be married." Her defense of him sounded shallow and lame even to her own ear.

"Well, that's his problem, not yours. If you love him, and I can't imagine that you do, that's one thing, but this is so fast, so out of the blue, that even you have to admit it seems pretty unusual."

231

"Yes, I know. However, it's fun to dream of living in the P Street house and then in the White House, but, of course, it has to be with the right man."

"And is Britt Holmes the right man?"

"I don't know," Dawn sighed and blushed. "But time will tell."

"Tell what?"

"How good he is in bed."

"OMG. Go home and take a cold shower."

CHAPTER 43

The next three weeks sped by quickly. Dawn was exceptionally busy with three new clients, but she managed to stop by P Street at least once a day, sometimes more. The restoration work was almost completed, and Carlos and his day and nighttime crews were making good progress.

The kitchen had suffered the least damage and was the first room to be worked on. The cabinetry had been hung. The countertops, the backsplash, and the oversized granite island had been set in place, and the appliances and light fixtures were due to be installed the next week. Dawn was thrilled by how the room was turning out and occasionally imagined what it would feel like to make cozy meals for herself and Britt on the commercial gas range or sip wine or drink cappuccinos together at the comfortable banquette. Then she shook off the notion and came back to her senses. This was not her house and probably never would be.

The catering kitchen was also almost finished, too, and the walk-in pantry shelves were stacked by the door ready to be hung. The library and dining room were next on the agenda.

Dawn spent evenings pouring through her design books looking for unique touches to make the house extra special. Then she cuddled up on her bed and called Britt. They talked endlessly about his political plans and campaign strategies. She tried to change the subject and tell him about her day and especially about her new clients. One of them had asked her to design the interior of their new 190-foot motor yacht. It would be her first attempt at nautical work and could open the door to a whole new range of customers if she did a good job. He half-heartedly listened, but the subject always returned to his presidency. He was also excited about his own physical therapy progress and returning to his congressional work – if only from his bedside at Walter Reed. He bragged that with Maggie's constant nagging, he had gained a few pounds. His transfer from Landstuhl was now only a week away.

He mentioned that since his "breakup" with Charlotte, he had not heard a word from her, except a brief text announcing that she was keeping the diamond ring. He also had only received one terse message from her father declaring that he'd talk to Britt in person as soon as he returned home. Britt was expecting that little "chat" to occur the moment he set foot on US soil. Then Britt asked if his cash payments were arriving on time from Owen.

"Yes," she answered in a strained voice. They come every few days. She did not tell him that she had not deposited any of the recent ones and that they were accumulating in her home safe. She had refused the last few ones. She kept putting off a visit to the bank for one reason or another. "I have over four million dollars from you so far, and I still don't understand why you think that's necessary. You must stop sending me money. I won't accept it anymore. The Kennedys and Bushes had mansions and second homes, and no one seemed to care...and look at Trump. I think you're being way too sensitive about this wealth issue. You'll have to reveal your taxes if you're president, and the price of the house will come out then anyway."

"Yes, but that's the point. I will already have been elected. I'm just being overly cautious," he countered. "And since you mentioned it...yes, look at 'the Donald' and all the trouble he got into when he overinflated the value of Mar-a-Lago and his condo in the Trump Tower. If he had simply paid cash for his real estate, there would have been no paper trail and thus – no lawsuits. For a smart businessman, he made a dumb calculation and misjudged the public's reaction."

"I guess I see your point," she admitted grudgingly, "but I'm serious. I will not accept any more money unless it's in a check."

He ignored her and did not respond.

"But getting back to Charlotte," she continued, "you've never made a public announcement saying that your engagement to her was off. Why not?"

"No, I didn't," he answered gruffly. "I thought it was a private matter between Charlotte and myself."

"Nothing is private when you want to hold the most powerful job in the world. Even I know that. But, as you said, there's nothing she or her father can do to hurt your campaign now except maybe hit you in the pocketbook. Is that right?" She was suddenly concerned. "They're no hidden skeletons in your closet, are there? No buried bodies in the basement or the backyard."

She had been joking, but she still knew so little about his past, and he also knew next to nothing about hers. The more she thought about it, the more she realized that he had never once asked her any personal questions and did not seem interested in her life before he met her. He had no idea where she went to school, if she went to college, who her friends were, when and why she had become a designer, or if she'd ever been in love or married. She could have six children for all he knew. He did not seem to care.

"I have no skeletons or dried bones of any kind in my closet." He sounded irritated.

"Well, that's good to know and I'm happy about that, but I must admit that I'm surprised that Charlotte went away so quietly. I thought she'd be vindictive and blame me, maybe even publicly like she did before. I've been a little on edge expecting it to happen…waiting for the other shoe to drop, you know. That's one reason I've kept Don around as a precaution."

"That won't be necessary anymore. You can let him go. I'm sure she's already on the prowl, with her daddy's help, searching for a more acceptable husband. I'm just a foolish mistake to her now, a dream – or scheme – of her father's that didn't pan out."

"I wouldn't be so sure about that. Wouldn't it be a smart idea to say something publicly before you come back here, and before we're seen anywhere together? I want to spend every free minute I can with you, but I do *not* want to go through another fiasco with the press."

"You're right and the timing to say something is perfect. I'm being interviewed tomorrow by a team from *60 Minutes* about the human toll of the Israeli War with Hamas and other Middle East problems. They're doing a human interest story on the tragedy of displaced families, the distraught and psychologically damaged relatives of the hostages, and the many innocent children and adults that were injured during the conflict. I'm sure I can find a clever way to slip that engagement tidbit in during my personal profile part of the story without drawing too much attention to it. I know the producers are interested in the timeline of my recovery and asked permission to film me during a PT session. It'll be the first time the American public has seen me since the explosion. I want to make a good impression, show vitality and strength."

"I'm sure you'll handle it beautifully and look as handsome as ever."

"Do you think I should exaggerate my limp, for the sympathy vote?" he joked. "*60 Minutes* has great viewership."

"Absolutely," she laughed. "Remember, a picture is worth a thousand words, and maybe thousands in financial contributions also. Be sure to hint about the well-known secret that you're making a presidential run."

"See, I knew you had good political instincts. I might hire you to run my campaign."

"No thanks," she answered swiftly. "One politico in the family is enough. But seriously, good luck with the interview. I'll be watching." When she spoke to him the next evening, he was cagey and refused to tell her how the *60 Minutes* piece went. He told her to tune in and see for herself.

She invited Lolly and Don over for dinner to watch the show with her. Lolly was still surprised and worried by Dawn's feelings for Britt, a man she barely knew. Dawn still had so much to learn about Britt: his favorite kind of music, his preferences for food, or what books he liked to read, and she knew nothing about his high school and college years, except what she'd seen on Google or Facebook. Lolly feared that her friend was caught up in the glamor of being associated with a possible president of the United States and was not really in love with him. *How could she be?* He was a virtual stranger, like an old-fashioned pen pal she'd never met and only exchanged letters with or someone she'd met on an online dating app, and she did not know if she could believe that his profile was accurate or honest. Britt was still very much a mystery.

Don agreed with Lolly's assessment and still felt a strong reservation about Britt. He questioned the man's commitment to Dawn and particularly his sudden profession of love with a marriage proposal. In his opinion, the senator was an opportunist and had no moral convictions of his own. He seemed like a perfect example of a puppet with someone else pulling his strings. *But who was doing the pulling and why?*

Charlotte, for all her faults, had not deserved to be treated the way she had been by him, and he feared Dawn was in for the same inauspicious, unhappy ending. Once she had served her purpose...whatever that was...she might become expendable too. Because he held Dawn in such high regard, he voiced his reservations only to Lolly, but he was always watching and listening and nearby in case of trouble. His gut told him that the senator was not who he appeared to be, and he always listened to its warnings. It had served him well as a Navy Seal and kept him safe since, so he trusted it implicitly.

Dawn turned on the television and the symbolic ticking clock was on the screen. *60 Minutes* was about to start.

CHAPTER 44

The program began with a segment on the dangers of pesticides in our water supply. The second was a piece about artificial intelligence and its use in various professional settings. The last was a story about the October 7, 2023, Hamas terrorist attack during a concert in Israel where approximately 1,200 innocent men, women, and children were brutally massacred. Senator Holmes's subsequent, nearly fatal injury during a subsequent congressional visit to the Middle East was featured.

The piece about him began with a short introductory narrative about his Midwest background and his rise to popularity in the ranks of the senate. He was described as being exceedingly handsome with a magnetic, Kennedy-like presence. His fervent followers were almost cult-like in their adoration and support. In the personal piece there were a few scenes showing him in various candid poses during his childhood and teenage years, and one of him accepting his college diploma from Brown University. There were recent videos of him walking statuesquely through the halls of congress and attending a meeting of the Homeland Security committee, of which he was a prominent member.

Then the narrative cut to pictures of the horrific scene at the concert and ended with pictures of the subsequent destruction of the senator's car after the bombing. There was a poignant picture of the medics placing him on a stretcher to be airlifted to safety and eventually to Landstuhl Medical Center for treatment.

One of Scott Pelle's colleagues sat down to interview Britt after showing an emotional clip of the senator struggling to lift himself out of a wheelchair and straining to balance and walk on a ramp. He held on to a set of parallel bars and took one slow step at a time with his surgically reconstructed leg, sometimes grimacing in pain. Each step was a miracle of the medical profession's expertise and was portrayed as a sign of the senator's grit and determination. When he reached the end of the ramp, he smiled and threw a triumphant fist into the air. The program cut to a commercial with a tease of an important upcoming announcement.

"He looks wonderful," Dawn commented happily. "Much better than when I left him in Germany." Her heart was overjoyed at the sight of him, but unhappy when she recognized Maggie standing in the background of the medical scene. "That damn woman never leaves his side," Dawn groused.

"Shh," Lolly warned. "The show's about to begin again."

"What has this experience taught you?" He was asked after the interviewer described the atrocities that occurred during that time and the ongoing situation.

"That life is very fragile, and that we can't take it, or our democracy for granted." He smiled tentatively. "We are so fortunate in the United States to have the freedom and expectation of safety and protection from acts by vicious terrorists, but we must never let down our guard. That's why I'm a die-hard advocate for a strong, well-funded, and powerful military. This experience has taught me that without an awesome military, and unquestioned support for our troops, our lives are at risk every day. That's why tonight I'm announcing the formation of the Britt Holmes for President Committee so that I can bring my views and philosophy directly to the American public."

The interviewer put down his notes and decided to explore the presidential announcement in more detail.

"So, you heard it here first, folks," he said, looking directly into the camera...a 60 Minute breaking news moment. The first official announcement in next year's election of a candidate running for the presidency." He turned his attention back to Britt. "I understand your prognosis is good now, Senator, although it was touch and go for a while, but do you really think you'll have the stamina to withstand the rigorous demands of campaigning?"

"Yes, absolutely. The doctors and nurses have been sensational, and they have led me to believe that with my hard work and my dedication to rehabilitation, I'll be as good as new in a very few months. I've had wonderful medical care and loving support from my friends. I'll definitely be ready to run."

"How will your future look?"

"I'll be transferred to Walter Reed Hospital in Maryland shortly. There I'll undergo intense PT, and once I'm completely mobile and able to navigate on my own, I'll be released for outpatient follow up. I can resume my congressional activities and move forward with running my campaign in plenty of time to enter all the primaries and caucuses in the winter and spring of next year. I'll be more than ready to make a good showing in New Hampshire."

"We know some of your political opinions and beliefs but not much about your personal life. Is there anything you want to share?"

"I'm afraid that my private life has become a little more public since my injuries. I was engaged at the time to a beautiful lady, Charlotte

Randolph. During the time of my hospitalization, we had time to reevaluate and realized that we had jumped into the idea of marriage prematurely. We mutually decided to call off our engagement. This is not the time for me to be consumed with romance or making wedding plans. I intend to devote myself full time to the pursuit of recovering my physical capabilities and running for the most powerful and important job in the world. I hope America will stand behind me." He looked fervently into the camera, mustering all his charm. "To be successful, I'll need all of your votes and your financial help. May God bless me and bless the American people."

"And there you have it. The first official announcement from a candidate for the presidency. More announcements will undoubtedly follow in the next weeks and months as politicians around the country seek to defeat our current president. *The Last Minute* is up next. But for now, Senator Britt Holmes has thrown his hat into the rink, and we will watch and see what happens next."

"Wow," Dawn smiled. "I think that went very well. He was articulate and compelling."

"Yes, he was unequivocal. I wonder what Charlotte thinks," Lolly asked. "I didn't think the broken engagement was by mutual consent. I thought Britt deep-sixed her."

"He did," Dawn answered truthfully. "He was being gallant by not throwing her under the bus. Hopefully her father will appreciate the gesture, too. According to Britt, Mr. Randolph was upset and very angry about the breakup. It ruined his hope of becoming the US ambassador to Paris or London."

"And he probably wanted to see his daughter living in the White House, with all the luxuries and privileges that implies," Don offered astutely. "I bet he was probably looking forward to being known as 'the First Father-in-Law.'"

Dawn chuckled. "Is there such a title? But at least he didn't say anything about me. I'm not ready to start up another paparazzi frenzy."

"Well, you might not be ready, but you should be prepared. As soon as your romance becomes public, you'll be every bit as much a target as your senator boyfriend." Don looked at her in earnest. "Seriously Dawn, what you experienced before is only the beginning and if Britt becomes the party's nominee, it will only get worse. I hope you've taken that into account. You'll be the American equivalent of Princess Diana, or Jackie Kennedy. Your private life will all but disappear. Are you ready for that?"

"I don't know," she answered honestly. "I just don't know."

CHAPTER 45

Dawn continued to supervise the P Street renovation, and in light of Britt's promise that it could be her home, too, she rolled the dice mentally and gambled that they would maybe one day work things out between them, truly fall in love, and that the house would become their home to share. With that in mind, she added a few personal touches of her own to the primary bedroom area...a gas fireplace, extra drawers, and much more hanging space in what might be her closet with a separate area for floor-to-ceiling shoe and handbag storage. She ordered a remote-controlled revolving rack for Britt's suits and sports jackets. It looked something like one would see in a dry cleaner's establishment, but it was attractive and would make selecting his daily wardrobe so much easier. She also added a dumbwaiter, a coffee bar, and a small refrigerator. In Dawn's mind, she pictured her and Britt spending an entire day or even a whole weekend in their bedroom retreat without ever having to see or talk to anyone else. If everything worked out between them, it was going to be a honeymoon Shangri-la, a dream come true.

Her trusting heart was trying to convince her that Britt's sudden and unexpected marriage proposal had come from his genuine love and devotion for her. She rationalized and told herself that millions of people fell in love at first sight. So why not them? However, her more logical and organized mind was not as easily persuaded. Common sense told her it was far too soon to be so involved, and she struggled mentally to separate the thrill of his attention and her attraction to Britt from the down-to-earth reality of making a lifelong commitment to a man she'd only known a short time – and never intimately. *Was she really deeply in love with Britt Holmes… or more probably simply in love with the idea of being in love?* Every time she spoke with him or made a personal design addition to the house, she felt happy and eager for their future together. Then, in quieter, more self-reflective moments, confusion and doubt set in. *Was she being foolish and acting only on her wishful thinking?* As much as she wrestled with the dilemma and talked it over with Lolly, the only answer was to play it out…wait and see what happened when they could openly be together. Time would make the final decision for her, but in the meantime, she was going to enjoy the ride.

* *

Britt's transfer to Walter Reed took longer than expected, but by the end of June he arrived in DC by military aircraft. He tolerated the trip well but was extremely tired. Maggie accompanied him from Landstuhl and was planning to stay at a nearby hotel until a more permanent living arrangement could be made. Owen met them at the airport and escorted them to the hospital in suburban Maryland. The press had not been notified of his arrival, so there was no coverage or fanfare surrounding his arrival.

Britt began his admittance procedure while Owen started to set up a makeshift office in the hospital suite. He senator's legislative obligations and campaign organization would occur in that space until Britt was well enough to travel to his own office on Capitol Hill and open his first headquarters somewhere in the DC area.

Dawn arrived at the hospital shortly after Britt with a cuddly "get well" teddy bear, and a bag of French fries and a Big Mac from McDonalds. She was so eager and excited to see him. However, he barely acknowledged her presence except for a quick peck on her cheek. She could never get him alone, not even a second. He was singularly focused on making sure that his hospital office was fully functional and up and running by the next morning, coordinating in-person and Zoom meetings for the week and scheduling his physical therapy and other hospital tests. Always clutching his phone or surrounded by nurses and doctors, he was too busy to spend any private time with her. She felt useless, like an extraneous third or fifth wheel.

Everyone, especially Maggie, hovered over him like he was some kind of rock star. She never left his side. His hospital room had become a beehive of activity, filled with computer technicians, telephone installers, and other office personnel bringing in computers, printers, collapsible tables, and boxes of files. Finally, the charge nurse clapped her hands together loudly to gain everyone's attention and announced firmly that it was time for everyone to leave. The senator was a patient, and he needed his medications and to rest. She pointed at the clock on the wall and gave them half an hour to finish up their business and depart.

"In the future," she announced with authority, "there will only be two visitors allowed at a time and only then for short periods of time. This is a hospital after all, and we must respect the privacy and needs of our other patients as well. They deserve peace and quiet." Then she asked permission to take a selfie with Britt. Even she, for all her bluster, was caught up in his aura of power and magnetism and ended up asking for his autograph.

And so it begins, Dawn thought in despair. She watched Maggie solic-
itously hand him a glass of apple juice and hold the straw for him like
he was her baby. *Was she going to have to fight that woman and the whole
frigging world for his attention from now on?* She was not at all sure she
could or would want to.

Dejectedly, she slipped quietly out of the room with her wounded
pride and her percolating anger…not that Britt noticed.

CHAPTER 46

"How was Britt?" Lolly asked Dawn the next morning. "Did he handle the trip home well?"

"He seemed good but there was so much going on in his room that I never got any private time with him. His staff came and they were setting up an office there for him. It was total chaos. I thought he'd call me last night, but I haven't heard a word."

"He was probably exhausted. I'm sure you'll hear from him soon. Are you planning on going to the hospital today?"

"I was, but after yesterday, I'm not sure what to do. He had so many people vying for his attention, and he was giving orders to them right and left and had no time to spend with me. It was not the way to treat someone you love and supposedly want to marry."

Dawn was disillusioned and felt let down. She had expected a different scenario. Upon reflection, she realized that had often ignored his former fiancée in much the same way and had treated her shabbily. *Was this how he treated the women in his life? Everyone but Maggie.* "I guess I'll hang out here at work until he contacts me."

"That's probably a good idea. Maybe he just needs time and space to get the logistics set up and then he can devote some time to you." Lolly did not believe a word of what she was saying and could see that her friend was visibly upset. Ever since his proposal, Dawn had been anticipating a romantic reunion with Britt and gotten a virtual kick in the pants – a virtual dismissal instead.

Don was furious at Britt, too, but not surprised. He had never trusted that Britt was the man he claimed to be, and now he had proof…another example of his narcissism and that he and he alone was the center of his own world. Britt was interested in one thing, promoting himself and his candidacy. Dawn was a pleasant diversion but hardly a priority. He worried that she was due for real heartbreak, and he and Lolly had no way to prevent it.

He left the showroom and returned a few minutes later with an armful of bagels and containers of Starbucks coffee. "I thought you two might like a treat," he smiled. "What's on the schedule for today?"

Dawn's irritation was evident in her tone of voice. "I'm going to P Street. Do you want to come with me?"

"Yes." They both answered in unison. Neither wanted her to be alone with her thoughts and her foul mood. Maybe they could do something to cheer her up.

Britt finally called an hour later. "Hi Sweetheart," he began apologetically. "Sorry about the chaos yesterday. I didn't realize setting up my office was going to be so disruptive. When everyone finally left, I collapsed and fell asleep. Maggie went to her hotel, and I didn't wake up until a nurse came in to give me my medications this morning. That's when I found a soggy burger and a bag of limp fries in the trash. I'm sure they came from you. Thanks for remembering. I guess someone decided they weren't good for me or my cholesterol. Sorry."

"That's okay." She felt a little better. "I'm glad you got a good rest. Are Owen and Maggie there with you now?"

"Yes, he's teaching her a little bit about how my office runs so that when she switches from being my nurse to becoming Owen's aide, she'll be ready. From what I've seen so far, she's more than up for the job. The two have a good rapport, amazing chemistry, as if they've known each other forever. Their collaboration should work out fine and will help me in so many ways.

"I'm glad. I'm sure Maggie will be a big help." Dawn was clamping down her resentment. *Did he have to mention that woman in every sentence? That was going to have to change.* "What's on your schedule today?"

"A PT session in a few minutes and another this afternoon. I have a meeting with a prospective big donor at 2:00 p.m. and then Charlotte's father is coming by at 5:00. I'm dreading that conversation, but I have to face him sometime, so I might as well get it over with. Are you free to join me later tonight for dinner? I can order meals sent to my suite. They actually have a chef who caters meals here to patients not on restricted diets. How about two rare steaks? We can finally have some alone time. I need it."

"I'd like that too," she said wistfully. "I'll be there by 7:00."

After talking with Britt, she felt much better. She had probably overreacted about yesterday. He had simply been overwhelmed and distracted by so much activity after so many quiet weeks in Germany. Everything was going to be fine as long as Maggie stayed out of her way and Mr. Randolph did not cause any trouble. Those were two big "ifs."

CHAPTER 47

Dawn was ready to leave for the hospital to have dinner with Britt. She was bringing an excellent bottle of Pinot Noir but was not sure Britt would be permitted to drink the wine because of all the medications he was taking. If not, more for her, she thought happily. The anticipation of "alone time" with him was palatable. Her pulse was racing at the thought, and she could not wait to fling herself into his arms. It had been a long time since she'd left his bedside at Landstuhl, but the tortuous wait was finally about to be over. All the troubles with Charlotte and the press paled in comparison to being with him again.

She grabbed her keys and was almost out the door when her phone rang. She glanced at the caller ID and did not recognize the number. Agitated that anyone or anything might delay her reaching Britt, she was tempted to let the call go to voicemail. But if it was a client crisis, they would only call back again and again until they reached her. She sighed and answered with a sharp "Yes. Dawn Sutter speaking."

"It's Maggie. I'm calling from Britt's suite on a staff person's phone. He asked me to tell you not to come to the hospital tonight...or anytime soon. He had a violent argument with Mr. Randolph an hour or so ago. I could hear a lot of shouting and accusations being hurled around. Frankly, I've never seen Britt so upset. His blood pressure soared, and the doctors had to give him a shot to calm him down. He's sleeping now and will be out cold for the rest of the night. I'm going back to my hotel and will check on him first thing in the morning. Good night."

Dawn was stunned. She angrily carried the bottle of wine back into the kitchen, opened it, and poured herself a hefty glass. Sitting at the kitchen table she wondered what could have happened. What could Charlotte's father have said that upset Britt that much? He had been expecting Ralph to lose his temper and withdraw his financial support but not a violent encounter. She did not have to wait very long for the details.

Her phone rang again. "Dawn, turn on the nightly news, any channel. Don, and I are on our way over there now." Lolly sounded strange and extremely upset.

Dawn grabbed the remote and flipped on the news. She watched in surprise as Mr. Randolph, his arm protectively around Charlotte's shoulder, took a position behind a podium in front of the Walter Reed Hospital logo and began to read from a written script.

"Ladies and gentlemen, my name is Ralph Randolph. I am a lifelong donor and fervent supporter of political causes and candidates aligned with my way of thinking. I've been an ardent supporter of Britt Holmes since his first run for local office in Wilmington, Delaware and then when he ran both times for his present position as US Senator. Until recently I had planned to continue my advocacy and was pleased by his recent announcement on *60 Minutes* that he would be seeking the office of the President of the United States.

"I have changed my mind since coming into the possession of some irrefutable evidence that Senator Holmes is a fraud, a liar, and a serious risk to our democratic way of life. As many of you may know, I also have a very personal relationship with the man. I considered him 'family' and expected him to become my son-in-law later this year, the husband of my only daughter, the lovely Charlotte."

He reached down and kissed her on her cheek. "But in good conscience," he continued, "I can no longer allow my family's good name to be associated with such an immoral, lying, criminal. This is not the time or the forum to lay out my proof of his illegal behavior, but suffice it to say, I have willingly, but with a heavy heart, passed all the pertinent information onto the proper authorities. The Justice Department will be looking into recently discovered alleged illegal payments made to the senator from dubious high-ranking Chinese officials. They were quid pro quo for specific introductions and favorable trade favors he granted China by way of his powerful position on the Homeland Security committee. The evidence will show that he revealed sensitive confidential government information in return for huge sums of money and he has cleverly lined his own pockets and laundered his dirty money through several legitimate American enterprises. I am also bringing this disgusting behavior to light because he was pretending to be engaged to my daughter, while secretly married to another woman, his interior designer, Dawn Sutter. She is now pregnant with his child."

Bedlam broke out in the room. Reporters charged the podium, their cameras flashed, and they shouted questions. Charlotte took cover behind her father, sobbing and dramatically wringing her hands in despair.

"I won't say anything more at this time," Ralph said, trying to restore order. "The eyewitness testimony you're about to hear from a completely disinterested third party will prove my accusations. I'm sure you will agree that Senator Holmes should be brought before the ethics committee, stripped of his positions on any and all committees, and unanimously impeached. And I demand that he immediately withdraw his candidacy for our great country's presidency. We do not need and cannot afford another self-serving, crooked, money-grabbing politician in the White House. "

Ralph stood completely still as he smugly pushed the play button on a video, and watched as it ran on a makeshift screen set-up behind him. The tape was of an interview with a pleasant-looking, middle-aged British widow, Elenor Blaine. She was standing in front of her quaint, vine-covered cottage in the Cotswolds looking frightened and shell-shocked. A reporter thrust a microphone in her face and handed her a photograph. "Do you know this woman?" he asked.

Elenor was surprised and nodded "yes."

"Mrs. Blaine," the interviewer aimed her camera directly at her. "Under what conditions did you meet Dawn Sutter?"

"I met her at the Landstuhl Medical center about a month or so ago, but she went by the name of Dawn Holmes. She was there to visit her gravely injured husband after he was wounded in the Middle East, in Gaza, I think. We were staying at the same hotel, so we shared a meal or two and became friendly. The senator was in awful shape and Dawn was very concerned. Poor thing, I worried about her and her baby. Stress is so hard on a pregnancy."

"Who told you she was married to the senator and that she was pregnant?"

"She did. Of course. Why? I don't understand what all the fuss is about. She was such a nice young lady, and we shared a mutually traumatic time together. Things like that bond people, you know. Why are you here questioning me? "Oh," she had a terrible thought. "Did something awful happen to her – or to the senator? Did she lose the baby?"

"No. Nothing like that," the reporter replied and began to move away. "Thank you for our time. We are simply verifying information we were given anonymously."

"I see." Elenor looked bewildered. "Please send my regards to Dawn and her husband," Elenor said innocently and turned to go inside her cottage. She had no idea the flood of recriminations her innocent remarks had unleashed and the horrific, life-changing consequences that would follow as a result of her words.

CHAPTER 48

awn's eyes remained glued to the television set. One commentator after another remarked on Senator Holmes's callous treatment of Charlotte Randolph, his naïve and trusting fiancée, when he was secretly married to Dawn Sutter. Her pregnancy was another nail in his political coffin.

The journalists and newscasters, one after another, berated and chastised Britt and called for him to withdraw from the upcoming election. They cited his clear lack of everyday decency and astounding moral corruption. Then a round table of talking heads, looking somber and perplexed, discussed the seriousness of Chinese allegations and their implications for the country. They were opinionated and unforgiving.

Don and Lolly came running into the kitchen, alarm written on their drawn faces. "Dawn, did you really tell that woman that you were married to Britt and having his baby?" Lolly demanded. "What were you thinking?"

"Yes, I did but," she hung her head in shame as her friends stared at her in silence. "When I tried to visit Britt, I was turned away. The lady at the reception desk said that only family was permitted inside. I didn't know what to do, so I left and then returned a few hours later hoping for a better outcome – a chance to speak to a supervisor or someone else in charge, so I could plead my case. A nice man, Holgar something, was at the reception desk this time, and that's when I told him I was Mrs. Holmes. Even then, he was not going to let me in because my name was not on Britt's visitors list. I was so frustrated and tired after having flown all the way there that I lied. Honestly, I was simply determined to see Britt. I told Holgar that I'd come there to tell my husband that he was going to be a father, hoping that hearing the wonderful baby news would give him the incentive to fight for his life. I never in my wildest imagination thought that the press or anyone else would find out. I guess I never stopped to think at all. But once I'd started to lie, I had to continue the pretense with all the doctors and nurses and any other people I met there."

She looked at her friend's shocked faces and before they could disapprove, she continued. "When Britt broke off his engagement to Charlotte, her father, Ralph, was royally pissed. He wanted revenge for his daughter and boy did he get it. I can't believe my stupidity…my stupid lies might cause Britt to be impeached and force him to withdraw from the presidential race." She put her head in her hands and began to sob. "How could I have screwed up so badly?"

"Maybe it's him, not you, who screwed up," Don said bitterly, putting a comforting hand on her shoulder. "Lying was a silly thing to do, but I understand why you did it. It must have seemed like your only recourse at the time. But, unfortunately, that's only one part of this terrible revelation. The accusations about a Chinese connection and laundering money are ten times worse. And how did that reporter ever find that woman, Elenor Blaine?"

Dawn suddenly felt lightheaded and tried to explain about receiving the cash payments and depositing them in her business account.

The more she said, the more she realized the terrible error she had made. "Andrew warned me not to accept any more money, and I haven't…but it looks like the damage is already done. And," she looked at him in total disbelief. "I have no idea how the reporter knew about Elenor Blaine. I had completely forgotten about her and have never talked to her since she left Landstuhl. She's a sweet person, and I can't imagine that she would have initiated that interview on her own. Why would she?"

"Maybe someone paid her to talk," Don suggested thoughtfully. "Did she ever mention needing money?"

"Yes, but not in the way you're implying. She was a widow living on a small pension and struggling to make ends meet. She made a point of telling me that she did not want to be 'on the dole,' as she called their welfare system. Who in the world would ever make the connection between me and her?"

"Maybe that Holgar fellow," Lolly suggested. "Suppose Ralph Randolph believed Charlotte's accusations about you and Britt, and he paid someone to go to the hospital and snoop around. In the process, he found Holgar and his big mouth."

"I guess that's plausible," Dawn furrowed her brows. "Holgar is the one who told the whole hospital that I was pregnant."

Don could no longer hide his distaste for Britt. "I have to be honest," he said firmly. "The plain and simple fact is that I believe Britt is dishonorable and set you up from the beginning. It's so obvious now looking back. He used you and Sutter Interiors to launder his dirty Chinese money. To be perfectly blunt, he never loved you. You were only a convenient means to an end, and he took advantage of your good nature and naivety. He only pretended to care, so he could exploit your innocence and use your company to cover up his crimes."

"Oh my God! That can't be true?" The heartbreak Lolly had predicted for Dawn was actually coming true. Dawn was devastated.

Tears streamed down her face. "Why didn't I see it? Why didn't I trust my own intuition? I knew something wasn't right. I even asked Andrew about it but then I did nothing. I guess I didn't want to face the truth. I'm such an idiot. Now, what?"

"Now you call your lawyer, Dawn. And don't waste another second."

CHAPTER 49

Dawn was too shocked and upset to call Andrew yet. She needed some time to think and digest what she had just learned and decide if she really believed the horrible accusations about Britt. She did laps, pacing around the kitchen table, trying to control her increasing panic and the bile rising in her throat. Finally, she ran to the sink and threw up, furious at herself for being such a simpleton and allowing Britt to manipulate and trick her.

"He never loved me," she moaned aloud as the truth of her statement finally sunk in. "I was an easy, lovestruck jerk." She stopped stone-cold when she had a stunning epiphany. "If I had followed my heart and married him, would you realize that I couldn't legally testify against him? I wonder if that was his plan all along...to set me up and then keep me from revealing the truth."

"And, if you were married," Lolly said angrily, "he could continue to give you money and then help himself to it at any time. I've always thought he was a little shifty and a smooth operator. He's conned half the country with his charm. I'm sure that eventually he would have convinced you to put his name on our business account as another signee, probably in the guise of protecting you from God knows what...maybe me? Then he could continue to move money in and out of our business account indefinitely. It was ingenious, but his plan depended on convincing you that he loved you. He not only put you in legal jeopardy, but me too." She was beyond furious. "We've worked so hard to build Sutter Interiors into the success it is today. We cannot let Britt ruin it. Please Dawn, do as Don asked. Call Andrew right away...or I will!"

Don started to agree with Lolly, but before he could utter a word, he heard a loud commotion at the front door. Looking through the peep-hole, he saw a huge crowd of neighbors, curious spectators, and the press with their cameras and microphones gathering around. The frenzy was happening again.

Andrew Hawkins plowed his way through the throngs of people and rushed inside Dawn's house. "By God. This is much worse than the last time. I just watched the news and knew that I had to come." Exasperation showed on his tense face. The bloody news hounds and gossip mongers are back in full force, and you're trapped inside here again. I swear," he said trying to be funny, "I will never live in a place without a back alley or a secret entrance, even if I have to dig a tunnel myself."

Dawn stopped crying and smiled weakly through damp eyes. "Thanks for coming. I brought this all on myself. I'm going to have to find a way to fix it." She knew she was going to need all her strength to muster through the coming hours and days. Who knew how long it would take to straighten out this debacle...but she would...whatever she had to do. Damn Britt Holmes...damn, damn, damn him!

* *

Don and Lolly took turns explaining to Andrew everything they had just discussed. Dawn was too distraught and angry to trust herself to speak coherently. She could see that Andrew was clearly disappointed in her, and she was too ashamed to meet his gaze. She felt like she was under an intense spotlight, and the heat from it made her feel vulnerable and uncomfortable. Finally, she found her voice. "If you, my best friends and my lawyer, are rocked by this, how am I going to ever convince the world that I'm innocent and not a part of Britt's scheme?"

"Well," Andrew spoke slowly. "I do not believe you did anything illegal, at least not knowingly, but the appearance of impropriety is certainly there. I'll need to review all the evidence, watch the tapes of all the news broadcasts, and speak to Elenor Blaine myself. Do you have any idea how she was drawn into this sordid mess?" He watched Dawn closely. "And have you kept a strict record of all the cash payments you received? Remember, I asked you to be very accurate."

"Yes," she mumbled as a new wave of shame washed over her. "I have it all written down."

"That's good. I'd like a copy, and for the time being, I don't want you speaking to the press, to Senator Britt, or to anyone associated with him. After I've reviewed everything, we'll come up with a plan. If you can work from home until then, it would be optimum, but if you must leave the house, please take Don with you, and absolutely refuse to respond to anything that anyone might ask you. The press wants you to make an incriminating statement...something they can splash all over the front pages in or put on television, and they'll do almost anything legal or otherwise to get it. Do you understand?"

"Yes," she answered solemnly. "But what should I do about P Street? Because of the fire, we are not nearly through with the renovations and the furniture is several weeks from delivery. I still owe the vendors and the construction crews their money. I can't just disappear."

"No, you can't. That would make you look guilty. The senator entered into a legal contract for your services as an interior designer. It's your obligation to make good on your end of that agreement. How you were paid and whether the transactions were illegal is another matter entirely. The government, if they pursue the case, will have to prove that you accepted the money knowing it was illegally obtained. I don't believe they can do that, so eventually I think you'll be okay, and I'll do everything in my power to ensure that happens. Continue to work as if everything is completely normal, but try to finish the house as soon as possible, please."

"What if more money arrives?"

"I doubt, given the publicity, that will happen, but if it does, refuse to accept it again. Turn the courier away."

"Alright." Dawn sighed wearily. "But I've already done that. A payment came yesterday, and I refused to sign for it. The courier simply shrugged, ignored me, and dropped the package at my feet. I had to bring it inside. I couldn't leave thousands of dollars lying on my doorstep. It's in my safe now with all the other cash." She nervously reached into her pocket for a tissue and pulled out a crumpled piece of fabric. "Oh," she said, startled. "I forgot all about this. I found this in the kitchen right after the fire, but I didn't recognize it. I meant to ask you about it, Lolly. Does it seem familiar to you?"

"No. I've never seen it before. It's not from anything we ordered for that house or any other job that I can remember. That's odd." She took it for a closer look and handed it to Don.

"Do you think it's important?" Dawn asked. She was tempted to throw it away.

Don jumped up, suddenly looking very pleased with himself. "Humor me. Can you play back Ralph's speech? Look at Charlotte. I think she's wearing a scarf like it."

They reran the tape of Ralph introducing his daughter. "Oh my God," Dawn cried. "This is from her scarf. Does this tie Charlotte to the fire? Why would she try to burn down her own house?"

Don grabbed the fabric and handed it to Andrew as evidence. "That's what we need to find out. Maybe if we figure that out, we can piece together the rest of the puzzle."

Andrew looked pensive. "Let me do a little investigating and I'll need to speak with Ralph Randolph and his attorney to sound them out about what it is he really wants. I'll explain about the circumstances at Landstuhl and that you were neither married to the senator nor pregnant by him. Your only mistake was in going to Germany to visit him. I doubt after he learns the truth that he'll continue to blame you. It's the senator's head he wants."

"I hope you're right." Dawn prayed.

"In the meantime, I guess I'd better plan on moving back in here," Don grimaced playfully but then grinned. "Is it okay if I bring my room-mate along?"

"Of course," Dawn smiled for the first time since the news broke. "The more the merrier."

Andrew left and Don went to his bedroom to make some calls. It was time for him to step up and become proactive in Dawn's defense. He had an idea but wasn't ready to talk about it yet. If the fabric swatch belonged to Charlotte, it would place her at the scene of the fire, and he'd have a powerful bargaining tool with which to confront Ralph Randolph. He left the two women temporarily alone and fought his way through the reporters to his car. He was on a mission and time was of the essence.

Dawn and Lolly sat in stunned silence trying to absorb and understand all they had learned about Britt. Then they pulled out the P Street house paperwork and sorted through it to see how they could speed up its competition. Neither had their hearts in the project anymore and both simply wanted it to be over.

"I know a few things off the bat that we can eliminate." Dawn bristled. "I won't be needing the dumbwaiter, the coffee bar, or the extra closet space. I'm never moving into that house."

Lolly smiled and high-fived her.

They set to work with vengeance.

"I'm going to nail Britt for what he did to Charlotte and to me," Dawn promised, "and more importantly – for what he did to hurt our country."

CHAPTER 50

Dawn felt like a virtual prisoner in her home. The press kept her afraid to leave, so she stayed housebound for five days and was so grateful for Don and Lolly's company. The three of them spent countless hours on the phone and with Carlos, changing as many things as they could to make the renovation happen faster. They dodged all calls and kept to themselves.

In hurrying up the project, Dawn had to be careful not to shortchange anything. She had agreed to provide top-of-the-line equipment and workmanship in every aspect of the renovation. However, there were degrees of excellence from which she could choose and use her professional discretion – in everything from dishwasher and garbage disposal brands to wallpaper and fabric selections. She chose what was in stock and readily available.

Bookkeeping was now a migraine headache. It meant hours spent canceling orders, applying credits to others, and buying completely new items, but after three days, Dawn had saved what she calculated to be six weeks' worth of time. Without any further glitches, the project could be finished within a month, maybe even sooner. It was a miraculous achievement and under normal circumstances she would have been thrilled to turn over a job to a client ahead of schedule, but this was not the usual situation and Britt was not her normal client.

Every day that she was involved with P Street increased her anxiety and her fear that Britt would show up and try to talk her into marriage to silence her about the cash payments and save his scalp. The more she thought about it, the more she realized how foolish she had been to believe he could fall in love with her at the same time that he was stringing Charlotte along for her father's money. *What kind of a man did that? What kind of woman fell for it?* She wondered if he ever intended to move into P Street, or if it was his idea to modernize the house and put it on the market all along, to make a huge profit at her expense…a perfectly legal way to profit from dirty money, and she and her company were the key to its success.

During her five-day self-enforced isolation, Dawn had not heard a word from Britt, Maggie, or Owen Marshall. The number of reporters holding vigil at her door had decreased and they were instead hounding Britt at Walter Reed. The hospital administration protected him, as they did all of their patients, but they could not keep the FBI or the CIA from questioning him in private. He was forced to make his one and only statement through his attorney. "Senator Holmes denies committing any crimes and is innocent of all the charges against him. He will have no further comments."

A few days later, Dawn felt compelled to visit the P Street house. So much had gone on there in her absence and a dozen change orders had been completed. She needed to approve everything for herself. She and Don snuck out at 5:30 a.m. before any reporters had time to congregate on the street in front of her home. They drove to P Street, and he parked his car in the garage. The night shift was finishing up and Carlos and his day shift were due to arrive soon.

Dawn used her key to let them inside. They wandered from room to room as she made copious notes and checked items off a long list. They ventured upstairs and were surprised to see that everything was almost complete there too, and the place would soon be ready to accept carpets and furniture. A few missing pieces of hardware on the closet doors and bathroom cabinetry, an occasional misaligned light switch, and the wrong faucet in the master soaking tub were the only faults Dawn found. "Remind me to give Carlos a huge bonus," she said happily. "I can't believe how much he's done."

"The place looks great." Don was impressed. "I can see why Britt fell in love with it and why you were so eager to move in. It's a virtual palace within the city limits."

"Maybe it could have been our Shangri-la, but no more. Now it represents everything bad and hurtful…betrayal, heartache, and criminal activity. I want no part of this place and can't wait to sign off on this project. In the future, I have to seriously evaluate my gullibility and understand why and how I was so easily misled. This can't ever happen again."

"It won't, Dawn. You've learned a hard lesson…to implicitly trust your gut. From the beginning you thought Britt's cash payments were suspicious, but you let your heart overrule your head."

"Never again." She folded her arms over her chest and stomped her foot with determination. "I'll never let a man get that close to me again. I will not be anyone's victim."

"You'll soften in time," he said gently. "Not every man is a scoundrel like Britt. There are plenty of decent, sexy men like me out there."

"Yes," she grinned at him affectionately, "but you're taken."

"That I am. Thank you. But don't worry. I know a few you might consider. Your knight in shining armor will come along at the right time."

"I don't want a knight or any man in my life right now after what I've been through with Britt, but I won't rule one out in the distant future. Just let me tag along as a third wheel with you and Lolly for a little while."

"No problem. I'm going to leave you here now to work with Carlos and I'll be back in a few hours. The press has no idea you're here, so you'll be safe."

"Okay," she smiled distractedly and was already concentrating on rechecking her measurements for the guest room drapes. "See you later."

When she returned to the kitchen, she heard a sound at the side door and expected Carlos and his men to be coming inside. She was startled instead to see Charlotte Randolph, decked out in a bright yellow sundress and teetering on yellow stiletto heels, looking like Big Bird. She wore a signature Hermes red and gold scarf around her neck. Her eyes blazed with hatred, and she was clutching a small revolver in her hand.

"I thought you and I should have a little chat sweetheart," she hissed in an exaggerated southern accent. "Lordy, do you have a girdle on? Because you don't look the least bit pregs to me…or did you use the oldest trick in the book to trap a man – my man – into marrying you?"

"Charlotte." Dawn's voice was as steady as she could manage while a crazy woman pointed a gun directly at her stomach. "Come in. Sit down. Please put the gun away," she begged. "We need to talk. You don't have all the information. We've both been misled."

Don had already left, and Carlos was not yet on the premises. She would have to use all her wits to handle Charlotte until help arrived. "There's been a huge misunderstanding. And you're right. I am *not* pregnant, never was. Haven't you spoken to your father? I know Britt told him the truth. Hasn't he said anything to you?"

Charlotte seemed momentarily surprised, but she did not trust Dawn. "I haven't seen or spoken to my father since his press conference about

Britt. He's been too busy meeting with reporters and consulting with his attorneys. I think he plans to sue the world on my behalf and ruin Britt's political career. Anyway, what I have to say doesn't concern him. My beef's with you…our high and mighty interior decorator. You're really a two-faced bitch, stealing my fiancée right out from under my nose, pretending to be my friend and promising to make this monstrosity of a house into a home for me. But the whole time, you were plotting to take him for yourself and move in here yourself."

She was yelling and so agitated that she started to sway back and forth on her high-heeled sandals, as she waved her arms and the gun wildly in the air. Losing her balance, she stumbled forward and fell with a thud against the counter. Dawn grabbed her other arm, steadied her, and wrestled the gun away.

"Women like you are evil. You're a menace to sisterhood." Charlotte shrieked and watched as her gun tumbled to the floor and Dawn wisely kicked it out of reach. Dawn tried to grab Charlotte by her shoulders to restrain her and shake some sense into her, but she only succeeded in ripping the scarf off Charlotte's neck and pushing the out-of-control woman to the floor.

"Violence isn't going to settle anything, Charlotte. Please, let me explain." She reached down to help her enemy up and was stalling for time until Carlos arrived. She forced herself to speak slowly and calmly. "If you listen to me, I think you'll see that we have a lot in common. Britt is the real enemy here…not me."

Charlotte looked dazed and actually surprised to find herself in the P Street kitchen lying on the floor with her dress hiked up to her panties. "I hardly remember coming here," she mumbled almost incoherently. "One minute I was watching a rerun of yesterday's *The View.* Joy and Whoopi were droning on and on about you and Britt and poor gullible little me. My blood boiled and I saw red. The next thing I knew, my car practically drove itself here." She held her throbbing head. White lights behind her eyes blinded her. "I don't know what I was thinking. What's wrong with me? As much as I hate you, I promise that I would never shoot you."

Dawn was wary and concerned that anything she said could set Charlotte off again and topple the distraught girl over the edge. Britt's former fiancée was obviously experiencing some kind of emotional crisis, maybe even suffering a mental breakdown. Dawn reacted instinctively. She stuffed the scarf in her pocket and gingerly reached for Charlotte's clammy hand, anticipating a violent reaction, but Charlotte allowed herself to be helped up and led out of the room, confusion clearly shown in her dazed eyes. Dawn detected the smell of bourbon on Charlotte's breath. *Was it possible? It was barely 7:00 a.m.*

"Sit down." Dawn indicated two metal chairs placed near a drafting table loaded with floor plans and fabric samples. "I'll get you some water and we'll try to figure this out together." She took a serendipitous glance at her watch. *Carlos, where the hell are you? I can't do this much longer.*

Charlotte complied. She was like a naughty student being ushered into the school principal's office and waiting to be punished for some unknown infraction of the rules. Her confrontational demeanor instantly disappeared, and she seemed limp as a noodle, transformed into a sniveling, apprehensive child. Her hands fell heavily to her lap as she looked at Dawn with a blank stare. "How could Britt do that to me?" she whimpered.

After giving Charlotte a bottle of water, Dawn took a seat opposite her. Speaking calmly, she prayed that Charlotte would listen and really hear her. She knew that logically she shouldn't be comforting her when she needed comforting herself, but life was strange. They were like two wounded birds huddling together for protection against a raging storm.

"I don't blame you for being upset at me. I'm furious at myself as well, for being so gullible, and like you, for believing everything Britt Holmes told me. He's a pathological liar, and he duped us both. I'd even go so far as to say he has every intention of fooling the whole country about what kind of a person he is. The only one who saw through his fake veneer was your father. In the beginning, he believed the gossip about me, but now he knows the truth. Let me tell you what really happened and see if we can't agree to unite against Britt and not against each other."

Charlotte looked at her wide-eyed, gulping some of the water, but did not interrupt.

CHAPTER 51

Carlos and his crew arrived at the house a few minutes later and began their tasks. Electricians, plumbers, drapery installers, and wallpaper hangers spread out everywhere, moving purposefully like black ants at a Fourth of July picnic. The city building inspector was due for an onsite visit to issue the crucial occupancy permit, and there were last-minute tasks to complete before his arrival. The whole team was in a frantic final countdown mode. Carlos saw Dawn talking to Charlotte and started to approach them, but Dawn waved him off. She was totally engrossed in Charlotte's unexpected visit and wanted to hear her out.

After initially skirting around the truth, Charlotte finally found the strength to speak from her heart. She raised her head and looked soberly into Dawn's eyes. "I never really loved Britt and marriage to him was totally my father's idea," she whispered softly, ashamed by how weak and spineless she had been. "Father begged me to help him, to be clever and use all my charms to seduce the senator. He told me marriage was the only way to save us from bankruptcy and humiliation and that I was his only hope to restore the family's good name."

"But why? I thought your father's a wealthy man."

"He was, but not anymore. In the last few years, he's blown through all his holdings and now our lives are all smoke and mirrors. He has a terrible gambling problem and owes a bunch of very nasty people a lot of money. He thought by marrying me off to the future President, it would force his creditors to forgive his debts. His secondary plan was for me, as the First Lady, to convince Britt to steer lucrative government contracts to our family businesses and make us solvent again and then father could pay off his debtors. Our family name and its place in the South's history is very important to my parents, and my father's insane addiction to poker and roulette has tarnished it forever. We're going to lose our home and Mama's going to have to sell all of her jewelry."

"Oh, my word. How long have you known about this?"

"Since I began to see overdue and late notices coming in the mail, and one time the electricity was turned off." She looked ashamed and twisted her hands together nervously. "My father's very clever. He has so many different bank accounts, loans, mortgages, and lines of credit, and he's always kiting checks and claiming there's a new deal around the corner that will make us rich again.

"To this day, he keeps making one bad bet after the next, hoping for the big jackpot, but he never wins. No one, not his accountants, bankers, or even his closest friends realize that he's so overcommitted and on the brink of bankruptcy. He'll do anything to keep his gambling debts from becoming public knowledge, even sell his own daughter," she said in disgust. "He's much like Donald Trump when his real estate empire nearly toppled. He's been overinflating the values of his assets, and robbing Peter to pay Paul. Some of Mama's credit cards have been denied and she's not welcome to charge at our county club anymore.

"My father is really an egotistical man, driven by delusions of grandeur. He's always dreamed of becoming a famous billionaire, surpassing the likes of Warren Buffett or Mark Zuckerberg. He also has always dreamed of being an ambassador and promised my mama that when I was First Lady, Britt would appoint him, and they would have an exciting life abroad. But, when COVID hit, his shopping centers, malls, and office buildings became vacant, cash-guzzling eyesores. Tenants refused to pay their rent. People worked and shopped from their homes, but his mortgage payments were still due, and the banks were unforgiving. His businesses suffered. His customers were too scared to venture into his stores for fear of catching the virus. Nonetheless, Father refused to accept reality and kept writing checks, but nothing reversed the trend. He's desperate now." She let out a huge sigh. Telling the ugly truth had been embarrassing and exhausting.

Dawn looked at Charlotte with a new understanding. Her father had put her through an emotional wringer and had tried to force her into a marriage purely to save his own skin. It was deplorable. She found herself feeling sorry for her. "That's a terrible way to treat a daughter and an unforgivable burden to put on you and your mother."

"I thought I was doing the only thing I could to help him," Charlotte whined, "so I went along with my father's stupid plan. I even came to like Britt and fantasized about us raising a family together in the White House. Many people live in loveless marriages and manage to be happy. Why not me? But that was never Britt's intention. It's obvious to me now that once he got what he wanted from my father and his influential buddies – the presidency – he wouldn't want me anymore. You conveniently came along at the right time, and I was out before I was ever really in."

"Oh Charlotte. I never intended to hurt you," Dawn stammered, instantly overwhelmed with shame and guilt. "I can't begin to justify or even explain what went on. One minute Britt was my new client and the next, he was declaring his love for me. I was so flattered and taken with him and his presidential aura that I never gave much, if any, thought to how this would impact you. I foolishly convinced myself that you were just a silly girl and that you two were never going to last. I'm so sorry."

"You know," Charlotte perked up a bit. "I'm not as dumb as I pretend. I graduated *summa cum laude* from college, but Father never told anyone that I went. He was actually ashamed that I was smart. He says men want whores in their beds, chefs in their kitchens, and saints in their children's nurseries but not brains in their parlors. He thought if Britt knew I had educated opinions on political matters that he would not propose. Father knew Britt wanted no intellectual competition in his marriage and he told me that Britt's first wife Taylor only finished the ninth grade. That's why they got on so well together. He was her king and she worshiped him."

Dawn shook her head in wonder. *How could she have misjudged Charlotte so badly?* "I admire you," she said honestly. "I went to Duke University myself, but never graduated. I had to drop out when my parents died. After paying all their bills, there was no money left for my tuition."

She handed Charlotte a Styrofoam cup of coffee. "I suppose you'd prefer sweet tea," she smiled weakly, "but this is all I've got."

Charlotte took the cup gratefully, breathing in the hot steam to steady herself. "Can we talk some more? I still have so many questions."

"Sure, and me too. You don't know half of it. Your father and Britt may have cruelly used you, but they did the same to me," Dawn said angrily, "and it might cost me my freedom and my career. I'll go to jail if I can't prove my innocence."

Charlotte looked aghast. "No way. Tell me. Maybe I can help."

"I'll share everything I know with you, but first finish your story. And I have to ask, although I'm ashamed to be saying the words, did you set fire to this place?"

Charlotte looked aghast. "Of course not!" She protested. "Since the day I was born, my father has programmed me to be obedient and follow his every whim. I was coddled and sheltered by her mother and surrounded by nannies and the hired help my entire life. I had no goals, real ambitions, or sense of my own potential or talents. I lived vicariously through books and movies. Until I went off to college, at my mother's insistence, my sole purpose was to please my father. I know he loves me in the only way he knows how…by throwing money at me and in return he expects blind loyalty. He essentially bought me and mama. When I excelled in college, he was not happy. It took the spotlight off him. He countered by making a huge donation to the scholarship fund there. They named the student center, the Randolph Pavilion, after him in gratitude. But he never attended my graduation or acknowledged my degree."

Dawn looked at her with compassion. Her own youth had been so different, and her parents had loved her unconditionally. She could not begin to imagine what Charlotte's bizarre childhood had been like. How was it possible to grow up so controlled by a parent that one lost her own identity and was told to hide her intelligence as if it were a fault, something to be ashamed about?

"When Father introduced me to the famous Senator Holmes," Charlotte continued, "it was the happiest day of my life. He was so handsome and important, and he showed interest in me. I was flattered and soon convinced myself that I was madly in love."

"I know how that goes," Dawn interjected, wanting to ask Charlotte more about the fire and how a piece of her scarf came to be in the kitchen but was afraid to interrupt her confession.

"So, I did as my father asked. I flirted and teased Britt until he was so horny that he proposed. With a wedding ring on my finger and the possibility of becoming the country's First Lady, I knew I was finally going to be free of my father's manipulation. I truly hoped Britt would help him get out of debt, but that was secondary to gaining my freedom from him. I was going to confess about going to college and hope that Britt would accept me as a true partner, a helpmate. But then he met you and started ignoring me. When I heard that he was secretly married and you were having his baby, can you imagine how betrayed and confused I felt?"

Dawn could not find the right words to comfort Charlotte or make herself feel any better. She had unwittingly become as much of a spineless puppet, pulled by Britt's manipulative strings, as Charlotte had been by her father's. "But what about the fire," Dawn persisted.

CHAPTER 52

Before Charlotte could answer, Don came barreling through the front door. He had recognized Charlotte's car parked haphazardly out front and had feared the worst. He had no idea what calamity he might be walking into and stopped short when he saw the two women sipping coffee together and appearing to talk amiably. That was the last thing he had expected.

"Hello," he said tentatively. "Is everything okay here?"

Dawn looked up and smiled. "Yes, Charlotte and I are comparing notes and getting to know each other." She knew Don was confused and she enjoyed seeing his surprised reaction. Under any other circumstance, his expression would be comical.

"Well, that's nice, I suppose." He did not know what to make of the new female alliance. It was a very unlikely pairing. "But I came back to tell you that the FBI wants to talk to you."

"The FBI?" Dawn gasped.

"Yes," Don answered solemnly. "Someone from the agency is coming to your house this afternoon, so I need to get you home. I've already called Andrew to meet us there." He looked imploringly at Charlotte. "Can you please resume this 'girl talk' at another time?"

"Oh sure." Charlotte, frazzled and feeling uneasy, stood up immediately. "We were just getting to the good stuff, but I guess the FBI takes priority." She looked at Dawn and frowned. "Good luck and call me as soon as you can. We need to finish this conversation." She picked up her keys. "By the way, you can keep the gun," she chucked on her way out. "It's only plastic."

"A gun?" Don was shocked. "What the hell's been going on here?"

"Well…" Dawn started to explain, but he cut her off.

"Never mind. We have to go. This FBI business is serious stuff, and you need to talk to Andrew before you speak to anyone from the bureau." He led her to his car. Hopefully everything he had set in motion would work out well for Dawn. He had done all he could. The rest was up to her.

* *

"Why does the FBI want to talk to me?" She asked Andrew.

"It's concerning the cash payments Britt made to you. They'll want to ask you about what he told you about them – what you might know about where the money came from – how often it came, how much and where you deposited it…all those kinds of things."

"But I don't know anything more than what I told you before. I never knew about any connection with the Chinese until I heard Ralph Randolph tell the world about it."

"I understand, but you'll need to convince the FBI of that. Sadly, in this country the idea that one is innocent until proven guilty is no longer the status quo. We need to show that you are an innocent person, tricked by a devious con man into laundering his dirty money through your interior design company. You'll have to open your books to the

THE HOUSE on P STREET

world. The bureau will question every entry that you wrote down and all aspects of your relationship with the senator. In order to indict you, their job will be to prove you were complicit in his crimes, and thankfully, I don't believe they can. You must answer their questions honestly but offer nothing else, no extraneous details. I'll be right here but the first impression you make will go a long way toward influencing how they regard and treat you in the future. Do you understand?"

She nodded sullenly. *How could this be happening?*

"Okay then. Go brush your hair and put on a decent outfit. Your clothes are full of construction dust, and you smell like fresh paint."

CHAPTER 53

Walker Brant strolled nonchalantly into her home as if he owned the place. He showed her his identification badge and his compelling brown eyes landed squarely on Dawn's face as they exchanged tentative, inquisitive glances. He raised an eyebrow, studying her carefully, and thought that she was far too attractive to be a criminal. Don had described her as "drop-dead gorgeous," but one never knew what treachery hid behind a brilliant smile and pouty lips. She greeted him politely before introducing him to Andrew.

"I'm Walker C. Brant," the agent declared in a deep baritone voice. "I'm a special agent with the FBI. Is there somewhere we can talk?"

"In here is fine," she answered primly, indicating he should sit on the sofa. She and Andrew took seats opposite him. "I have nothing to hide. Ask away." For all of her bravado, her knees were shaking. It was hard to be casual around the FBI.

Walker began the interview by verifying her correct legal name, address, and social security number. Then he got straight to the point. "I understand that you and Senator Holmes have or had a personal relationship?"

"Yes, we...." She planned to expand but Andrew cut her off sharply.

"Ms. Sutter was employed by Senator Holmes to renovate and redecorate a large home he purchased on P Street in Georgetown," Andrew stated candidly. "They subsequently became friends." He shot Dawn a warning look to remind her not to say anything more and to only respond to what she was asked.

"So, there was no romantic relationship?" The agent appeared skeptical. He watched Dawn's body language for signs that she was lying but saw none. "I was led to believe there was much more going on between you two…even a baby on the way."

"They had a professional relationship, one between a decorator and her client," Andrew answered sternly.

"I'd like to hear from Ms. Sutter, directly." Walker insisted, perturbed at the lawyer's meddling. "I don't mind you being here, Andrew, but you must allow her to answer my questions herself."

Agent Walker C. Brant was very handsome but stone-faced, and he sounded grim. From his serious posture, he must have believed she was involved in Britt's crimes. Her long eyelashes, heavy from recently applied mascara, framed her fearful, wide-open eyes. Her hands became clammy, but her voice and resolve remained strong. Sitting opposite her inquisitor, she looked like a beautiful heroine on the cover of some hot romance novel – but looks were deceiving. She was like Jello inside but determined to convince this man that she had done nothing wrong and was in fact another injured party in Britt's money laundering scheme. She would not allow him to leave her house until she had convinced him of her innocence.

"I can't really explain how it happened," she began tentatively. "But when I learned that Britt had been gravely wounded, I felt compelled to be with him. I know it defies logic but without giving it a second thought, I bought a ticket and flew to Landstuhl. In retrospect it was dumb, and I should never have gone." She jumped up and paced around the room. "Mr. Brant, haven't you ever done something ridiculous in your past that you regret to this day? This was one of those times for me. However, I assure you, once I was allowed in to visit the senator, all we did was talk."

The agent's attitude softened a bit. His years of experience in observing and questioning suspects led him to trust his instincts. He believed that she was telling the truth, but he remained incredulous that such an accomplished and obviously intelligent woman had behaved so spontaneously and with no encouragement or motive, solely from the desire to visit a sick friend. "Alright," he gave her a sideways half-smile. "Let's start at the beginning. Assuming you're telling the truth, can you tell me specifically how and when, and the exact amount of money that you've been paid for your services by Senator Holmes?"

Dawn hoped that he was not being sarcastic when he referred to her "services." She glanced at Andrew before answering, grateful for his previous sage advice to keep good records. "Britt paid me in cash, and I have kept very concise records." She went into her office and returned with a spiral notebook. "Here," she handed the agent the proof. "This is a list of all the transactions with the accompanying bank deposit receipts attached. There have been five accounted for to date, as you can see, and the total amount is written at the bottom of the receipts column. But I've received two more, and the money's in my safe here. With everything that's happened lately, I haven't gone back to the bank again."

Walker took the notebook and reviewed it carefully. "I'll need to keep this as evidence," he said, trying to ignore the growing attraction he was beginning to feel for her. "And I'll need to confiscate the money you have here." He had seen dozens of innocent women conned and duped by unscrupulous men before, but he felt particularly protective of Dawn. He had watched the news programs and seen the press viciously attack her. From experience, he knew that she would continue to be hounded until the Chinese accusations were either proved to be true or the senator was cleared of any wrongdoing. Britt Holmes had, with his greedy and nefarious behavior, jeopardized Dawn's business, her livelihood, and possibly her life by involving her in his crimes. He decided at that moment that he wanted to be on "team Dawn" and come to her defense. He had years of expertise to fall back on.

The more Walker listened to Dawn, the more he was enraged at the senator and the more he believed in her. "I'll do everything I can to help you," he said earnestly, "but this investigation and the legal system in general usually takes a long time to sort things out and come to a final resolution. I'll do my best to speed the process along but most importantly, please call me if you think of anything else that might be helpful. Try to remember if the senator ever mentioned any friends in China or any overseas banking connections. The smallest detail might help me. And Dawn, I'll need you to come to FBI headquarters tomorrow to make an official statement." He rose and handed her his card. "Shall we say 10:00 a.m.? And try not to worry. It's standard protocol."

Andrew watched the interaction between the FBI agent and Dawn. He was relieved that the interview had gone well, and Walker C. Brant had appeared genuinely concerned about Dawn and seemed willing to help her prove her innocence. It was the best outcome he could have wished for his client, but she was still under scrutiny and not cleared of any wrongdoing as yet."

"Oh, one more thing," Walker said as he was leaving. "Do not talk to Senator Holmes. There must be no further communication with him or with anyone in his office."

"You don't have to worry about that," she bristled. "I never want to see that horrid man again."

CHAPTER 54

Clutching Walker's card in her hands, Dawn stormed purposefully through the front doors of the FBI Headquarters on Pennsylvania Avenue at 8:00 a.m. – two hours early for her appointment.

She had awoken in the middle of the night, remembering that before he was injured, Britt had given her a key to his safe deposit box with his cryptic note. She had stuffed the note in her desk drawer and the key in her change purse and completely forgotten about them both. She rushed out of bed and, shaking with anticipation, scoured her purse and retrieved the key. Holding it tightly in her hand, she wondered if there might be something in the bank box that was incriminating, that could hurt Britt and clear her. Maybe there was a reference or a phone number for one of his Chinese contacts? She could not wait for the morning.

It was just past 3:00 a.m. No matter how conscientious he was, Walker would not be at his desk at this early hour. Dawn was too wide awake to fall back asleep again, so she dressed and wandered around the house nervously reading and rereading Britt's note. It still made no sense to her. Was he paranoid or really guilty of something? She wanted to see Walker and give him the key and the note as soon as possible.

Her agent was surprised when Dawn marched into his office so far ahead of their scheduled meeting. But he was happy to see her. His eyes twinkled. She looked very pretty and very excited.

"Couldn't wait to see me?" He grinned a crooked smile showing off beautifully straight, white teeth. "That's not the normal reaction I get from people being called in here. They tend to dread seeing me."

"Well, I thought of something in the middle of the night and thought it might be of interest." She showed him Britt's note and gave him the key to the Capitol Hill Bank box. "I have no idea what all this means or if I should have given the key to you, but as I said yesterday, I want nothing more to do with Senator Holmes. I intend to finish his house for him as promised, but he can have his lawyers sign off on it. No in-person meetings or phone calls ever gain. I hope I did the right thing by bringing you this key."

"I'm sure you did," he reassured her. "And as long as you're here, let's get your statement on the record."

As kind and solicitous as Walker tried to be, giving her statement was a lengthy ordeal. Two other agents also came in and interviewed her. They were not as compassionate or convinced of her innocence as Walker and made her tediously draw a precise timeline, naming every encounter and phone call she had ever had with Britt, including her visits to Germany and at Walter Reed. They asked her what she knew about Elenor Blaine, about Maggie, and about the senator's aide, Owen Marshall.

Dawn was as honest and as thorough as she could be, but trying to recall every detail about every conversation was difficult. There had been so many discussions about the house itself, the furnishings, and even some artwork that it was hard to remember which topic came up when. However, Dawn was adamant that Britt had never mentioned having any connection, friendly or otherwise, with the Chinese Government.

"Getting back to your impromptu visit to Germany," the female agent persisted. "Didn't you think it odd that none of the senator's family were there?"

"No. His parents are deceased and he has no siblings, at least that's what he told me." Now she questioned that too. "The fact that he was so alone was one reason I felt so strongly about going there myself."

"And what do you think now?" the male agent persisted.

"I think I was a fool but that even after this awful cloud of suspicion, one good thing might come out of this mess. My renovation is, if I may brag a little, excellent, and I hope it will be appreciated by the industry and be good enough to earn my company a gold or silver Prism award or even an Aurora. They are the equivalent of an Oscar or an Emmy in our profession. Something positive must come out of this disaster."

"So, you went to Germany in hopes of receiving some kind of design award." The male agent pressed her. "Not for humanitarian reasons."

"No. Not at all! You're twisting my words." Dawn was getting angry. "I went to Landstuhl out of genuine concern for Britt, not knowing if he would survive his wounds. All I'm saying is that now that the project is almost finished, I'm proud of how the house has turned out and the work I've done there. I believe it's excellent and should be a candidate for an award. Have we become so jaded in this country that having pride in one's work is politically incorrect?" She glared defiantly at the offending agent. Walker smiled in spite of himself and was impressed with Dawn's spunk in the middle of adversity.

"I think we're getting off track," Walker intervened, trying to stem the escalating tension but proud of Dawn's feistiness. She was not letting herself be intimidated. "Awards or the lack thereof are not pertinent to this case. If," and he stared at his two colleagues, "you have no more questions, I believe we can let Ms. Sutter go home."

"Nothing more at this time," the female mumbled. The male did not answer Walker but stood up, his temper barely in check. "You'll be hearing from us again." He slammed his notebook closed and left the room.

Dawn shook her head and frowned. "That went well," she said sarcastically, but then she worried. "Why was he so hostile?"

"It's the good-cop bad-cop approach we're taught in the academy," Walker admitted. "Sometimes they take it too far. Don't be upset. From what I've seen so far, you were an innocent bystander, not an accomplice, but I still need to do more investigation. Go back home or to work and leave this to me. I have an important date with a security box." He gave her a boyish grin and opened the door for her to leave. "My advice is to finish that damn house as quickly as possible and close the books on Senator Holmes once and for all."

"Yes. I will." She gave him a mock salute and a tired smile. "I certainly will." Then she looked at him and grinned. "Could I go with you to the box? After all, he did give me the key."

"Sorry, no," he answered lightly. "But it might have been fun."

CHAPTER 55

For the next three weeks Dawn spent most of her time on the P Street project and the rest working for her other clients. She personally supervised the completion of phase one, the renovation itself, and she paid Carlos and his crew for their work. She began phase two – supervising the delivery and installation of all the furnishings and accessories.

Lolly was by her side as much as possible, staging the furniture and equipping the closets with padded hangers, the bathrooms with fluffy towels, and the kitchen and pantry with dishes, pots and pans, stemware, and small appliances – a blender, espresso machine, and state-of-the-art toaster oven. There were sheets stacked neatly in the linen closet and beautiful duvets on the beds. Throw pillows of various sizes and fabrics were placed on sofas and chairs, and the table and desk lamps contained soft pink bulbs to cast the ideal light in the room so photographers could take flattering pictures of the presidential candidate in his own home.

In the end, the house was exquisite. No detail had been overlooked, from the chair railings and coffered ceiling to the sponges and dishwasher detergent under the kitchen sinks. The house was move-in ready, except for groceries. Dawn was as proud of it as any mother would be of her child, but being in it now made her sad.

She remembered Britt's many broken promises and his deceptions, and the only thing she wanted now was to lock all the doors, walk away, and never go inside again. And she would have, except that a representative from *Architectural Digest* called the senator's office and requested permission to film inside and do an article on the amazing transformation for an upcoming issue. It would be wonderful publicity for Sutter Home Interiors, as long as no reference to Dawn's personal relationship with Britt was mentioned. Andrew made sure to insert a clause to that effect in the written agreement before Dawn signed it. Then it went to Britt for his signature. He was torn between his desire to appeal to the middle-class voters as a down-to-earth man of the people candidate and his wish to brag about his superior taste and obsessive fascination with presidential history. In the end, his ego and preoccupation with promoting himself won out and he approved the publication of the article. If anyone questioned his extravagance, he was prepared to come up with some explanation and throw someone else under the bus to cover for him.

Dawn had not heard from him in weeks, but she read in a tabloid that he had been released from Walter Reed and was living in a posh hotel near his office until his new home was ready for occupancy. Maggie was always pictured by his side and so, surprisingly, was Ralph Randolph. *What had happened to bring about that strange reconciliation?* Dawn thought that relationship had been permanently severed after the broken engagement with Charlotte and then Ralph's searing verbal attack on the senator, but politics made for strange bedfellows. Her name, thankfully, was not mentioned, and the press seemed to have found another poor soul to torment. The streets outside of her home and office had returned to normal. Even so, she continued to be nervous, waiting for the other shoe to drop.

Walker called her from time to time to reassure that things were moving along in the investigation, but he said that he was not allowed to divulge what, if anything, he had found in the safe deposit box or how the inquiry into Britt's Chinese connections was proceeding. They had pleasant conversations about almost everything else and found that they had a lot in common. He admitted that Don had called him about her situation and asked for his help. They had been Navy Seals together and served in two deployments overseas together. Dawn and he were developing a friendship and enjoyed spending time with each other on the phone.

"When this is over, and you've been cleared, we'll have a celebration dinner and I'll share everything about this case with you. In the meantime, FBI policy states that an active agent cannot socialize with a person of interest. That's you," he joked. "You're definitely of interest to me."

Dawn grinned. Talking with Walker always made her feel reassured and that everything was going to be alright. She appreciated his devotion to duty and his keen sense of humor. Knowing he and Don were friends made it even better. However, she was not ready to let another man into her life. Having been badly hurt by Britt, she was in a self-protection mode. Walker was handsome, witty, and she knew she could rely on him, but she was still too wounded to trust her own judgment when it came to men. She was glad that his professional ethics kept them physically apart, at least for now.

Charlotte had called her several times, but Dawn, on the advice of counsel, did not meet with her. Andrew had warned her that she could not put herself in a position where she could be seen or photographed with anyone, including Charlotte, who was in any way connected to Britt Holmes. She explained the situation clearly to Charlotte and apologized.

She had come to like her as a friend and realized she was as much an innocent victim of Britt and Ralph Randolph's manipulations as she was herself, but she had to respect her attorney's advice. They agreed to meet again after all the dust settled.

"Mama and I are so upset about all this nasty business that we're going away for a while, to Europe actually. She's so furious at my father that she's considering divorce. She needs time to think about what's next for her. By the way, we have never discussed it again, but you do know that I was just testing you and maybe Britt with that ridiculous chicken coop and Barbie hot tub stuff. I never wanted either."

"Yes, I suspected as much." Dawn laughed, "and actually it was pretty funny. Please call me when you and your mother return. Take care, Charlotte. I wish you well."

* *

Dawn sent the keys to P Street and a "paid in full" receipt by messenger to Britt's hotel. She also opened another checking account for Sutter Home Interiors. The FBI had frozen her original one on the day they began their investigation so she would not be comingling her legitimate expenses and deposits with Britt's. It was inconvenient, and separating her other costs from those for P Street was tedious, but her accountants managed it. When they finished their internal audit, and everything had been paid, there was a balance of over three million dollars left on the house…money that Britt had sent her hoping to hide it from government scrutiny. It had been impounded by the FBI as evidence until all the legal matters concerning it were resolved and its rightful owner determined.

"Now that this chapter of your life is almost over," Don declared one morning at breakfast. "You can get on with your life. You don't need me as a bodyguard anymore."

"That's true," Dawn smiled wistfully. "I still have to get through Britt's trial, but that's a long way off. For the record, I've truly loved having you around." She hugged him affectionately. He had become like a brother. "Has Lolly mentioned how worried we are that there's been a distinct lack of new business? I'm afraid all the bad publicity has cost us future clients. They must have been scared off. And – even though the *Digest* piece was flattering, and should have generated a lot of new business, it has not. Britt's alleged crimes and the FBI investigation have brought my reputation into question and I've no idea how to resurrect it. Any suggestions?"

"No, but everything takes time. What's hot today is old news tomorrow. Remember, you and Lolly built your business by doing excellent work, and the news traveled by word of mouth, not via tabloids or the television news. It will happen again. You'll just have to ride this out and be patient, and maybe reach out to past and present customers and ask for referrals."

"Easy for you to say," she said in frustration. "But that's a good point, and as luck would have it, and I don't know why under the present circumstances, we're suddenly being considered for a huge new job today, refurbishing the public rooms in the historic Danelli Hotel downtown. If we get it, it would be a big feather in the company's cap. The Danelli is the flagship boutique hotel in their chain of twelve around the country. If their management likes our work, we might be considered for the other eleven. Wish me luck."

"You know I do. And tell that sexy girlfriend of mine that I'll take you both to dinner there if you all get the job."

CHAPTER 56

Lolly manned the showroom and handled the office problems while Dawn set out with a large portfolio of drawings the two had made to show their ideas for transforming the lobby, piano bar, and dining room of the iconic hotel. The Danelli was a popular watering hole for DC businessmen and women, particularly lawyers and judges and the legal community, as it was around the corner from the Justice Department. Its theme was Italian life through the ages, from the life-size roman statues that guarded the lobby to the delicious Northern Italian pasta, veal dishes, and fresh fish served in the highly acclaimed restaurant or the less formal, trendy Casa D trattoria.

Dawn was optimistic but anxious. Given recent events, this was the most important presentation she was to give since her original one to Britt. She began by complimenting the general manager, Giovanni Campari, and telling him how often she and her friends frequented the hotel's piano bar and restaurants. Then she brought out pictures of her most recent design work, including the before-and-after ones of the P Street house. It would have been impossible to leave those out, given that so many people knew about the scandal.

"Legally, because the house is involved in a government investigation, I can't discuss what's going on there at the moment," she said, honestly trying to meet any objections before they were voiced, "but I feel the design work is excellent and represents the true creativity of my firm. I hope you'll agree."

Giovanni took the pictures and slowly nodded his approval. "These are excellent. You have lived up to your reputation."

Dawn blanched and he clarified himself. "No, I mean that in a good way. You've always been highly regarded by your clients and your professional peers. I checked your references thoroughly. They were all very positive and glowing. That's why I am willing to consider your firm. I also heard about your amazing creative talent from my nephew, so I felt I had to give you a chance. What is rumored to have happened with Senator Holmes is no reflection on your talent. Now that we've addressed the elephant in the room, can you get on with this. I have another meeting in an hour."

She smiled in relief and wanted to ask who his nephew was. She didn't remember having any clients by the name of Campari, but he was eager for her to begin her demonstration, so she did not ask. She explained her concepts, one by one, with drawings and diagrams which showed changing the public rooms into softer, more inviting spaces. Everything would still remain distinctively Italian, but with a softer, more welcoming edge. Instead of fierce-looking Roman soldiers dressed in armor standing guard in the doorways of the lobby, guests would be greeted with elegant marble statues of the most famous Roman Goddesses: Juno – the Queen of the Goddesses, Venus – the Goddess of beauty and love, and Minerva – the Goddess of wisdom and the arts. They would be dressed in the traditional flowing garments of the time and would be holding delicate bouquets of fresh seasonal flowers. The softer look would carry throughout the various spaces...

evident in more comfortable sofas and chairs, creating more intimate conversational and seating areas. Dawn suggested translucent, billowy window treatments that would soften the room and invite guests to relax and unwind. "Everything about the interiors should suggest elegance and warmth."

"I like it," Giovanni said, but then he frowned. "Italian men are very macho. We pride ourselves on our masculinity. I can't sell upper management on frills or pink, girly touches."

"Of course, I agree." Dawn smiled and was secretly ecstatic. She could tell from the expression on the manager's face and the time he spent perusing the drawings that he was intrigued with her presentation.

She continued by showing a new design and table layout for the formal dining room, which featured colorful hand-painted murals on the walls depicting gorgeous Roman villas and their magnificent gardens. The table clothes, napkins, and even the chinaware followed the garden theme. The trattoria on the same floor was modeled after a classic pizzeria located near the Trevi Fountain and would serve casual fare late into the night. The newly designed piano bar was decorated in sophisticated, muted colors with throw pillows everywhere, and it exuded a mellow, sultry feeling – the perfect place to enjoy late-night cocktails or a crisp cold Limoncello.

"There you have it." she smiled triumphantly. "This is only a first look at what can be done. I'm open to any suggestions you and your board may have." She sat back, satisfied that she had done her best and hopeful that it had been enough, and that she had won him over.

"I'll need to speak with the board, and if they're interested, I'll ask you to come back and make the full presentation to them. And to discuss costs."

"Yes, of course. Thank you for your time, Giovanni. I hope to hear from you soon." She stood up and firmly shook his hand.

Dawn had not felt this good about anything or as energized in a long time. As she walked out of the Danelli, her phone rang.

"Dawn, it's Walker. I need to see you right away. Where are you?"

"I'm just leaving a client's place downtown. I can meet you anywhere."

"I'll be at your house in an hour. Ask your attorney to join us."

"Do I need to be worried?" She asked anxiously, her nerves once again on edge, but he had already hung up.

CHAPTER 57

awn called Andrew right away and rushed home to wait for him and Walker. Only minutes before, she had been so happy and hopeful about the Danelli job, but now, she wondered if outside forces were again going to upend her life. *Would this nightmare ever end?*

She tried to distract herself by calling Lolly. "The presentation went beautifully this morning," she said, trying to recapture her former enthusiasm. "Giovanni liked the drawings and our soft edges concept. I don't know if there are any other competitors vying for the job, but I got the impression that he really appreciated what he saw. He even said that he checked our references, and that the Britt scandal did not reflect negatively on our work...So, I'm hopeful."

"Then why do you sound so down?" She could tell from the tone of Dawn's voice that she was upset.

"Walker Brant is on his way over here and he asked me to have Andrew meet us. That doesn't sound like a positive thing."

"Don't be so sure. Maybe he wants to tell you some good news and let your attorney in on it at the same time."

"Maybe." She heard a knock on the door. "I'll know in a moment. Someone's here."

Andrew and Walker came in together, having met up on the street.

"Sit down, Dawn. I have some interesting information to share," Walker said. "You're not going to believe it."

She could not tell from his expression whether the news was good or bad. "Well, don't keep us in suspense."

He turned towards Andrew. "You knew that Dawn gave me the key to Senator Holmes's safe deposit box?"

"Yes," the lawyer nodded. "So, did you find anything important there?"

"I did." He looked pleased with himself. "Dawn once mentioned that the P Street house was not titled in Britt's name but rather in an LLC's. When I looked into that, I discovered that Maggie is listed as the majority partner of that particular LLC. She has a ninety-nine percent interest in it. That means she, not Britt, owns the house." He waited a few seconds for that surprising information to register. "I found that very curious."

"Is Owen also a partner?" Andrew asked, suddenly beginning to put the pieces together.

"Yes, but he owns only a small part. He owns a meager one percent share."

Dawn was dumbfounded. "Are you saying that Maggie has owned the house this whole time and neither she nor Britt ever thought to say a word to me about it? Why would they keep it a secret?"

"They were not only keeping it from you, Dawn, but more importantly, from Uncle Sam," Walker said. "The ownership of the house is yet another layer of deception perpetrated by Britt to hide his assets from the federal government. As you've said so many times, he didn't want any paper trail connecting him to the house or to the excessive money he put into it after the purchase. By titling the deed in an LLC with Maggie as the majority partner and Dawn paying cash for all the renovations and furnishings, his hands, paper-wise, are completely clean. But there's more."

He paused for emphasis. "I also found a side agreement attached to the deed and the paperwork for the LLC, and it's dated and notarized on the same day. It states that when the P Street property is sold, Maggie Chen is to receive twenty percent of the profits, Ralph Randolph twenty percent, and Britt gets the balance – the remaining sixty percent."

"Why Ralph Randolph?" Dawn was astounded. "I thought they were on the outs."

"I'll get to that later, but first do the math. What would you say the asking price for a unique property like it in Georgetown would be today? Take into consideration that it's been completely renovated and fully furnished, and supposedly would be advertised to buyers as being previously owned by the future President of the United States. What, Dawn, with your many years of real estate experience would you think the house will sell for?"

"I'd list it for a minimum of twenty million and expect that a bidding war might increase the price substantially, maybe even double it." Dawn did a quick calculation. "At the forty million price tag, that would be about eight million each for Maggie and Ralph Randolph, and over twenty-four for Britt."

"And there's nothing illegal about it." Andrew declared. "Except possibly the claim that a president once owned it. We won't know if Britt will win the election until a year from November. However, people exaggerate and fudge facts all the time. Do you have any idea how many houses George Washington is reputed to have slept in and how much US property the Chinese are said to own? As an example, I know that the Shanghai Shendi Group owns fifty-seven percent of Walt Disney Company and GE Appliances is owned by the Chinese Multinational Home Appliance Company. The list goes on and on.

"There's more," Walker continued triumphantly. "After I discovered that Maggie was the majority partner in the LLC, I wondered why and decided to do some more sleuthing. I put some of our best men on it and they found a marriage certificate dated four years ago from a wedding chapel in Las Vegas. It listed Margeart Chen – bride, and Owen Marshall – groom.

"So, Owen ran off to Vegas and got hitched. Why's that important?" Dawn asked.

"Because the bride, Margaret Chen is none other than your Maggie, or rather, to be more precise, Britt's Maggie – his private nurse – aka, the lady who recently went to work for his campaign as Owen's assistant."

"But why did Ralph get any part of the P Street profits?" Dawn was still confused.

Walker smiled patiently. "I'll explain everything, and I'm glad you both are so fascinated by the possible sales price of the house, and by the properties that the Chinese own," he smiled mischievously. "But I think you're missing the forest for the trees."

"In what way?" Dawn furrowed her brows in concentration.

"Haven't you wondered why Ralph Randolph was so desperate for his daughter to marry Britt? And what about Britt's Chinese connections? Who are those people and what does he do for them to justify being paid so much money? If you're not curious, I can assure you that Homeland Security, the CIA, and the FBI are."

Walker could not help himself from grandstanding a bit, knowing he was about to deliver mind-blowing information. "Let me clarify. Maggie Chen is not an ordinary nurse or anyone's personal assistant. She's a highly trained, Chinese covert operative, and her husband Owen is coincidentally Britt's top aide and closest confidant. If Senator Holmes does win the election, Owen would naturally become his chief of staff. That reeks of a very questionable, major Chinese presence in our White House, don't you think?"

"Yes. I suppose it does," Dawn said thoughtfully. "But getting back to Ralph, I don't understand why he would have tried to force Charlotte to marry Britt if he knew all along that he was due so much money from his share of the P Street deal."

"Because he's incredibly greedy. The approximately eight million from the house is only the tip of the proverbial iceberg of what he expected to gain from his close ties to the future president. Having Charlotte as the First Lady would have given him unprecedented and unrestricted access to the most powerful people in the world. His connection to the White House would open hundreds of new business opportunities. He could easily make millions as a paid consultant to foreign entities in return for sharing the classified information that Britt could provide. The Justice Department is convinced that Britt and Ralph planned to split the enormous profits from such a scheme. It was going to be a 'win-win' for both corrupt men…think Hunter and Joe Biden."

Dawn gasped, suddenly understanding. "And then the hope of all those deals fell apart when Britt broke off his engagement to Charlotte. That's why Ralph was so angry."

"That's it, exactly." Walker said. "Ralph's financial future dried up overnight, along with his hope of an ambassadorship."

"So, why then would Britt break up with Charlotte, knowing all of this? And why is Ralph suddenly back in the picture?" Dawn asked. "Was that news conference a hoax?"

"Yes. It was staged, but the reason is very complicated. Let me explain. The situation between Maggie, Britt, and Ralph was a true example of the right hand not knowing what the left was doing. Nobody in this convoluted plot was honest and each person was out for themselves and at the same time being blackmailed by the other. Remember, both men, Ralph and Britt, are desperate in different ways. Ralph needed money and wanted to recoup the business opportunities that the broken engagement cost him… and of course, his precious ambassadorship. Britt, for all of his bravado, still needed Ralph and his 'bought-and-paid-for' convention delegates to ensure his nomination and then their continued help fixing the final election results in his favor. He also wanted to keep the money he expected to make with Ralph from the Chinese. They were two symbiotic leeches feeding off each other…one more vile than the other."

Walker could not hide his disgust. "When Ralph thought he had lost it all and Charlotte began hurling her accusations about Dawn and Britt, he hired and sent a private investigator to Germany to find out the truth. When there, the investigator discovered the very talkative Holgar Schmitt, who was more than eager to provide the hospital's daily records of Dawn's visits to Britt and contact information for her friend, Elenor Blaine. That's how this all started."

Dawn looked dazed. "I think we could all use a short break." She stood up and stretched. "Let me get us all something to drink and we'll regroup in a few minutes. Can I please ask Don to join us? He's been such a help since this nightmare began. I'd like him to hear what you have to say."

"Yes," Walker grinned. "But he already knows. He's been working with me from the beginning. As a matter of fact, he's the one who asked that I be assigned to your case. We've been good friends and colleagues for years and were Navy Seals together in our two deployments. His security guard and Uber jobs were his cover. He's really with the FBI and my partner."

CHAPTER 58

The group reconvened with glasses of Chardonnay. Don was in the room this time. Dawn kept looking at him, wondering why she had never put two and two together about him and Walker being friends. She could clearly see it now, the same military posture, their similar attention to detail and commitment to doing what's right. She could not wait to get Don alone and ask him more questions but for now, she was more interested in what Walker had to say.

"Let me continue," Walker said, putting his wine glass on the table. "Ralph's investigator met Maggie in Germany. He checked her out, too, and subsequently learned that she and Owen had been secretly married a few years before. That's when it got really interesting.

"He reported his findings to Ralph and Ralph immediately saw an opportunity to make money and went to Owen. He threatened to reveal the secret marriage to Britt. Owen panicked and agreed to give Ralph Maggie's share of the P Street profits in return for his silence. He was in love with his wife and afraid of what would happen to her if their marriage became public knowledge, and he knew Britt would fire him. Also, the Chinese government would punish and recall her. He'd never see her again."

Walker looked at the shocked faces in the room and continued. "That was not enough. Then, behind Owen's back, Ralph went to Britt, who knew nothing about Maggie's marriage or her Chinese affiliation, but he had been sleeping with Maggie long before his wife's death. He kept making promises to her that they'd be together, but then reneged. When Ralph revealed the secret marriage and threatened to expose Maggie, Britt had nowhere to turn. He could not let the world know he'd been duped and allowed a Chinese spy to become his lover and his chief aide's wife. To keep Ralph quiet, and protect his presidential aspirations, he agreed to sell the P Street house immediately and give Ralph his sixty percent share of the profits. For all the money he had spent on it, Britt would not see a penny in return. Ironic, isn't it?"

Don piped up for the first time. "Let me make sure you all have this straight. Ralph was holding all the cards now. He had proof that a Chinese dissident was working in the West Wing and was married to the president's Chief of Staff. That information would raise more than a few eyebrows. Britt could not afford to let that damning information surface, so he did what he had to...he, like Owen before him, paid Ralph for his silence."

"That's quite some story," Dawn responded, wide-eyed. "But are you saying that Britt did not know that Maggie and Owen were married? And all this time I thought she was in love with Britt."

"Britt did not know about the wedding and Maggie wanted you to think that she and Britt were an item. She had to keep you from getting close to Britt in order to stay in her privileged position as his confidant and mistress. She was afraid of your influence on him. When you showed up in Germany, she was caught off guard. After you left, she did everything she could to prevent you from talking to him. Remember all the unanswered telephone calls and supposed medical emergencies?"

THE HOUSE on P STREET

"So, that makes sense in retrospect, but what do the Chinese want from Britt?" Andrew asked the question, although he was pretty sure he already knew the answer. "And how do you know all of this? Is it verifiable?"

Walker's shoulders stiffened and he continued in a grim voice. "Thankfully our government has many resources and spies of our own. We know that the Chinese want access to the White House and to all our state secrets and classified documents. Five years ago, they sent Maggie, one of their best operatives, to worm her way into Britt's life and into his confidence, first by taking care of his dying wife and then by making herself indispensable to him personally and sexually. Once he came to rely on her so completely, she used her position to learn important information from their pillow talk, all of which she relayed directly to her handler. The fact that Owen fell in love with her and was willing to keep their marriage a secret until after the election was an added bonus. Maggie had not expected that good fortune. Owen was another excellent source of information. China was very proud of her, and she thought she had the world by the balls."

"According to our sources," Don added, "from outward appearances, Maggie's marriage was solid. She was happy and content, at the same time, to keep stringing Britt along. He and Owen had no idea about her real agenda."

"And how do you know all of this, or is it just speculation? Andrew asked again.

Don smiled and stepped in front of Walker. "The FBI became suspicious that something illegal was happening in regard to large deposits Dawn made to her account. The Bank of America's branch manager became alarmed and notified the FDID who in turn called us. It seems he was a movie buff and had watched the same Tom Cruise movie many times from which Dawn derived her explanation for all the cash she was depositing."

Dawn paled. "So, I never fooled him, not even for a minute."

"No, afraid not. But the powers that be were very suspicious by then and sought a warrant for a wiretap and surveillance on Senator Holmes's office and his hospital room in Walter Reed. The information I just told you about was legally taken from those tapes, so they are admissible in a court of law."

"This is all riveting," Andrew was fascinated. "But Walker, what about my client? It's Dawn that I'm worried about. Is she legally off the hook? Does the government now believe she took the cash payments from Britt with no malice of forethought or with any intention of becoming involved in any international espionage or doing anything illegal?"

Walker's lips formed a wide smile and he winked at Dawn. "She's been completely vindicated, but I'm afraid the case is not closed."

Dawn was ecstatic to be cleared and wanted to celebrate, but Walker's last sentence stymied her. "What more could there be?"

"Nothing that directly affects you," Walker answered. "But the government still has to prove that Senator Holmes willingly accepted bribery payments in return for granting select Chinese companies special trading exemptions and deliberately overlooking certain business regulations and practices that gave them a huge advantage over their competition and thus made them very rich while doing enormous financial harm to American companies in the same spaces. It might take us years to sort everything out and come up with enough evidence to lock him up permanently. But rumors of pending charges against him for federal conspiracy to undermine the US government, bribery, money laundering, and many other felonies should be enough to force him to withdraw from the presidential race, and congress will likely vote to impeach him. A grand jury is meeting now, and I predict they'll indict him before the week is out. Then he'll be released on bond pending a lengthy trial."

"What about Maggie and Owen?" Andrew was curious.

"Maggie is toast! She's under close surveillance by Homeland Security and the FBI and pending the outcome of some delicate diplomatic negotiations, she'll either be arrested and imprisoned here for life or deported back to China. Either way, it will not be a good outcome for her. Owen will most certainly be indicted as her co-conspirator, although I personally think he was a pawn in her plan. It's our hope to turn him into a prosecution witness in return for a lighter sentence. In the meantime, the FBI will make a statement clearing Dawn later today." Walker's smile was as wide as the Atlantic City boardwalk.

His stood up, and before Dawn could react, his arms were suddenly around her waist as he pulled her tightly against him. "Your nightmare is over," he whispered in her ear and nuzzled her gently on her neck. "Remember, I promised you a dinner out when this was all over. How do you feel about tonight?"

She broke away, happy tears misting in her eyes, and gave him a playful grin. "That would be great. I'd love it – anything but Chinese."

CHAPTER 59

F all arrived in DC five months later, ushering in the sights and sounds of the season...brilliantly colored leaves, eager football fans crowding into stadiums rooting for their teams, and anticipation of the upcoming Halloween and Thanksgiving celebrations.

The presidential race was still a year away, and the earlier election frenzy had temporarily fallen off the radar during the late summer months of boating, picnics, and time spent at the beach. But now, politics was front and center again with the impeachment proceedings of Senator Britt Holmes underway on the hill. He had, under immense pressure from his colleagues and party officials, withdrawn his name from consideration for the presidency, but that was not enough. The government and his constituents demanded he be punished for bribery and other high crimes and misdemeanors. The nation was glued to the television broadcasts of his impeachment on Capitol Hill.

Not since the O.J. Simpson trial in the 1990s have so many people tuned in to watch the justice system at work. The public hung on every word from those in charge. They were as familiar with the senate's cast of characters as the previous generation had been with Judge Ito, Marcia Clark, and Christopher Darden representing the prosecution and Johnnie

Cochran, F. Lee Bailey, Robert Shapiro, Alan Dershowitz, and Robert Kardashian for the defense – the so-called "Dream Team."

There was no ill-fitting leather glove this time, no bloody murders, but allegations of corrupt activities and possibly treason ran rampant. Dawn's meticulous records and her bank receipts substantiated the government's claim that the money the senator had sent to her for renovations matched the specific times, dates and amounts that he received by electronic transfers from Beijing. They were a key piece of evidence against him, as was Dawn's emotional testimony that Britt had insisted there be no paper trail tying him to the P Street house. FBI forensic accountants had been able to follow the money trail from a bank in Beijing, to Britt's account in the Grand Cayman Islands and then to Dawn's business account at the Bank of America. She had testified to receiving all the payments in cash increments because of Britt's obsession with looking middle-class and pretending to be fiscally conservative. She also emphasized that Owen was the one to package the cash and arrange for the messenger services.

She had been extremely nervous during her appearance before congress but vowed to tell the truth, no matter how stupid her actions in the past made her look now. Britt must pay for his treachery to her, to Charlotte and of course to the country. He had betrayed them all.

During her lengthy testimony she avoided looking at Britt, keeping her eyes focused only on Walker, Lolly, and Don, who sat in the first row of the gallery to support her. When she finished speaking, she started to walk out of the room, but her curiosity got the best of her. She turned around briefly and snuck a quick glance at the man she had thought she loved.

Britt was a mere shadow of his former self. His hair had gone completely gray. His beautiful expressive eyes were hooded in fear and guilt, and he had lost at least ten pounds. She thought ironically that he had looked so much more handsome after suffering through all his injuries and surgeries than he does now. *How the mighty have fallen. Maybe it was true that guilt could eat you up.* It certainly looked like it had in his case. She thought she saw him briefly try to engage her, maybe to ask for her forgiveness, but it was a silly hallucination – a fleeting wishful moment. In fact, he openly stared at her with profound hatred, as if *she* had been the one to betray *him*. She turned back around and left the courtroom with her held high and her good name restored.

* *

Charlotte Randolph was called as the next witness. She took the stand looking like a buttercup, dressed head to toe in yellow with a yellow and white headband holding her hair primly off her face and a bold patterned neck scarf tied under her chin. She looked innocent, sweet, and naïve...exactly as her lawyers had intended. Her mother watched proudly from the gallery and smiled encouragingly at her daughter.

Charlotte answered question after question about how, when, and where she met Britt and about under what circumstances the senator had proposed. She started to tell the senator who was questioning her that the marriage had been all her father's idea, not hers, but Britt's lawyer cut her off immediately. He accused her of being a frivolous child, a spineless, spoiled dilettante and unable to make an adult decision for herself.

"No," she stammered. "That's not true. I was just trying to please my father."

"Why?" He smirked. "Why was your father so involved in your love life?"

"It wasn't that he cared about that," she stated defensively. "I don't think he even understands the concept of love." Peggy Randolph nodded in the gallery and mumbled her agreement from her seat. "I was trying to spare him and my mama the embarrassment of their friends finding out that he was a fraud and had gambled away the family businesses. He was – is, bankrupt. We're living check to check."

There was a loud murmur from the spectators as all eyes were on her. "Father convinced me that I had to help the family. He said that I must convince Britt to marry me. Then as his wife, and eventually as the First Lady, Britt would feel obligated to see to it that my father's debts were paid off or forgiven and set him up in a cushy new job. It would not be good publicity for Britt – as the president – to bring dishonor and ridicule to his wife's parents."

"So, you went along with this alleged plan of your father's with no qualms, no hesitation?" The inquisitor was skeptical.

"Yes," she answered meekly. "But of course, I had qualms, and I knew it was wrong, but my father can be very persuasive."

"I think we've heard enough from this witness. Her clear lack of a moral compass makes anything further she has to say about Senator Homes irrelevant. We must simply consider the source. If she was willing to flagrantly lie and toy with a man's heart and career to further her own family's personal financial gain, anything else she has to say cannot be trusted or taken seriously. Ms. Randolph," he said pretentiously, "you are dismissed."

Charlotte looked shocked and dismayed. This was not how she expected her testimony to go at all. She had not been given the chance to say how deceitful Britt had been to her, or to discuss the emotional agony he had put her through and the cruel way he had treated her in the end. He was not, she had planned to say dramatically...presidential material.

"That will be all." The chairman said. "Ms. Randolph, you may go."

Charlotte stood up as a hot rage began to build inside of her. She shot her mother a quick glance for reassurance and suddenly felt a burst of renewed determination to set the record straight. "There's one more thing you gentlemen need to hear. Have you thought about the fire at the P Street house? Do you want to hear about that?" She glared defiantly at Britt.

It was at that moment that Dawn, watching the proceedings with Walker on a closed-circuit feed in an anteroom, gasped in horror. Charlotte was about to incriminate herself and it wasn't necessary. The committee had enough evidence on Britt to impeach him without her confession. Dawn looked at Walker in panic. "You have to stop her. Call for a recess or something. Charlotte should not have to pay for her father's crimes. Doesn't she have a lawyer, someone who can object?"

Walker bolted out of the anteroom and ran into the chamber where the inquiring panel and the congressional members had been listening to the witnesses' testimony. There was complete confusion in the room. Everyone was talking at once, pointing fingers and looking at Charlotte. The chairman banged his gavel repeatedly on the table, trying to regain control of the room and bring the impeachment session back to order. Charlotte faced Britt with a steely glare, a "gotcha by the balls" look of self-satisfaction plastered on her genteel face. She held her ground, afraid to move and afraid not to. Her southern backbone had stiffened like concrete at just the right time.

Walker rushed up to and whispered something into the Chairman's ear. Once again, the Chairman banged his gavel, demanding order. "In light of the new information Charlotte Randolph wishes to have entered into the record, we will recess until tomorrow morning at 10:00 a.m. to give the accused time to confer with his council. Miss Randolph," he looked at the southern beauty with renewed interest. "You'll be called to testify again in the morning. Please be here on time. This impeachment session, granted to us under Article One, section 5 of the Constitution, is adjourned."

CHAPTER 60

Charlotte sat huddled with her mother and her attorney. Everyone looked grim. "I'm so sorry," Charlotte cried, furious at herself. "I shouldn't have said anything. Now, I suppose, I'm in big trouble."

"I guess it depends on what you have to say," Erwin Ranzinni, her attorney, answered solemnly. "Tell me exactly what happened and why you never mentioned any of this before."

"Yes, go ahead darling. Tell the truth. You no longer have to protect your father or anyone else for that matter," Peggy Randolph patted her daughter's hand. "The important thing is that you are not charged with a crime."

"I understand," Erwin said sympathetically. "That's a hell of a way for a father to treat his daughter, but what about the fire?"

"Father was moaning and groaning that the money he and Maggie were expecting from the eventual sale of the P Street house would take far too long to materialize. His anxious creditors were browbeating and harassing him daily, demanding full payment immediately or threatening that physical harm would come to him, and to me and my mama. Father needed the money right away, so he went to Britt's office in desperation to beg him for a loan. As much as he hated Britt now, he knew he would not willingly put me and Mama in danger. But Britt turned him down. He said that he had already sent all his cash to Dawn."

"Go on, tell him the rest," Peggy urged. "It gets worse."

"That's when Owen overheard the conversation and came up with a plan. Since there was no way to get the money out of the house until it sold, the next best thing would be to make a bogus insurance claim. Owen suggested starting a fire. It would have to be large enough to do significant damage to the property but not burn the place down. He, Britt, and my father worked out the details. Owen agreed to set the fire for one third of the insurance money and he made an agreement that when Britt became president, he would pardon Maggie and himself if any charges were outstanding and give her a cushy job in the White House. Father stole one of my Hermes scarves and told Owen to leave a scrap of it behind where the fire department could find it. That's what kind of man Father is. He set me up to take the blame – his own daughter. Britt had no choice but to go along or Ralph would go through with his threat to expose Britt's Chinese connections. But his clever plan was foiled. Dawn Sutter found the scarf instead, not the fire department. May I have some water?" Charlotte asked. "And could we take a break, please? This is exhausting."

Peggy handed her daughter a bottle of Evian. "Best to get this over with. Go on, tell the rest."

Charlotte fingered her scarf nervously but plunged ahead. Her story was becoming more interesting with each sentence. "Owen bought some off brand of paint thinner and snuck into P Street. He placed old rags doused in flammable liquid all around the kitchen and then lit a match. Running through the garage, he thought he had accomplished his mission and would get away, undetected. But he was wrong. I saw him. I had come to the house hoping to find Dawn, and I watched helplessly as the flames began to take over the first floor. Most of the crew had left the house by then but a few stragglers, including the construction manager, whom I recognized from an earlier visit to the property, were still inside. As soon as the fire started, he called 911 and tried to put the flames out himself. I think he was injured," she said. "The house was enveloped in flames almost immediately."

Erwin pulled his chair closer to Charlotte. "Go on. And?"

"And Owen, in his hurry to escape, ran right into me. He panicked and tried to kill me, choking me and bruising my neck." She reached up and touched the spot, painfully reliving the moment. When he finally came to his senses and let me go, he warned me that if I ever said a word to anyone about him starting the fire, he'd kill my mama. I was so scared and didn't know what to do, so I ran. I hid in some bushes down the street and watched as Dawn and her friends arrived and a construction person was eventually taken away by ambulance. After what seemed like hours, everyone left, and I was able to creep to my car and drive home."

She started to cry softly. "I never told anyone but my Mama about what happened. As much as I hate my father and Britt, I don't want to be the one to send them to prison. I knew that if I told anyone about Owen's part in the fire, the whole house of cards would come and crumble. What's going to happen to them now…and to me?"

Mr. Ranzinni answered calmly. "You're going to write down, word for word, everything you've just told us, and I'll give your statement to the judge. He'll decide whether it's admissible or not, but don't worry. The only thing you can be charged with is the failure to come forward with this information sooner. The judge will consider the circumstances and what your father's put you through. You'll be fine and nothing will come from this for you, but it's another major problem for Britt and

Owen's defense. You'll likely be subpoenaed to testify in Owen and Britt's trials, probably in two or three years, but that's it. Maybe they'll even settle for your written deposition. You're not to blame for any of this."

Charlotte picked up a pen and began to write furiously.

CHAPTER 61

The impeachment proceedings continued for another two days and resulted in a split vote along party lines. The Chief Justice refused to step in and break the tie. There was no law that compelled him to, but it did not matter. Britt's reputation was forever ruined. His illustrious career, the aura of power and mystique that had surrounded him for years, ended abruptly. He had become a pariah, and no one wanted to be associated with him. He was removed from his committees and on strong advice from his legal team, he resigned from the Senate effective immediately. Retreating to his Delaware home in disgrace, he was seen at local bars popping tranquilizers and washing them down with his only remaining friend – Jack Daniels. Fearfully, he waited for the final FBI findings, which could land him in prison for the rest of his life, and especially with the addition of Charlotte's unexpected bombshell about his complicity in an insurance fraud on P Street.

Every knock on the door, every phone call could potentially signal the end and his imminent arrest. On Christmas morning, two years later, his Delaware home was raided. He was read his rights and unceremoniously carted off to jail in handcuffs.

Maggie had been anxious ever since the impeachment hearings, waiting for the government to come after her. Every day they didn't was a gift.

She watched Britt's arrest play out on television and panicked. She knew Owen and she would be next. A year before, in anticipation, she had stashed a duffle bag full of clothing and some money in her basement in case something like this happened. When she saw the telltale unmarked black FBI van pull up in front of the house, she slipped out the back. Hiding as a fugitive in the US was better than being deported to China and facing the consequences of her failed mission. But she had not fooled Homeland Security or the FBI. They had been watching her every step, and they knew exactly where she was. They were biding their time while a delicate prisoner exchange was being worked out by the State Department for the return of some American prisoners. Then her deportation would happen. The Chinese government did not take well to their operatives being unmasked and embarrassed before the world and their clandestine missions were exposed. It was only a matter of time before everything ended for her – one way or the other.

Ralph Randolph was arrested that same Christmas morning for his numerous crimes and misdemeanors and sat forlornly in the DC jail awaiting trial. Humiliated, defeated, and lonely, he reached out to Charlotte with his one phone call, begging her to post his bail. His message went unanswered.

Charlotte and Peggy moved to Charleston, South Carolina immediately after Britt's impeachment hearing ended. They were happily living their lives there, occupied with gardening, decorating their new home, and establishing themselves in the community.

Charlotte was seriously considering using her business degree knowledge to open a Pilates studio and health spa. Last year she had met and fallen in love with a handsome physical therapist, who owned his own thriving practice in town. She was trying to convince him to join forces with her and create their own new business together. He was more than eager, and they made a great couple.

Peggy Randolph was hopeful that a marriage for Charlotte might be the future, and while she waited to plan it, she was busy writing a titillating novel about her daughter's experiences in Washington. It was tentatively entitled...*Sweet Tea Revenge.*

EPILOGUE
Six Years Later

Lolly and Don pushed Tiffany, their rambunctious two-year daughter, in a stroller around the Tidal Basin. The landmark cherry blossom trees were in full bloom, painting the two-mile walking loop with soft splashes of billowy pink color. Their shimmering beauty reflected off the water, making the sky appear almost pink itself.

Lolly gazed at the iconic scenery around her, and at the obelisk marble tower, the easily recognized Washington Monument. It stood in all its refurbished splendor as an awesome symbol of remembrance to the country's greatest founding father. Don picked up his daughter and pointed out all the tourists sitting or standing on the steps of the nearby Thomas Jefferson Memorial, which glistened in the April sun when the sunlight bounced off its roof. The statue of Jefferson was situated so that his eyes gazed at the White House.

"There's so much history here, so many stories of sacrifice and greatness," Lolly said softly. "I can't wait to teach Tiffany about our American history. She's a lucky little girl to grow up in a free country amid such inspirational examples of our past."

"And she's so lucky to have a wonderful mother like you." He looked at his wife fondly.

"You're not a bad Dad yourself," Lolly smiled at her husband. "I think Tiffany's getting tired. Should we leave and put her down for a nap?"

"Sure, but like we do every time we come here, let's do our nostalgic driving tour on the way home."

He fastened Tiffany safely into her car seat, and they took off slowly past some of the most famous landmarks in the city, the Smithsonian Museums, the United States Capitol Rotunda, the FBI Headquarters, and down Pennsylvania Avenue to the White House. As they passed in front of the president's home, they both looked at each other and smiled. The former occupant had been replaced by a popular, moderate third-party candidate and the country's wounds had begun to heal from the scandals of recent years.

Britt Holmes and Owen Marshall had been convicted in separate jury trials by unanimous decisions for numerous crimes including trea- son. Although Owen's prison sentence was ten years shorter than Britt's, neither man would ever experience freedom or see life outside a federal penitentiary again. Ralph Randolph was languishing in the same federal prison faced with a twenty-year sentence himself. He would be an old man by the time he was released.

"When you think of what could have been," Lolly shivered. She did not need to finish her sentence. Don understood. They had been through a harrowing time together and were grateful for everything they had now...a loving marriage and a healthy, adorable child. Sutter Interiors had rebounded from the P Street scandal and was flourishing as never before. Dawn had made Lolly an equal partner and the company was continuing to grow in profits and prestige.

Don had overcome his fear of commitment and married Lolly. He worked a full-time job at the FBI but no longer accepted undercover assignments. He was happy and content to be with Lolly and Tiffany and to leave the cloak and dagger stuff to the younger agents.

As a jumbo jet flew overhead on its departure pattern from Reagan National Airport, Lolly and Don looked up at it and grinned. The last time they had watched one of those enormous planes take off, they had been standing on the tarmac with Dawn and Walker and many high-level government officials as they witnessed a broken, shamed Maggie Chen, being led in handcuffs towards the plane. Her fate, her final destination, would never be known to them. But she was gone from their lives forever. Lolly hugged Walker just a little tighter and silently thanked God for her good fortune.

Don drove down M street, past Sutter Interiors. The lights were on, and they could see Walker and Dawn huddled closely together in the showroom. They were picking out furniture for their new home on the twenty-first floor of the city's trendiest hotel/condo building...the Danelli. It turned out that Walker C. Brant's uncle was none other than Giovanni Campari, the hotel's manager. He used his considerable connections there to put their names first on the list of prospective buyers to choose one of the apartments when they became available.

Dawn knew the building well. She and Lolly had designed the public spaces and the upper floors that the hotel's board of directors had decided to convert into luxury condominium apartments. Sutter Interiors had been instrumental in helping to design the floor plans and selecting the finishes, cabinetry, and appliances for the units. Dawn felt right at home there. The building was selling out quickly and was expected, in real estate terms, to rival the Plaza Hotel in New York City or the Ritz in Miami for its hotel/condo innovation.

Dawn kissed Walker tenderly when they finally decided on a beige, tufted leather king-size headboard for their bedroom. "I can't wait to move in," she said contentedly. "That place and our life together is every-thing I've ever dreamed about." She rarely thought about Britt or Maggie anymore. They both seemed like part of a bad dream, and she had awoken from it long ago.

"The only thing that would make it more perfect is if you would agree to marry me," he said for the hundredth time.

"You know I love you, but things are so perfect the way they are now, I don't want to jinx it."

"Never say never," he grinned at her affectionately. "Look at how Don came around and how happy he and Lolly are now."

She smiled back. He had a point. "I'll give it some serious thought, I promise. And just so you know, I prefer pear-shaped diamonds and I like them big!"

"I'll keep that in mind," he smiled knowingly, fingering the little blue jewelry box in his pocket. "But, in the meantime, what do you say if I close the showroom shades, lock the doors, and we initiate our new bed?"

"I say, yes. Absolutely 'yes.'" She began to undress.

* *

Two weeks later the four close friends were joined by Charlotte and her new husband at the official ribbon cutting ceremony. The Federal Government owned the P Street house now. It was a fine arts museum, also to be used as an overflow facility for the American embassy to house their guests and visiting dignitaries. The gorgeous grounds and beautiful home were a tribute to Dawn's interior design talents and to American presidents and first ladies. Dawn and Lolly glowed with pride as the mayor cut the ribbon and made a short welcoming speech.

"I never thought I'd ever want to come back here," Dawn commented. "But this is a wonderful use for the property. Some very prestigious galleries are going to rotate their American history exhibits through here," she said proudly. "And schools will take annual field trips here."

Dawn looked at Charlotte and winked. She pulled a gift from her newest red Chanel bag. "A little wedding present from Walker and me."

Charlotte looked surprised and happily tore open the wrapping. She started to giggle and then broke into a full-scale belly laugh. It was a framed charcoal drawing of a two-story chicken coop with a small, birdbath-sized pink hot tub sitting in the middle of the upper floor. It was personally signed by the artist – Elenor Blaine.

Charlotte held it up to show everyone. "Should we hang it in the portrait gallery?" She laughed.

"No, I don't think so, but maybe you can find a place for it in your Pilates studio." Dawn smiled and hugged her friend. "We've come a long way together, haven't we?"

Charlotte nodded and hugged her back.

Walker pulled Dawn close to him. "This story has a happy ending after all. Does anyone want to venture outside and look for eggs?"

The mayor's security detail looked at the happy group of friends and had to come over to shush them up. They could not stop laughing.

ACKNOWLEDGEMENTS

Thank you to all the interior designers who use their creative talents and work so diligently to make their clients' dreams come true.

And special thanks, as always, to my wonderful loving husband, Bart, for his constant support and encouragement and for giving me the time and space to write. It was not always easy. We had things to do and places to go but he allowed my writing to come first. I love him for that…and for so much more.

Although my parents, Ed and Kay Ferriday, sadly did not live to see my success as a writer or have the chance to read any of my books, I thank them profusely for the educational opportunities they gave me and my sister and for the privilege of allowing me to make precious memories while growing up in beautiful Washington, DC and Chevy Chase, Maryland. I tried to capture their ambiance in the setting for this and in many of my other books.

And last but not least, thank you to my creative colleagues in Texas – the publisher, Monkedia, and especially to Noah Curran for his wise advice and guidance and to Hannah Bagley for her responsiveness and her unending patience.